MW01042964

EMERUS:
THE
WONDER
OF
WINGS

Benjamin Deer

CONTENTS

Listen to your inspiration.

P.S. It's rad having such a cool friend.

Benjamin Dee

For Hilary, my beloved wife, without whom this book would not have been possible.

<u>CHAPTER 1</u>

Sunday, 4:03 am

Time was a foreign concept. A black hole sucked up the seconds, minutes, and hours like a vacuum. Rick Engleheart sat atop the dirtied, gray-colored cloth passenger-seat, staring out the half-opened window with half-opened eyes. Lacey was lying across the sedan's dusty and aged back seat, asleep. It had been nearly three hours since they had left the Engleheart house, and Gabe had not revealed much, at least not to the extent Rick Engleheart and Lacey had hoped. He spoke about life in every regard - whether it was sports, film, vacation spots, animals, even the dwindling stock market - Gabe seemed to know a little about a lot. After about a dozen valiant, but failed attempts to evoke important information from him, Lacey had given up. However, it had only been two minutes since Rick Engleheart had last pleaded for Gabe to impart any knowledge regarding the *who, what, when, where, why,* and *how* questions that circled his mind like vultures. The highway's lights lining the side of the road every few hundred feet took turns dimly illuminating the inside of the old, slightly beat-up sedan. After losing count, Rick Engleheart began to uncomfortably shift in his seat. He thought he might go insane if he didn't find out exactly what was going on. In fact, he was surprised he had even made it this far without escaping his life's nightmare and rolling out onto the shoulder.

Survival wasn't a necessity anymore, he thought. Finally, he spoke up. "Gabe, can you please tell me what is going on? I've asked countless times. It is my right to know. I've been through so much. I don't even know why I'm here," Rick Engleheart begged, frustratingly. An exhausted sigh escaped his lips. "Please."

However, he didn't get the answer he wanted because just like every preceding time, Gabe calmly replied, "In due time, Rick. In due time."

The sadly frustrated father turned toward Gabe as another streetlight extended its long, yellow beam, pushing the car along the road to hand it off to the ray waiting in line. For the first time during the ride, Gabe saw the overwhelming hurt in Rick Engleheart's eyes. He grimaced. After the pained father sighed once more with nothing other than a tiny glimmer of hope, Gabe slowly looked away. He breathed deeply three times as if preparing to meditate. Closing his eyes and resting his hands on his lap, Gabe kept the car straight with his knees, although Rick Engleheart failed to notice. Seven seconds later, he spoke.

"We are getting close to our first pickup, Rick. Soon. I promise."

"What do you mean first pickup?" Rick Engleheart asked, frustratingly confused.

"Someone you know is coming with us, Rick. He is going to help us get your son, and he is so incredibly gifted, you won't believe your eyes," Gabe replied, smiling.

"What? Who?" Rick Engleheart was becoming more and more confused from every one of Gabe's words to the next.

Gabe let out another incredibly deep sigh. "Easton," he finally said.

For the next few minutes, Rick Engleheart's mouth did not stop moving. Perplexed as to why they were going to pick up his eighteen year-old nephew, Easton, the stressed-out father's mind became a boulder rolling down an endlessly steep hill, picking up more and more speed as time let on. Gabe sat, calm as a pond, listening and smiling.

"We're two minutes out," he said, after luckily finding a break between his passenger's words. "Lacey Sleepy Head, wake up."

Lacey let out an annoyed and tired groan.

"We're close."

"Okay," Lacey replied, opening her eyes and slowly trying to sit up.

"Now that I have both of your attentions, listen to what I have to say," Gabe said, in a serious tone.

Both Rick Engleheart and Lacey held their breath in anticipation.

"There is quite a bit going on in regards to Johnny. A lot of what I am about to tell you may sound confusing, and I don't expect you to understand it all. But, all I ask is that you trust me. When Johnny fainted at his baseball game in June, that was not random and it was not natural. A government drone about the size of an old Gameboy targeted him and fired a miniscule metal chip into the back of his neck. It was found by EMTs, pulled out, and authorities took it away while Johnny was in the hospital."

Gabe stopped as if to answer any questions, but his two passengers were silently staring with their mouths slightly agape.

"This was the beginning of something," the driver continued. "Something big. Johnny was the first successful pilot study of a top secret government program. Its primary focus is to take away freedom of thought to create a more sustainable future for the human race. The iron chip forced Johnny into a coma and conducted some sort of test using an unknown foreign technology. I'm not sure what it was, but I can tell you that it worked. Otherwise, he'd be dead."

"How do you know all of this?" Rick Engleheart asked, skeptically.

"We'll get to that later," Gabe replied. "So they have him."

"Who has him?" Lacey asked. "The government?"

After wrestling with himself to find the appropriate answer, Gabe addressed her inquiry. "Sort of."

"What the hell does that mean?" Lacey rudely requested.

"A secret branch of government has him. But it's not like the government we see or hear, or learn about in school. It's an underground extension of the U.S. government that deals with quantum leaps in technology. This is their new leap, and it is dangerous, beyond your most horrifying imagination."

"Why have you waited three hours to tell us this?" Rick Engleheart asked.

"Probably because if he told us back in Windsor, we would have jumped out of the car thinking he's crazy, which for the record, Gabe, I still think that you are insane," Lacey voiced.

Gabe laughed. A remnant of a smile twisted Rick Engleheart's face into something that he had not felt in days.

"Seriously though," Gabe continued. "They have Johnny in Wyoming, deep underground, and they plan to keep him there alive. But they're not counting on us. And we're going to rescue him. We all have an incredible destiny to fulfill, and this is only the beginning. Like I've said, all I ask is that you trust me."

"Bang! Bang! Bang! Bang!"

Before Rick Engleheart or Lacey could reply, four well-placed bullets blew out all four tires of the beat-up sedan one by one, sending the car skidding out of control.

CHAPTER 2

Lacey and Rick Engleheart instinctively ducked down, covering their heads while Gabe did his best to keep the car from abruptly flipping into a violent seventy mile-per-hour roll. Surrounded by small clouds of the rapidly escaping compressed air, the old sedan skidded off to the right, crossing the double rumble strip, the discourteous sound of which alarmed the passengers. The car continued drifting off to the right toward the two hundred-foot cliff that lined the right side of the road. Luckily, the guard rail contained the old sedan and its passengers, absorbing some of the impact as the car's six airbags deployed simultaneously. Finally coming to a stop, all that was heard inside the vehicle was silence.

Gerald Green was kneeling behind a thick, three-foot tall pine tree stump half a mile from the highway when his receiver began to vibrate. Green had been a sniper in the National Guard for five years and was home with his family when he obtained a strange, but specific mission to shoot out the tires, then murder the driver of a sedan traveling on I-95 when the car crossed exactly 1 mile north of Cove Island Park. According to intel, the driver was armed and dangerous, and Green's orders descended from the highest authority. Green had learned not to question such jurisdiction; however, the random orders still forced him to scratch his head. He thought it better not to think about it. His receiver's vibration was the signal. Green peered through the scope of his McMillan Tac-50. Sure enough, the lonely vehicle was exactly as described. There was his confirmation. Green inhaled and then exhaled slowly. Four consecutive shots - one to each tire. He watched from the hill, invisible behind the veil of the night-darkened emerald forest, as the car slid out of control into the highway's guard rail. Green peered through his scope once more to observe the situation.

Gabe was the first to move. "Everyone safe? Everyone alright?"

"Yeah," Lacey and Rick Engleheart answered, frightened and confused at the same time.

Lacey, who was not wearing her seatbelt, was the most banged up, with scrapes and cuts slowly leaking blood. Her forehead looked the worst as it had slammed onto the center console. Rick Engleheart quickly suggested she needed medical attention, which was just as quickly refused by Lacey.

"Everyone just stay put," Gabe commanded through a cough. "Thank goodness for airbags, huh Sleepyhead?" he asked Lacey, exiting the car.

The beautiful eighteen year-old rebel was tough and would normally not listen to what anyone told her to do. This time, however, she was in too much shock to move. She only watched as Gabe stood five feet from her with his arms stretched wide as he gazed up to the stars.

"Wingspan of a condor," Lacey muttered.

Rick Engleheart laughed through his nose at Lacey's quip. Just when he was about to open his mouth though, his sentence was intercepted by the horrifying sound of another gunshot. This time, aimed directly at their strange, but honorable driver. Lacey shrieked and turned towards Gabe, not wanting to keep her eyes open. However, he stood still, in the same position as before.

"Bang!" Another shot. The bullet's impact against the opposite guard rail echoed throughout the valley.

"Bang! Bang!" Lacey and Rick Engleheart ducked for cover. "Bang!"

Gabe stood upright, unmoved. Then, he spoke in a soft, quiet whisper. "You do not have to do this. We are good, and so are you. There is much more going on than you know. Turn around, walk away, and you will not be harmed."

"Okay, now you're really freaking me out," Lacey vocalized to anyone within ear-shot.

No more gunshots were fired. The buzzing of insects commandeered the middle of the night's soundwaves as Gabe retrieved the keys out from the ignition and went back to open the trunk where he pulled out four donut tires. Rick Engleheart unbuckled his seatbelt and offered help.

"Why do you have four donuts in the trunk?" he asked.

"I thought something like this may happen," Gabe replied, matter-of-factly.

"I'm sorry, but you're going to have to explain what in the world just happened. That was not normal," Rick Engleheart stated, perplexed.

"I'll explain everything soon. Now let's get these donuts on.

We're very close to Easton's house."

"We're gonna drive around with six deployed airbags?" Lacey rudely asked. "Good idea," she said, nodding with sarcasm.

"We'll change vehicles when we get there," Gabe replied. "And after we pick up Easton, I'll explain everything. I promise."

Driving slowly with four donuts and six deployed airbags tickled Lacey. Though the sedan did finally roll into the middle class home's driveway, it was a miracle no police cars had seen the contents of its insides. All three of them quickly climbed out of the car, Lacey and Rick Engleheart following Gabe's lead. It was the middle of the night, and the house was dark - mysteriously spooky in a way, but Gabe calmly rang the doorbell as if it was 5 o'clock in the evening and he was inviting his neighbors over for a barbeque.

Rick Engleheart stood behind Lacey, hesitant. "They're going to think I'm crazy. They're going to think I've completely lost my mind," he stated, embarrassed.

Lacey respectfully stood silent.

"No, they won't, Rick," Gabe reassured his new friend, looking back with a smile. "The news story about Johnny's kidnapping was contained only to Windsor's news stations. No one else knows anything about it. This type of stuff is done more than you would think. The national news stories are for the most part real, but another purpose they serve is to distract everyone from what goes on in front of their own eyes. Usually local stories, unless extremely heinous, are forgotten rather easily because the mainstream public gets absolutely bombarded with other stories - some with meaning, most with none."

Gabe rang the doorbell once more, which prompted slow steps from inside the house, descending down the nearby staircase.

"Gonna break this door down too?" Lacey quipped.

Pete, Johnny's uncle, answered the door. Slowly opening it an inch, his big eyes appeared in the tiny opening. "Rick, is that you? Who are *these* people? What are you doing?"

"We need to come in, Pete. It's important. Johnny has been kidnapped," Rick Engleheart told his brother-in-law.

Pete hurriedly undid two locks and a chain before inviting the two strangers and Rick into his home. After brief introductions, Pete briskly walked upstairs to wake up his wife, Deanna. As the humble matriarch of the family, Deanna was a hard worker and best friend of her sister, Eileen Engleheart, who had tragically and suddenly died two months prior. Deanna was grieving as well as someone could under the circumstances. To the Englehearts, family was an unbreakable bond - one which could not and would not, under any situation, break for anything. So Rick Engleheart was not surprised when Deanna came running down the stairs in her white, silk night robe in a panic with tears welling up in her eyes.

"Who the heck is this?" she asked, frightened, as she slid to a stop on the hardwood floor hallway.

"This is Gabe. And he is going to help get my son back," Rick Engleheart replied, surprised by his own confidence in the man he just had met three hours earlier.

"It's probably best if we sit down," Gabe spoke for everybody to hear. "And we need Easton."

It was an awkward feeling to be obeying a virtual stranger's odd requests. However, there was something about Gabe's presence that calmed everyone around him. It was as if he had an aura and it was naturally encompassing people around him. True, he was strange. And he had already staged some incredible performances - from killing the government agent at Rick Engleheart's house James Bond style to having a sniper's bullets go directly through him - he was not normal. In his demeanor, in his appearance with his long and flowing hair - in any sense of the word, Gabe was not normal.

Easton looked like any eighteen-year-old would a few hours before dawn on a warm summer's night. After an initial hug to his uncle and confused, fast-paced greetings to the strangers in his house, Easton joined the group by taking a seat at the large, wooden dining room table. Rick Engleheart spoke first, explaining to everyone he was not crazy. Next, he told his sister-in-law, her husband, and their son what had happened when Johnny went missing, graciously thanking Lacey, whom he introduced as his son's girlfriend (it was the first time Lacey had been called that, which prompted a wide, lip-only smile). Hands went up to eyes, foreheads were rubbed, the words "I can't believe this" emanated from mouths. Everyone sat in silent thought under the flicker of the half-lit chandelier. Then, Rick Engleheart spoke of Gabe and what he had said and what he had done. Easton shifted in his seat, shooting Gabe a look, which the tall, ridiculously in-shape man returned with caring eyes. After Rick Engleheart finished what he had felt compelled to say, a feeling of idiocracy came over him. What he had just said, almost all of it, sounded like something out of a movie - a completely fake, made-up series of scenes. However, it was very real. And there was no escaping it. Everyone at the table simply stopped their frustrating thought processes and turned toward Gabe. Anticipation was building. He had answers, and everybody, especially Rick Engleheart, was dying to find out what they were. One by one, they took turns directing their gaze on the strange man who sat among them who was perched with impeccable posture and a peaceful smile on his perfectly smooth face. He sighed deeply.

"There is so much that humans do not know. You may think you have most of it figured out. But even the top of any scientific or mathematical field knows virtually nothing compared to the truth."

"Humans? What are you talking about?" Rick Engleheart asked, confused and frightened, fearing Gabe's answer.

"I'm an angel," the strange, long-haired man replied. "And I'm just one. There are countless angelic beings all around us. Isn't that right, Easton?"

CHAPTER 3

The silence was deafening. If a pin fell, it would reverberate like an abrupt thunder clap. Pete and Rick Engleheart began questioning Gabe while Deanna and Lacey simply stared at Easton as if had they deserted their gaze, wings would appear and he would fly away out of sight. Before long, the dimly lit dining room transformed into a frantic question and answer session - mostly just questions. As some of them began to subside and voices started to lower, Deanna's speech stood out above the rest, surviving on its own momentum.

"Are you Gabriel, the archangel?" she asked, as the room once again fell silent directly after her serious inquiry.

After another long sigh, Gabe responded. "Yes I am."

"This is freaking me out," Lacey said, getting up from the table. "I don't even believe in this kind of crap."

Gabe looked up at the beautiful brunette and pleaded with her to stay. He promised he would explain, so she sat down. He had a way of being quite persuasive when needed. As Lacey reluctantly returned to her chair and crossed her legs in frustration, eight eyes simultaneously shot Gabe their looks.

"Everything is not as it seems," he stated, like a professor on the first day of class. "What you know, what you think - it is probably wrong. I am an angel, like I said. I am Gabriel. Some of the mainstream moronic population think of my kind as either nonexistent, freaks, and most commonly, extraterrestrials. But I prefer to refer to my kind as extra-dimensionals. We can transcend the countless dimensions that surround this universe in the blink of an eye. Surely you cannot think humans were the only intelligent beings the Creator designed. What you see of me now is an angel, yes - but in human form. In other dimensions, I look completely different. What only one of you knows, Easton…" he said, pausing for comedic effect, "…is that I have visited this residence a few times before. Usually in the middle of the night when everyone is sleeping. And most people when they see these types of visits in movies, or hear them on idiotic television shows think that aliens are visiting and sometimes abducting. Well let me enlighten you with something. They're not. According to Einstein's theory of relativity, the faster you travel - we're talking super super sonic speed here - the more your mass increases. And if any extraterrestrials were to come to Earth, they would need to travel the speed the light or it would take them so long they would die. That's how far away the nearest planet containing intelligent life is. And Earth is twice as far from the next, and so on and so forth. That is how the Great Designer arranged it - not one species of intelligent life can visit the other. And due to the fact that the speed of light is the fastest anything can travel, if an actual extraterrestrial did travel at that velocity, then their mass would become infinite. And that's impossible - across a whole spectrum of sciences."

"But it's only a theory," Lacey interrupted. "Einstein's thing is not proven. How do we know you're not just an alien feeding us bullcrap?"

"It's not proven yet, but it will be in about two decades," Gabe replied, nonchalantly, ignoring the laughable fact that Lacey was attempting to argue with him on such matters.

"So," he continued, "What many of you think of as extraterrestrials making appearances on this planet or abducting humans are actually spiritual beings - angels or demons - transcending one dimension and coming to this dimension. They can give gifts - we call them gifts of the guardians - and do so much more. However, only to certain types of humans. Some for evil purposes and some for the opposite. Right, Easton?"

Gabe ceased talking and directed his sharp blue eyes at Easton, and everyone else followed suit. Easton looked around the room and smiled shyly. The truth was Gabe had been visiting his dreams for as long as he could remember. Sometimes they would fly, other times they would simply talk, but the two knew each other from the inside out. Easton tried to explain it to his parents, but they were skeptical. Without saying it, both Deanna and Pete thought that they might need to call the authorities.

"I can assure you," Gabe announced, "There is no need to call anyone. I have been bestowing gifts on your son for quite some time, specifically the temporary gift of immortality."

The confusion meter had broken off. Rick Engleheart and Lacey kept their thoughts internal, but Pete and Deanna were now grilling their eighteen year-old son so much so that he couldn't even get a word of response in. When they stopped to take a breath, he finally spoke up.

"Show them," he told Gabe, who was sitting directly across

from him.

Gabe, who was becoming frustrated with Pete and Deanna's skepticism, knew time was of the essence. Oh, you of little faith, he thought. "You two," he interrupted, loudly, "Will not believe unless you see. Well, pinch yourselves now if you think you're dreaming." Without hesitating, the long dirty-blonde haired rugged-looking man quickly retrieved the silencer-equipped pistol from his side, reached across the table and fired it at Easton's chest. The black-haired teenager didn't even flinch.

"Where'd the bullet go?" Pete hastily inquired.

"I stopped it from going through me," Easton replied. "Wouldn't want it ruining Mom's museum-like walls."

"But how…" Deanna was beside herself with perplexion.

"How did this happen? Why did it happen? How is it even possible? I can only answer when it happened, and it's been happening ever since Easton was little. I've visited him many times in the middle of the night, giving his soul gifts of the guardians, particularly the short-term ability to be immortal for the specific task to help rescue his cousin, Johnny. As for the rest of your questions? I am a high ranking angel, and even I don't know the answers. I just deal with fact, and the fact is that your son is special, and I was sent to give him a gift. And now my mission is to collect him so we can retrieve Johnny. Now let's go," Gabe said, pushing his chair back from the table.

There was another wave of silence that descended over the table. Family members shook their heads and blinked their eyes, but nothing changed. Lacey had mentally checked out of the whole situation, not wanting to believe what was clearly right in front of her eyes. Rick Engleheart hunched his back and lowered his body until the cold wooden table caught his forehead.

"So, my son has been kidnapped by a secret branch of government; Gabriel, the archangel is here to help; and my nephew is immortal for the purpose of helping save my son. Pete, Deanna, is this correct? Am I going crazy? This can't be happening. It just can't," Rick Engleheart spoke, with his head down and his eyes closed.

Even though Pete and Deanna were just as befuddled as their widower brother-in-law, they tried to comfort their despondent family member. For the next five minutes, the three of them spoke to each other while the other three misfits in the room remained quiet. After hard convincing from Deanna, who was one of the wisest and most spiritual people Rick Engleheart knew, he decided to trust the situation and go with his gut. It was his only hope. Deanna believed in faith, and there was something about Gabe that made her trust him, unlike anything she had ever felt before. Successfully, she instilled a little of that hope in her brother-in-law, one of the countless good deeds she carried out on a daily basis.

"Now we're all on board," Gabe announced, "Right, Sleepyhead?"

Lacey had been staring for the better part of two minutes, her flawless soft skin carrying no emotion whatsoever. Finally she spoke up. "Why do I have to come?" she asked. "I mean, I'm not immortal. I'm not an angel. I like Johnny a lot, but this seems like it's going to get real dangerous, and I'm just a normal human. I don't want to die. If that is what I'm signing up for, then I'm sorry. It's just too much."

Lacey had never been shown much love in her life. Sure, before her mom had died. But since then, no one - not her so-called fair-weather friends, not her teachers, not her family, not even her own father had showed her any sort of love. When her life collided with Johnny's a few months prior, it was a new sense of care that stirred a fire inside of her. But she had not seen him or heard his voice in days. So when Gabe's eyes met hers, Lacey's soul melted. It was not a romantic feeling or any sort of lustful sensation. Simple and untouched love. It was like nothing she had ever felt before in her life. She felt like crying, but stopped herself before her throat tightened and raw emotion passed the point of no return.

"Lacey, you matter so much more than you surmise," Gabe said, with a soft tenderness in his voice that could evoke emotion from even the most heartless of humans.

"You're just lucky that I don't have a life and that I have time to do this," Lacey replied, with a half smile.

"We all are," Gabe replied. "We have three days. That is all. Rick, Easton, Lacey, and I will leave shortly. Oh, we need to borrow your minivan, if that's all right," he said, more of a command than a question.

Deanna and Pete nodded like they were in a trance.

"All right then. Everybody ready to go?" Gabe asked, with a semblance of excitement.

After answering more questions calmly and politely, Gabe started to become slightly impatient. He had been sent on a mission, and even he was unaware of some of its parameters - and the information he did know, he had not planned on sharing until well into the thirty-hour trip. Deanna hugged her son, Easton, goodbye while giving him a few looks of confused astonishment, as did Pete. They squeezed him tightly and told him good luck. Deanna made Gabe promise her son would return safe and sound, which he did. Rick Engleheart hugged his in-laws, Lacey said goodbye, as did Gabe, and they were off. Gabe climbed up into the forest-green minivan's driver seat. Rick Engleheart claimed the front passenger seat, even though Lacey proclaimed, "Shotgun!" as the group walked off the cobblestone front porch. She instead frustratingly slid open the side door, climbed into the potpourri smelling van, and gracefully flopped onto the light gray seat directly behind Rick Engleheart. Easton replicated her movement on the opposite side. Even though the van afforded room for three seats across the middle row, Deanna had had Pete remove the center seat some time ago, which made the middle-row passengers feel as if they were on an airplane.

Four o'clock in the morning on a warm summer's night consumed every aspect of the terrain and atmosphere. In the distance, Lacey could see the New York City skyline. She let out a sigh, wishing that at some point in her life, she'd grace its boisterous urban beauty. There was something strange about viewing the city skyline at a distance, especially soon before dawn. The tops of buildings stretched tall toward the skies like blades of grass, each a different size and shape towering over the pebbles and dirt at their bases. As the concrete towers of midtown Manhattan rose from the ground, resolute, then dipped down as the bedrock was unable to support the skyscrapers' density, the superstructures downtown ascended into the heavens with high hopes and big dreams. The Freedom Tower climbed the atmosphere like a beanstalk. It was truly a breathtaking sight exhibiting the achievement of man. Photographs did not do it justice, not even close. A smile commandeered Lacey's face the longer she took in the unprecedented view.

Almost ten minutes had passed, and no one had said anything. Rick Engleheart, Lacey, and Easton were deep in thought. They wrestled with ideas in their heads until finally surrendering to the fact that there is a lot going on behind the scenes and like it or not, they were caught up in the middle of it, and it was big, real big.

"Mr. Engleheart?" Lacey asked, breaking the silence she could no longer stand.

"Just call me Rick, hunny."

"Do you really believe all of this?" she asked, apathetically ignoring the van's other two passengers.

Moments passed before Rick Engleheart replied. The truth was he didn't know what to believe anymore. He pondered, sighed, and then answered.

"Lacey, I don't know. I guess I can give you a full report on my beliefs when my son is rescued."

That was good enough for Lacey. She nodded in agreement as she nonverbally signed on with Rick Engleheart's line of thinking, adopting it as her own as she did. Much thought was given to the situation by everybody in the van, but no one spoke. It was as if they silently speculated on one matter for a few minutes, then immediately considered the next in the long line of questions. As time slowly inched by, the numerous inquiries began to fill up the van's empty space until question marks began bumping into capital letters, mostly Ws. At first, they would freely float about the van until finally finding a place to rest, but the more that time relentlessly pressed on, the less space newborn questions had to settle. Eventually, as soon as they were born, the queries were forced to remain right where they had popped into existence, above passengers' heads, for there was no room any place else. The roads were eerily empty, but if anyone had shot a look at the interior of the minivan, they would not be able to see anything inside except a dark, dense nebula of countless letters and question marks.

"What exactly is our plan here, Gabe?" Rick Engleheart asked, opening the window, letting the clusters escape. "I mean there are four of us - half of whom are umm...gifted, the other half only normally human," he said, looking over his shoulder to the back seat.

"I can't tell you the exact plan yet, but there will be others. Many others. We will meet up with them along the way, and they will follow us there. We will get your son back, Rick. I promise. He has quite the destiny to fulfill."

Easton sat silently, as if preparing for battle. He gave a serious nod.

"When are we going to get there?" Lacey asked, mimicking an annoying child on a road trip.

"Sunrise on Wednesday morning," Gabe replied, without thinking. "We must. Three days is all we have. Three days."

"Three days until what?" Rick Engleheart loudly asked, frustrated with Gabe's vagueness and ambiguity.

"Until the beginning of the end."

CHAPTER 4

Sunday, 5:12 am

"The time to talk is now," he said, with a glimmer of pleasure in his eyes. It had been over five hours since Victor last heard a sound emanate from Johnny's mouth. The truth was that Victor and many other of the various high ranking authority figures in the underground inverted super silo beneath Wyoming's barren wasteland already knew at least some information. However, they did not know all of it. And Johnny, after being kidnapped from his therapy session, drugged, and brought to the "real Area 51" was not about to comply so easily.

"Listen to me, boy," Victor continued. "It has already begun. There is nothing you or anyone else can do about it. Soon, we will have the ability to influence thought processes across the globe. It will make for a better, more sustainable future for the human race. Now," he said, pausing to allow his capture to think. "Don't you want that?"

Johnny stood, staring off through the ivory walls, allowing Victor's reasoning to go in one ear and out through the other. Johnny was intelligent for an eighteen-year old. In fact, his English teacher had told him that he was well beyond his years in wisdom and in thought. And he knew and believed that not one person, or organization, or any entity for that matter, should have the power to control other people's minds. Even with good intentions, it spelled disaster. So when Victor attempted logic and existential reasoning with him, Johnny simply stared and even though he didn't mean to, a smile may have crept onto his face. It had been over twelve hours since Johnny had seen the light of day, and even though he was being held captive, he started to accept his situation. Maybe when one is completely hopeless, there is a dormant pool of latent optimism that surfaces, he thought. When there is no light at the end of the tunnel, a man can learn to become his own light, to make a life among the darkness - to adjust, to adapt. And that was what Johnny was naturally learning to do - on the fly, like he always did. He was thankful that Victor and his cohorts finally removed him from the upright cold-to-the-touch metal apparatus he had been bound to for the first few hours of his stay. Johnny had been moved to his own living quarters, and he knew one thing was for sure. They were going to keep him alive - at least for now. His room was simple - a 10 x

16 bedroom could not fit much, after all. The walls, ceiling, floor, and furniture were all a spotless shade of white, like nothing Johnny had ever seen before. It almost seemed as if the material was self-cleansing in a way. A twin-size bed, a small nightstand, and a miniature dresser consumed most of the humble room's space. Johnny was a prisoner, but at least he wasn't in the trunk of a car, drugged, or rigged up to a Hannibal Lector-esque apparatus. He was told he could not leave his room unless supervised. Food and water were brought to him when desired, and when he wasn't being interrogated, there was nothing else to do but sleep. So when Victor walked away frustrated and in doing so slammed the metal door, the sound of which would make an unsuspecting person jump, Johnny unaffectedly laid back down with his arms crossed behind his head.

To say the least, Johnny's life had been tumultuous during the past few months. Fainting at the baseball game; the strange visit by "extra-dimensionals" in the hospital; his mom dying tragically and unexpectedly; Lacey coming into his life and everything the two of them encountered together; getting kidnapped from his therapy session, being brought deep underground to discover that everything that he ever thought he knew was wrong and a secret branch of government had been pulling the strings on the world stage for decades - yes, tumultuous was an understatement.

He had been told multiple times that his father was en route to Wyoming, but somewhere in the back of Johnny's mind, doubt had begun to creep in, multiply, and grow as the hours passed. The more he thought about it, the less he cared, which was a strange and foreign mindset for the eighteen year-old. For some reason, he had been chosen to be the subject of a pilot study to test a type of new technology on the human brain. So far so good. But that is relative, he thought. What is good for the people down here is bad for the rest of America as well as the rest of the world. Johnny shrugged his shoulders. He was still adapting to the darkness. A head shake and slow blink later, he was one step closer to not caring about the quality of his life anymore. He was trapped, and there was nothing he could do about it. But he'd be damned if he gave in and helped the people that did this to him. No, that was not going to happen. A question that continued to burn like an orange ember in the back of his mind was one that perplexed him the most. Why was *he* chosen? And that sparked another glowing question. What did they want from him now? Johnny pondered on addressing these thoughts with Victor, but did not want to seem weak. So, he let them enkindle in his mind, hoping that at some point the questions would simply burn out.

Overall, Johnny was surprised by his own rigidity given the situation. His mom had always told him that he had an innate inner strength. His level headedness, his tough hard-to-crack aura - maybe she was right. They were keeping him together, certainly protecting him in the game. There was something that his captors and all of the people secretly working and living here deep underground wanted from him. Johnny had not the slightest clue as to what it was, but that did not matter. In fact, it probably helped his cause, he thought. Whatever information they wanted, they definitely had means of forcing it out of him - these were very powerful people working for an extremely authoritative organization and Johnny was just an eighteen year-old kid. Maybe his ignorance was for the better.

After comfortably lying on the soft cumulus cloud called a bed for too many minutes for the average person to not tire, Johnny's eyes became heavy. Maybe it was the lack of real rest, but something about lying down on what felt like the most comfortable bed Johnny could ever imagine put him to sleep rather rapidly. The bed consumed him as he turned over on his right side - the upper half of his right arm behind the puffy and distended down pillow, his left arm clutching the front, almost hugging it as if it were his friend. It felt so good to close his eyes. Pleasurable. Sheer and utter pleasure. He let out a comfortable sigh.

***

Sunday, 9:37 am

They were halfway through Pennsylvania, and thankfully, things had become less awkward as time pressed on. The group had become more talkative and the ceiling of maladroitness, which had been caving in since the trip began, was raised up high above the passengers' heads, creating a new world of breathing room in their atmosphere. Gabe had been less strange, much to the delight of Lacey; Easton acted like a normal eighteen year-old; and even Rick Engleheart slowly began to break out of his hardened and embittered exterior. Lacey, loud and brash per usual, kept inside the confines of her extremely large comfort zone - cussing, poking fun at the other three members in the carpool as well as at herself, controlling each and every situation. Naturally and with finesse, Lacey gradually began to appoint herself the group's leader. She had a way about her. Men simply seemed to listen to her and do what she wanted. However, it was on an unconscious level rather than on a bossy, commanding one. She felt in control of everyone, everyone except Gabe. But he wasn't human - or so he claimed. Many times Lacey would be speaking and Gabe would interrupt - a big no-no for anybody; however, Lacey let it happen without wrangle. Just as Lacey assumed natural jurisdiction of everyone within earshot of her acid tongue, Gabe instinctively surmised natural regimentation over her. As visible as the clear blue sky, that was just the way things were.

Gabe was in the middle of a fun-loving sports argument with Rick Engleheart and Easton about the New York Mets, a quarrel Lacey quickly checked out of. Just when he was about to arrive at the zenith of his point, Gabe abruptly stopped speaking. The unexpected silence stood out. Even Lacey took note.

"Uhhh Gabe? Aren't you going to finish your point about that thing that no one cares about?" she asked, with her head down as she played a game on her phone.

Gabe kept driving, but his focus was somewhere else. After forty more seconds of silence, he finally spoke, much to the relief of the other three in the van.

"I have to go somewhere," he said, bluntly. "Rick, take over driving for a bit."

Gabe pulled the van across the highway's rumble strip and over to the right shoulder. Rick Engleheart unbuckled his seatbelt in prepared compliance.

"Why? What's going on? What do you mean? You're leaving us?" Lacey asked, angrily.

"You'll see," Gabe replied, frustrated. "It's Johnny. I have to visit him."

CHAPTER 5

The amount of comfort enveloping Johnny was unlike anything he had ever felt before. And, given his immensely unusual and nearly hopeless situation, he remembered feeling puzzled by the armistice of his emotions. Bewilderment was the last, faint stream of consciousness he recalled before trailing off into stark nothingness - before unseen, unconscious thoughts usurped his mind.

As Rick Engleheart took over the helm, Gabe laid down across the bench seat in the back of the van. He preferred to complete his arduous task in a different, more peaceful setting; however, time was of the essence and they had to keep the wheels spinning over the pavement. The atmosphere inside the van was silent and mysterious, almost supernaturally so. Easton sat still, facing toward the front, directly behind Rick Engleheart - the van's new driver. Lacey, who was fascinated in a somewhat skeptical sense, was facing the back of the van with her arms crossed on top of her seat as she looked down with analytical eyes to watch Gabe. His eyes were tranquilly closed, but Lacey could tell that he was concentrating hard. She shook her head with perplexity, not knowing what exactly was happening, but also not wanting to miss a millisecond of it.

***

Johnny left the towering hotel skyscraper with frustration. He was ostracized. All for not wanting to see a movie where you take a pill beforehand to enhance your viewing experience. The rest of his family complied, but his refusal meant isolation. He could care less. Apathy soon took over as he sat calmly on the stone edge of a fancy fountain. He noticed a woman walking briskly toward him from a distance of about a hundred feet. He could barely make out the expression on her face, but she was clearly looking directly at him, and closing in fast. Johnny looked down, noticing the beautiful cracks in the surface of the alabaster cement. Three seconds had gone by. He felt a presence, looked up, and saw the woman patiently standing over him - her shadow long and lanky in the late afternoon light.

"Take this bag. Take it to the fifteenth floor," the old blonde woman said, innocently but directly.

With nothing else to do for two hours, Johnny agreed, not knowing or even caring what was inside. His own cooperation surprised him. Walking past the endlessly long transparent check-in desk and hanging a right down the next hallway, Johnny found the elevator bank and since the strangely attractive woman did not specify on which one to take on his ascent, Johnny patiently waited for the next one available, which was the elevator directly behind him. The absence of life in the perpetually busy hotel had no effect on him. Quite the contrary. He delighted in the quiet calmness surrounding him. Solitude and loneliness are two conditions not to be confused, after all. As the doors smoothly closed, Johnny peered into the oversized black shopping bag for the first time. He felt the elevator begin to lift off the ground. Johnny noticed a normal size shoe box to one side of the thick plastic bag and other smaller boxes stacked to the other side. Four of them. 12, 13, 14. The numbers flashed red, violet red on every wall in the perfectly square room. 15. The doors remained closed. Johnny's head jerked back with confusion. Seven seconds passed, then he finally heard the bell signalling that he had arrived at the desired destination, the fifteenth floor. However, the doors he entered through held still while the back wall of the elevator split open. Turning around in consternation and curiosity, Johnny took one step but then abruptly stopped every muscle in his body - for three feet away, a 180-foot sheer drop awaited him. He stumbled backwards, the bag's long plastic straps still entangled around his right hand, the closed doors behind him graciously catching his floundering panic. He and heights did not get along. As he gathered himself between short, heavy breaths, Johnny noticed that a distinct yellow light was emanating from the diminutive crack between the two still-closed elevator doors. Something inside Johnny was telling him to open the bag, so he listened to his instincts and took out the perfectly assembled boxes. They were a pristine white in color, carrying an innocence that made Johnny hesitant to handle them. The opposite wall still remained wide open and the wind that swirled around the confines of the small open room flew in over and over again to deliver a chill dividing Johnny's bones from his head to his toes. For just three feet away, a death-delivering drop down to the hotel's lobby was staring at his back and would not look away.

Soon, the smallest box began to shudder on the cold tile floor. It started slowly at first, but then its vibrations grew stronger and stronger with every second. Johnny listened to his instincts once again and picked it up, and simultaneously, the trembling box subsided its movement. Johnny opened the little one inch by one inch box and found a miniscule black hand tool. It was so small that it could be carried by an ant. Still in tune with his intuition, Johnny used the gizmo to pry open the elevator doors. It was difficult at first - with the object being so small - but with careful precision, the eighteen year-old slowly created enough space to walk through with the puny, but extremely dense object. After stopping with a satisfied grunt, Johnny kept the doors opened with his hands and kicked the boxes through - first the four small ones and then the larger breadbox-size square. Tumbling and rolling to find random spots on the floor, they came to an eventual halt as Johnny walked through, the doors quickly closing shut behind him. As he wiped some sweat off of his brow, he took in the sight of a place that took his breath away.

***

Rick Engleheart had the van's cruise control set at 73 miles per hour on Interstate 80 as the group of four pushed through Pennsylvania. Lacey was still curiously fixed on Gabe's peaceful body lying across the back seat. Silence consumed the car like an invisible fog. It was unearthly to say the least. Rick Engleheart could not stand it anymore.

"Hey Easton," he said, looking in the rear view mirror to meet his nephew's eyes. "If the government is so powerful and trying to take away the freedom of thought and everything, why can't they locate us and just kill us? Like an ambush, you know? We were shot at on the way to your house, but Gabe put a stop to that. I know that you two are immortal, but Lacey and I could easily be killed. And it wouldn't be all that difficult either."

Easton refrained from answering for a few seconds. The onlooker would naturally assume that the temporarily gifted eighteen year-old was pausing to think. However, he was simply making sure that his uncle was done speaking.

"Somehow, I think we're protected," Easton finally replied. "Like flying under the radar or something like that. Maybe even invisible."

"You gotta be kidding me," Lacey said aloud, joining the

conversation but still focusing on Gabe's deathly still body. "Invisible. Yeah, that's happening," she asserted, sarcastically.

"Lacey, it's possible. If the past day has taught us anything, you gotta believe that it's at least possible," Rick Engleheart reasoned.

"He's got a point," Easton said, turning his head over his right shoulder to address Lacey. "I mean if they wanted to stop us, they could. So, we're either part of the conspiracy and they want us to show up for God knows what reason or they are trying desperately to stop us, but are unable to find us."

"I wouldn't be surprised either way," Rick Engleheart announced.

"Maybe we'll ask weirdo when he wakes up," Lacey said.

***

Johnny's feet stopped moving as his eyes took in a sight they had never had the privilege to see before. Endless levels of living quarters. As far as the eye could see and in every direction. Johnny's hand found its way to his chest as his mouth tried to drop to the floor. If comfort and peace could be manufactured, they would look exactly like what was in front of his face. Merely by looking at his surroundings, Johnny's mind discovered pure and utter peace.

"What is this place?" he asked aloud.

Beautifully thick carpet enveloped every level like foliage in the forest. Each level bore a different color carpet - colors which Johnny never even knew existed. It was like he had been transported to a different dimension, and soon he started to think that it wasn't like he had been - he legitimately was in an ethereal habitat. The furniture, the walls, the decor - they breathed life. Johnny couldn't tell for sure, but he swore that he saw them swaying in an invisible breeze of tranquility touching the thick but soft rays of light that shone through every room. As Johnny stood still, mesmerized by this strange place containing countless livable level lofts of pure contentment, the sight of a person sitting just ten feet to his right startled him. There was a man sitting on a couch watching television, facing away from Johnny.

***

Lacey thought she heard a faint humming sound coming from

Gabe. She leaned in closer, lifting her knees off of the seat. Her face scowled. She didn't know what it was, but it was strange - that was for sure. She accepted it with a quick raise of her eyebrows. Peculiarity was par for the course with Gabe. Suddenly and without warning, Gabe's body became no longer undisturbed. He became tense and rigid, almost wooden-looking.

"Uhh, guys?" Lacey spoke to call attention to what was eerily happening.

Then, Gabe slowly began to levitate off of the soft gray back bench seat. Lacey's eyes widened.

"What!" she exclaimed, in a whisper. Gradually, she mysteriously began to believe. Maybe he was who he said he was after all. Almost as an uncanny response to her thought process, a smile crept across Gabe's face, which made Lacey let out a short, closed-mouth sigh as she squinted her big brown eyes. Silently, she thought to herself, "Well played."

**

Johnny only saw the back the man's head. He had brown hair, and was glued to the television because when Johnny called out, the man didn't even flinch. After one more unsuccessful try, Johnny decided to approach the man on the couch. Before he got halfway there, the man turned and Johnny stopped in amazement. It was him. He was looking at himself - or some version himself in another world. But every feature - the face, the hair, the eyes, the stature - everything was exactly the same. Before Johnny began processing the complexities surrounding the unexplored territory he found himself in, he heard a noise in the level above. Footsteps. He quickly glanced to his left at the two-tiered emerald carpeted staircase. Someone was walking down it. Only the person's shoes could be seen at first, next their legs, then their waist and torso - it was another man - and finally his face. Johnny's chin hit the floor with a bang. He was looking at himself again. His eyes went back and forth between the two people who were motionlessly staring back at him. They were in different clothes, but all three of them were clearly the same person.

All at once, a single idea began to grow in Johnny's mind, and not just in his own - he could sense the thought processes of the other two versions of himself grow as well. Before long, the idea grew from a strange hypothesis to a theory, and eventually arrived at its final destination of a perfect exactitude. The whole thought development from start to finish lasted three seconds. The end understanding caused goosebumps to form on the back of Johnny's neck to his toes like mountains rising out of the sea. The id, ego, and superego existed in this place and all had become personified. And for the first time, all three of them were working together. Next, Johnny's hands moved out in front of his body, his palms facing him as his fingers formed a loose fist. The other two in the room mimicked his motions like a mirror. Then, all thirty fingers stretched up toward the sky simultaneously. Fingertips turned a beautiful and deep variety of vibrant neon lights and became elongated, reaching all the way to the dimpled white ceiling so Johnny and his counterparts could run their now-illuminated and extended digits along the countless dimples like they were reading braille. Their fingers retreated, and then prolonged again. This was repeated multiple times as Johnny found a new delight. Each time it was repeated, a sweet sound of freedom rang through his ears, but he swore it could be heard for miles and miles.

"Johnny," a voice louder than the freedom song whispered. "Johnny."

All three versions stopped looking at their neon lights in awe, simultaneously.

"Johnny," the voice whispered again, as if it were preparing to give a secret message.

"Who's there?" the confused and fearful teenager asked.

As an answer to his anxious question, a being suddenly appeared in the unusual room, standing equidistantly between the three versions of Johnny. The two original dwellers stood still, stoically - they were clearly waiting for it to show up. Johnny, however, trembled in wonderment. The being was facing him, so Johnny could see every last bit of the exquisite creation. He was tall - abnormally so. He wore flowing white pants that beautifully blew in the same invisible breeze as every other inanimate object in the bizarre place. He had no shirt, and his body was extremely muscular - from his abdominals to his chest, from his biceps to his upper traps, to his triceps - he had muscles stronger than Johnny had ever seen. There was something different about the way they protruded from his skin, which was eerily a translucent white, almost transparent. It certainly wasn't human. But the distinct muscular build and skin type are not what gave it away. It had wings. Majestic, white wings. Possibly each twelve feet when fully stretched out, the wingspan was enormous. The color of the wings was a white that was so pure, Johnny thought he should bow before it. A thousand times whiter than any flawless snowfall. Human eyes were not meant to see such a sight. It was nearly blinding. The being did have traces of a human design to it though. His face looked human, besides the strange skin tone, and his hair, although ridiculously long, was dirty blonde in color. He had a mouth, a nose, ears, and eyes. With an elegant smile that brought peace to Johnny's soul, it was the most magnificent thing he had ever seen. It exuded radiance. Pure and untouched brilliance.

"Are...are you an angel?" Johnny asked, with hesitation.

"Some people call us that," the being replied. His voice was calming, giving Johnny's heavy heart rest with every word.

"What is going on? What is this place? Am I dreaming?" Johnny asked, looking forward to hearing the angel's voice and feeling its effects again.

"You are in a dream. This is paradise, well, not thee paradise, but pretty close to it. I have been sent here to give you a message. I am Gabriel, the archangel." Every word re-energized the teenager's beaten down and dragged-through-the-mud soul. "Stay strong. You are not lost. You are not forgotten. You are exactly where you are supposed to be. Look within yourself, and find the means by which to discover your deliverance. What you need is already in hand. Awaken your mind and find your soul. We will be coming for you. You will be rescued. And your enemies will be defeated. What they dread will overtake them, and what you desire will be granted to you. Take comfort in knowing that the fear of the wicked is really all they can be sure of receiving. We will come like wildfire. Stay strong. We are on our way."

"I...I don't understand," Johnny stuttered. "What's going on?"

"This is how humans were meant to live. In harmony with themselves and with others. Death entered the world a long time ago, however. And things have come to a head. Now you are caught up in a monumental fight. A fight that will decide the fate of everyone. Do you believe in other worlds?" Gabriel asked.

"You mean like extraterrestrial?"

"More like extra-dimensional," he replied.

And just as quickly as he came, he was gone. Vanished from the room. Soon Johnny realized the room was gone too. The levels, the magnificence of it all, the chills that ran up and down Johnny's spine. Everything was gone. He opened his eyes even though it was the last thing he wanted to do. He let out a sigh. Back in the depths. Something was different though. The walls were still the same ivory color - dull and boring compared to the unearthly shade of white his eyes had recently grown accustomed to in his dream. But he was looking at the room from a different vantage point. As Johnny looked around in confusion, he noticed that his bed had been moved to the other side of the room. The small nightstand that was normally adjacent to the bed remained untouched, as did the dresser. Only the bed had moved. Johnny scratched his head. He did not know how long he had been asleep for, but it was the most rested he had ever felt in his life. How had his bed moved? Was it something to do with the dream? *Was* that a dream? Confusion clouded Johnny's mind like a smoke bomb.

Parts of the dream felt so real. Had an angel really visited him? Because it was in a dream, in his head, does that make it less real? The angel, Gabriel seemed eerily familiar. And what he said also sounded familiar.

"More like extra-dimensionals."

That's it! Johnny's mind began to race. Those are the exact words that Victor used when Johnny had first been taken to this underground testing facility, part of the inverted super silo chain. The amplitude of the situation began to scare the eighteen year-old. How had he become a vital part to his? The angel in the dream told him he was exactly where he was supposed to be. What did that mean? The underground government's diabolical plan was being carried out with alien technology for sure, but were there good extra-dimensionals and bad extra-dimensionals. It's possible, Johnny supposed.

He concentrated, trying hard to remember everything the angel had said. It was quite easy to recall. He scrambled to the nightstand across the room and opened the drawer. A smile commandeered his face. He knew for a fact that a pencil and a piece of paper were not in there before he had fallen asleep. He'd looked. They sure were there now though. Johnny hastily began writing everything down - from beginning to end. Every minute detail of the dream. He flipped over the paper and pencilled every word Gabriel had said, verbatim. After he was finished, he folded the worn out piece of looseleaf four times and carefully placed it in his pocket, telling himself that it would be his mission to read and memorize every word, every emotion, and every detail. Just as he had heard and felt a freedom song in his dream, the memorization of what it was in its entirety would become a new freedom song in the real world - the instauration of his mind and his spirit. Johnny was energized with anticipation. And for the first time since his arrival, Gabriel's words rang true. He was exactly where he was supposed to be.

CHAPTER 6

Gabe awoke with a deep inhale, startling Lacey. She shot him a look of confusion, which he returned with the same smile he showed her when she started to believe.

"Creep," Lacey joked, with a half smile of her own.

"Listen, Sleepyhead," Gabe replied. "I know you have your doubts. That's understandable. All I am asking is that you give it a chance. Give faith a chance. For once in your life, trust what you don't see. Amazing things will happen."

Lacey looked down at Gabe, who was still lying on his back across the minivan's back bench seat. "Just because I'm starting to believe, don't get all mushy on me. It'll make me puke," she responded.

The other two passengers, caught up in an argument about the new virtual strike zone masks umpires wear in the Major Leagues, did not even notice Gabe was awake.

"Sports?" Gabe asked Lacey.

She answered with a sarcastic eye roll. Gabe laughed through his nose and shook his head. He cleared his throat. The two fanatics were still stuck in their trivial quarrel. Somewhere between, "He sees the true strike zone through his virtual mask!" and "He could easily give borderline calls to one team and not the other. We should see what he sees!", Lacey spoke up.

"Hey ding-bats, Gabe is awake and he has news. You done arguing about nonsense?"

With Lacey's words, silence struck the vehicle like lightning. Rick Engleheart had been discussing baseball to take his mind off of the difficult matter at hand, but now he could not delay or ignore it any longer.

"Are you alright to drive, Uncle Rick?" Easton asked.

There was a long pause. Finally, he replied. "Yes. This is good. I like this. I'm happy here. I'm focused."

Gabe spoke from the back seat loud enough for everyone in the minivan to hear. The mid-morning sun's rays that shone through the windows illuminated his face in an attractive yellow glow. What would make the normal human squint seemed to have the opposite effect on the strange being claiming to be an archangel, as his eyes widened in the light. After explaining what he told the eighteen year-old captive in his dream, Gabe went on to reassure the group that Johnny was safe for the time being. After a plethora of questions, much of what the angel was saying began to sound redundant. He could only tell them so much to the extent they would understand, and some of what they were inquiring about he did not have the answers for.

"I plan on visiting him at least once more before we get there, so I will have more answers for you after that." Gabe's tone implied that the torrid question and answer session was over with. "Rick, let me take over the wheel until the next time I visit Johnny."

Rick Engleheart obeyed Gabe's wishes and pulled the minivan over to the right shoulder at the foot of the Ohio border. The sun was not yet at its zenith, and the day's high temperature was still a little less than six hours away, but it was incredibly warm outside. Two car doors were opened for merely seconds, but Earth's heat rushed in and smacked Lacey in the face. She scowled. It was the type of heat that made you instantly sweat.

"Thank God for air conditioning," she said, nudging Easton. "If air conditioning wasn't invented, I would have stayed home."

Easton let out a chuckle as Gabe clicked the left hand turn signal downward after Rick Engleheart jumped into the passenger seat and shut the door.

"So I'm curious," Lacey said, turning toward Easton. "How come you seem so calm, cool, and collected with all of this? It's strange and the fact that you're cool with it makes it even stranger."

"Well, when I was a kid, weird things started to happen to me. Like I started to control my dreams in a mysterious kind of unconscious way. Like if I woke up from a dream and I wanted to go back into it, I could. And vice versa. If I was having a bad dream, I could wake myself out of it, fall back asleep, and not worry about drifting off into the nightmare again. In the dreams, I felt like I could consciously control my actions, but it was all being done on an unconscious level. Rarely are humans in control of their unconscious mind, but for some reason I was. Then, even stranger stuff started to happen. Like I would have a dream - a random one about nothing big - then whatever I dreamt of would occur the next day. For instance, if I had a dream about a character on a TV show, somehow at some point the next day, I would be watching television, and that character would do exactly what I dreamt of."

"Well that's not too weird. That sort of stuff has happened to me too," Lacey replied, skeptically.

Gabe let out a chuckle. Lacey ignored it.

"What seemed to happen on a random basis but for as long as I can remember, I started to get visited in my dreams. It was freaky. And at first, I thought it was aliens or something. It really freaked me out. I was scared to tell my parents or anyone for that matter. Then one night in a dream, I told what I thought was the alien that kept coming that I knew what he was and I wasn't afraid. I yelled it, like I was angry at it for haunting me. And then, a huge sense of calm came over me, and it showed me what it really was. An angel. It was Gabe. After that first revelation, I loved going to sleep because Gabe began to impart the gifts to me. It was like a drug. I would hate to wake up."

"What exactly did Gabe do? I mean, how did he give you the gift of immortality?"

"Temporary immortality," Gabe said, correcting Lacey. "The last thing the Creator would want would be immortal humans. Could you imagine?" he pondered, laughing and turning to his right, trying to elicit life from Rick Engleheart. Half a success, but Gabe accepted it with a smile and a nod.

"It's not like you think," Easton replied.

"You mean it's like in Mario when Toad feeds him a mushroom?" Lacey sarcastically joked, evoking a laugh from Easton.

"It's hard to explain. He mobilized something within me. Like it was always there, but I never even knew it existed."

"Sounds pretty simple. Gabe, why couldn't you just snap your fingers and give us these gifts?" Lacey asked.

"There's a lot that goes on in the ether of existence that you don't know, Sleepyhead. Heck, there's a lot that goes on that even I don't know. But trust me. Things will get explained in due time."

"We're all kind of going on faith here, hunny," Rick Engleheart expressed.

Lacey disappointingly accepted what was being presented to her with a long and deep sigh. "I'm doing my best," she said.

Off in the distance, a large thunderstorm was brewing in the sky. And the road seemed to be going right through it. It was interesting to feel the sun shining and to see the rain coming. Two opposite weather patterns happening at the same time and in the same place. It was eerie. With the sun behind the foursome, pushing the minivan along, their immediate atmosphere became darker and darker with every second. The light green grass that enveloped the meadows met their dark green cousins in the towering pine trees. Their tops spiked toward the dark bluish gray flanking line of the growing supercell system. Heavy rain could be seen from miles away. Lightning began to flash periodically from the anvil down through the shaded gray cumulonimbus clouds. Gabe had increased the van's cruise control four miles per hour, but they were still at enough of a distance to see the whole storm system - even the overshooting top as it peaked its head through the top of the anvil. The atmospheric superstructure seemed to grow in size as they sped toward it - probably perception, possibly not.

"A storm is brewing," Gabe slowly and seriously announced.

"You think it's going to cut into our time at all?" Rick Engleheart asked, analytically.

Gabe responded with a stern look of deep thought, keeping his eyes fixed on the road and the threatening storm ahead. The clouds had converted to a petrified pale color, as if they too were dreading what was about to come. "I'm guessing that might be the least of our problems."

"What are you talking about? It's just a thunderstorm. I don't think northern Ohio gets many really bad tornadoes or anything like that," Lacey said.

"Powerful thunderstorms don't usually happen this early in the day," Easton stated quietly, as he looked out his window.

Gabe was glaring at the supercell's shelf cloud as if he was expecting to see something that only showed itself for a second and then disappeared forever. What went unnoticed as the group took in the sight of the rapidly developing storm was that the highway fell abnormally quiet for a weekend's last day. I-80 was usually bustling with cars; however, in this moment, whether eastbound or westbound, the forest green minivan was the only vehicle for miles and miles.

***

It had been hours since Johnny had woken up from his strange dream - a vision as he decided to aptly call it. The events occurring over the past few days opened up that tiny space in the back of the mind that says 'I want to believe', and now Johnny was almost all in.

He was ready for whatever came his way. And after what the angel had revealed to him, he was looking forward to it. However, not knowing exactly what *it* was made him ponder. Johnny retrieved the folded up piece of looseleaf from his right pocket once more. The strokes of hand writing seen on the side opposite his eyes seemed more neat and artistic - like the Declaration of Independence. The letters were slanted differently and possessed a contrasting spacing of what Johnny was used to seeing in his hand strokes. In turning it over however, the writing took on its normal non-mirrored form. Reading it for the fifth time in the last hour, Johnny had nearly memorized every word. A smile slowly crept across his face, starting back by his left ear and zigzagging down his cheek to the outer edge of his lips, then across to the other side returning to his right ear. His face completed this every time he neared the end of his description - every time he read Gabriel's words. Stopping his tears from falling before it was too late, Johnny nodded and folded the piece of paper back up and returned it to its resting place in his deep right pants pocket.

A mere two seconds later, Victor stormed in the room. Out of instinct, he turned toward to his right, expecting the bed to be there. After a couple embarrassing double takes, which Johnny took delight in, Victor shot a look of angry confusion across the room.

"Why?" he asked, as if he wanted the answer to be as short as the question. "It doesn't matter," he remarked, disallowing Johnny to answer and shaking his head to forget about it. "So my boy, since you are down here and the world is up there..." Victor clarified with his index finger, in case his captive forgot the basics of two dimensional direction. "...I can share this with you. But I care to know something first. What do you know about Lacey Hassle?"

***

Gabe had slowed the car down six miles per hour by pushing the minus sign on the cruise control panel three times. He clearly was anticipating something - something that the rest of the passengers were not. Rain began to fall. Loud and large drops struck the van's metallic shell with slaps and spanks. They completed their direct hits slowly at first - the front line pawns. But the rest of the rain was close behind, and soon the van was driving straight through an all-out downpour. The windshield wipers mechanically sprinted through their fastest setting so Gabe could see the road every two seconds.

"Lacey. Get down," Gabe commanded.

"What?" she asked, over the sound of the heavy rapidly falling rain.

"Get under the seat!" he screamed, in a panic.

But it was too late. A cloudy gray mist swiftly and suddenly appeared right where she was sitting and engulfed her. The sound of its arrival was unlike anything Easton or Rick Engleheart had heard before. It resembled a substantial gust of wind, but was extremely abrupt and awfully eerie. Less than two seconds after the ugly gray smoke appeared it was gone, and Lacey as well. It left behind a residue of its vaporous material for a couple of seconds, but that dissipated into the air along with Lacey.

"No!!" Gabe yelled at the top his lungs, which was a lot louder than any human had the capacity to scream. He stepped on the gas until the pedal hit the floor as the van raced further into the storm.

CHAPTER 7

Johnny was being forcibly carried through the transparent tube-like hallways. Apparently Victor did not like his answer when asked about Lacey Hassle. "I know everything about her, and you will never find out a single word," was not good enough for "The Doc," as people working in this particular inverted super silo called him.

Two men, whom Johnny had never seen before, were at each of his sides pulling him as his feet haphazardly hit the thick plastic-like floor. Victor led the way down the intricate and twisting labyrinth as if he had walked this exact path countless times. He could probably do it with his eyes closed, Johnny thought. It seemed quite silly to Johnny that the men were carrying him the way in which they were. It was not as if he could find his way out of the meandering maze he found himself in. Even if he somehow managed to escape, he was still thousands of feet underground, and all that the surface contained was hundreds upon hundreds of miles of desolate land. The thought of men manhandling him entertained Johnny. Where was he going to go? He held in a laugh with a smile.

"Here. In here," Victor pointed to his right, notifying the men.

They tossed Johnny into the room, sending the eighteen year-old tumbling forward. On the surface, the room seemed like just another interrogation room; however, something told Johnny that it was much more sinister than that. Maybe it was the way that the solitary chair was tilted backwards or the fact that there was a tray with sharp metallic utensils on it. Johnny took a gulp of impending worry. He tried to remember what the angel told him. His next swallow was one filled with confidence. It was like taking a pill of poise, and now he felt ready for whatever Victor was going to do to him, taking comfort in the fact that he knew they weren't going to kill him. Victor had made a potential mistake when he told his captive that. Nonetheless, Johnny knew the next part of his life was not going to be a picnic.

***

"Where'd she go?" Rick Engleheart yelled, in a panic over the sound of the torrential rain.

"They took her. They freaking took her!" Gabe angrily

screamed, as he wrestled with the steering wheel.

"So what do we do now?" Easton asked. "Where are we going?"

"We have to get through this storm. If we don't get through in time, we'll lose her forever."

Both Rick Engleheart and Easton sat in silence, confused.

"It's like this," Gabe continued. "A portal has been opened. I thought the storm looked strange, and I was right. I just noticed it too late. So they took Lacey, and now we have to get to the other side of the storm before it ends or else she'll be gone for good."

"Wait a second," Rick Engleheart said, raising his hand. What portal? What's the storm have to do with a portal? And who took her?" he asked, beyond perplexion.

Gabe let out a sigh. "The storm is the portal."

"So every time there is a thunderstorm, it's a portal to another world?" Easton asked.

"No, not every time. But some of the time, this being the case in point. This time!" Gabe replied, getting frustrated. The two ignorant humans understood his irritation and responded with submitted silence, allowing him to continue. "If we don't get through the storm to the other side before it ends, the portal will close - never to open again. This particular storm is of the large variety, so it will take us a while, which gives me more time to save her, probably something they didn't think of."

"Can you explain who 'they' are?" Rick Engleheart asked.

"They are the fallen angels. Demons. You humans probably refer to them as aliens or extraterrestrials. They exist in a different dimension and they have taken Lacey for reasons I do not know and failed to prepare for," Gabe responded, with guilt.

"So if we don't get her back, then she'll be with them in that dimension forever?" Easton asked, trying to understand the ins and outs of this new logic.

"Unless the Creator steps in, yes. This might be a battle he wants us to fight on our own though. I don't have the time to think on it. When we get further, Rick, I'll need you to drive. I have to go and rescue her. For now though, take this," Gabe commanded, giving Rick Engleheart his gun. "Easton, there should be one in your bag. It's loaded."

"What are these for?" Rick Engleheart asked.

"My guess is that they're going to send out some troops to prevent us from getting to the other side of the storm. They'll be in human form, so if you shoot them, their bodies will die just like any human. Except, they'll be sent back to where they came from, returning to their true form. When extra-dimensionals are in human form and die, they can't return to this world. So think of them as humans. Kill them. Kill them all."

"But what about when you were shot on the way to Easton's house from the woods? Why didn't you die?" Rick Engleheart inquired.

"Because angels are stronger than demons. Much stronger. And besides, I am one of the most powerful angels created, so although I am an extra-dimensional, I cannot die and be sent back to my original dimension in my original form. Only I control where I go and what form I take. Listen, I would love to get into the metaphysics of all of this with you, but let's just focus on the task at hand, alright? They'll come in trucks and SUVs. Shoot on sight."

Lacey felt as if she was dreaming. Had she fallen asleep during the thunderstorm's roars? That seemed odd to her - she was a very light sleeper and one can only get so comfortable in a car. Confusion plagued her mind. Then, all of a sudden something stirred inside of her. It was as if she felt that she might burst into a million tiny beautiful pieces. It was a feeling like no other. She held her breath - not really knowing why; it was like she could not help it - until she couldn't hold it any longer. As soon as she let out a big, heavy exhale of air, she felt her feet lift off of the ground. Lacey's eyes widened at the view. It was eerie. She struggled with the invisible molecules surrounding her, and then realized why she was so frightened. It was pitch black. She thought that her eyes were closed, but she was wrong. Even the darkest nights she had experienced out in the woods on the dawn of a new moon or underground on a caving trip when her father suggested they turn off their flashlights just to see how dark it really was - these types of pitch blacknesses were nothing compared to what her eyes were desperately trying to adjust to in the strange place she found herself in. If a new, exponentially darker shade of black existed, this was it. This was not an earthly place - that was for sure. Not even close. She tried to scream for help, but no sound emanated from her mouth. She pinched herself to wake up. It didn't work. In fact, it hurt so much more than usual. It was like she was bitten by a viper or an asp. The stinging sensation crept from where she pinched herself on her left wrist up her arm and soon began to spread throughout her entire body. She hurt, but she couldn't cry. The exploding sensation she felt before was starting again. Lacey didn't know if it was because her body was trying to force out cries of pain or because of something else. But it was becoming more and more intense. She shut her eyes tightly and covered her ears. She swore she heard a noise with every heartbeat. A loud, deep horn sound. It too became louder and louder. Lacey tried to scream again, but just like before, her vocal cords failed her. The feeling that she was about to burst coupled with the deafeningly creepy horns that coincided with her every heartbeat made her want to die. Again she cried for help. Nothing. And then a voice spoke through the darkness.

"Lacey Hassle."

She took her hands off from the sides of her head. She was about to answer, but the raspy voice stopped her in her tracks.

"Don't try to speak. It's no use. Humans can't talk here. But how would you know that?" the voice let out a menacingly low laugh.

Gabe noticed two SUV's approaching in his rear view mirror. They were black and coming up fast. Gabe quickly commanded Rick Engleheart and Easton to shoot out their tires. Both miniature TAC 338s possessed military grade long range scopes. Before the SUVs showed their ugly faces, Gabe taught Rick Engleheart and Easton the basics.

"Easy enough," was their answer.

Easton pulled the minivan's side door open. The storm had cooled the air considerably. And the rain that came down in sheets slanted its way into the van, making cold direct hits on their skin. It was loud with the side door open. Between the intermittent shouts of thunder, the abounding downpour, and the roar of the van's tires on the cold wet ground, both Easton and Rick Engleheart had to yell to hear each other even though they were kneeling right beside one another. Gabe screamed that the guns packed quite the kick, but he doubted either of them heard him due to the roar of the elements.

"Bang!"

Rick Engleheart took the first shot, but missed the front SUV completely. Gabe watched from the rear view and side mirrors as he sped forward. The two SUVs were in the same lane three hundred feet back. The back one seemed to be hiding behind the front one. Gabe could not tell for sure, but they didn't seem to be gaining much ground.

"Get down!" he yelled as loud as he could.

Easton and his uncle ducked behind the seats. A bullet hit the back window, blowing it out completely.

"They must have silencers!" Gabe screamed. "Keep shooting. Shoot out their tires. If you can't after a few tries, shoot out their windshield and then shoot to kill."

***

"So you've gone out on a limb and now you're off on a cross-country adventure. Wow," the voice remarked, with sarcasm.

"What do you want with me?" Lacey thought, as she tried to use her voice, but to no avail.

"What do I want with you?" The voice was obviously reading her thoughts. "You're special, Lacey - beyond your wildest dreams. You didn't know this? I can't believe he hasn't told you yet. Makes sense. Do you know who you are?" the throaty voice said, before making creepy ticking sounds of disapproval with his tongue and the roof of his mouth.

***

After two more unsuccessful attempts each, Easton and Rick Engleheart began shooting at the leading SUV's windshield. Gabe sped forward with the van's wipers on their fastest setting. "They're starting to gain on us, hurry up!" he yelled.

"Crash!" Rick Engleheart's first attempt at the windshield was a direct hit and shattered the glass completely. They ducked down behind Easton's seat, awaiting return fire. Its location forced adrenaline up their midsections as a bullet ripped through the back bench seat and tore a hole into the seat they were using as a shield. Their eyes widened in fright.

"That was lucky!" Gabe yelled over his shoulder. "Easton, finish them off. If they hit you, you'll be fine. Rick, get up here and crouch down in front of the passenger seat. We can't afford to lose you."

Rick Engleheart quickly obeyed Gabe's commands while Easton provided some cover fire. The minivan sped forward, dodging debris that had been tossed into the road by the supercell's strong winds. Tree branches, power lines, and uprooted maples that used to line the side of the highway, even a half of an industrial wind turbine made up the oversized items on the long list of debris to evade.

"Easton, when you use the scope, aim three feet higher than your target," Gabe shouted, over an abrupt and heavy thunder crack.

Easton fumbled with the gun as he wiped the cold rain from the corners of his eyes. He tightened his grip on the gun's hand points as he took a few breaths, then swiftly aimed the gun toward the driver of the black SUV and fired, obeying Gabe's suggestion. The driver's face exploded, and almost instantaneously, the vehicle veered off to its left and began an end-over-end roll after sliding down the five foot embankment at nearly eighty miles-per-hour. Easton anticipated that the driver of the identical SUV trailing directly behind the one he just crashed would be ready to fire, so the eighteen year-old beat him to the punch.

"Bang!"

Even over the heavy rain, Rick Engleheart could hear the abrupt sound of one of the SUV's tires getting blown to bits. Gabe sped forward as the the SUV in pursuit began to fall behind. Even though they were most likely safe, Gabe commanded Easton to kill the driver. Not knowing what exactly it was - a shape shifter, a flier, a mind manipulator, or a soldier demon - he was not ready to take any chances. Easton's next shot was not a direct hit on the windshield, but indirectly struck the wide pane after bouncing off of the hood, causing it just to crack, not to break.

"Boom!"

The sound of lightning striking a tall and lonely roadside pine tree was deafening. It began to fall towards the road from the left.

"Hang on!" Gabe yelled, as he sharply jerked the minivan's gray steering wheel to the right, in an instinctive attempt to avoid the falling tree.

"Crash! Snap!"

The nearly one hundred foot tall pine tree fell merely a foot behind the speeding minivan as the two passengers and Gabe intuitively covered their heads. Easton did everything he could to stay inside the van, desperately clutching to the driver's seat in front of him; however, the gun slid out the open side door and was lost in the darkness and debris of the supercell storm. Easton hurriedly asked for the other gun as the approaching SUV slammed on its breaks to eschew the fallen tree that spanned across the entire width of the road. Gabe, who saw it all unfold in his mirrors sent the minivan on a side skid using the emergency break like a professional stunt driver. Five seconds later, the van was at a dead stop. It was alarming to hear the thunderstorm without the immediate humming of the vehicle's engine. The rain's speed had reached past its climax, but was still falling at an incredibly fast rate. They had passed the eye of the storm because looking back to where they had come from, lightning flashed throughout the cumulonimbus clouds with the immediate bellows of rolling thunder. They were not out of it, but they were close. Gabe got out of the car with anger after he picked up the other gun from the passenger seat.

"You can't win!" he shouted through the steady rain. "No matter how hard you try, the battle is over. The fact that you don't know this by now is embarrassing. Show your face, you coward!" Gabe was screaming with disgust.

Gabe walked closer to the SUV, which was shaded by the long pine needles that stretched out from the tree's crumbled branches. He continued forward with slow heel-to-toe steps, with the gun ready to fire. He smiled slyly.

"Go where the dead go."

"Bang!"

As soon as the driver showed his face, it became a bloody mess dripping down the SUV's windows. After the mayhem of the chase, the atmosphere, although still murky, was surprisingly tranquil. Raindrops slowed and fell like peaceful pieces of liquid alleviation, and both Easton and Rick Engleheart exited the the van to experience the refreshing sensation. Although they no longer needed to, the van's windshield wipers were still moving back and forth at their fastest setting. Gabe continued walking towards the fallen tree.

"Where are you going?" Rick Engleheart asked, in a yell.

"I like that gun," Gabe replied, not knowing or caring whether anyone heard him.

After retrieving the undisturbed gun from under the tree, Gabe told the two passengers to return to the car, letting Rick Engleheart know that he'd be driving once again.

"We made it through to the other side of the storm. Take over the wheel. Now I need to find Lacey and bring her back before it's too late."

Rick Engleheart obeyed silently with a nod of his head. Easton returned to his seat and shut the open side door, while Gabe crawled through to the back of the van to lay down across the damaged and wet back seat. The minivan pulled away as Rick Engleheart clicked the speed setting for the windshield wipers down a couple of notches. Many thoughts passed through his mind, but none more prevalent than just how capacious the conflict he found himself in had become. He thought of his son. Tears welled up in his eyes and tribulation tightened its grip on his throat. He thought it silly, but he began to pray.

CHAPTER 8

"Johnny, my boy. Why do you continue to resist your purpose in life? Down here - where amazing things happen - this is where you belong. After all, you were our first successful pilot study. You and your mind will pave the way for millions of people to make the right decisions in their lives - eating healthy, exercising, being kind to others, making sound financial decisions, doing what is right for the common good. Hell, even influencing the grandiose stage of world diplomacy. You were the first. And we thank you. So that is why we are offering you a wonderful life down here in this underground city. Everything you could ever want. All we ask is that you allow us to run tests on you twice a week. That is all. Now, come on. What do you say?"

Johnny did not hesitate. "You know nothing of what I want. Where is my father? I was told that he was en route yesterday and haven't heard a peep about it since."

"Surely I didn't tell you that," Victor replied, insinuating something heinous.

Johnny sat silently in horror as heart-stopping and stomach-turning thoughts raced through his mind and attacked his heart.

"The people who brought you here," Victor began to understand, as his eyes widened. He slowly started to walk backwards while keeping his perpetually thoughtful eyes fixed on his subject.

Johnny thought he might throw up. "Where is he? Where's my dad?"

Victor turned his back away from Johnny and faced the ivory wall. He smiled, knowing that it would go unnoticed. For the first time, he had leverage. And he could use it against Johnny. Victor turned back around.

"You know Johnny, I had a father once. We were very close. But he died when I was about your age. I never got a chance to prepare for it. I never got a chance to tell him how much I appreciated everything he did for us. But my biggest loss was never again being able to see his big smile when I told him that I loved him."

"What's your point?" Johnny asked, without looking up from the lucite table.

"My point," Victor continued, impatiently, "is that I don't know what you've been told, but I can assure you that your father is alive. And I can reunite you two. All I ask is that you cooperate with us. Don't you want to be of help to the greater good? Make your family proud? Hmm? I am a powerful man, Johnny. And I can bring your father here. What do you say?"

For more than a minute, Johnny sat in silent thought, weighing his options. He didn't have many. After trying to decide what was best not for himself, but for his father, he came to a decision. "If you bring him here, I'll cooperate. But until then, you won't get a word out of me."

Victor let out a laugh through his nose. "Johnny my boy, you have made a good decision. But you listen here." His tone suddenly became stern. "I can get you your father. But right now, you need to tell me about Lacey Hassle. If you don't, we will send out a simple sniper drone, and you will never see your dad again. It is entirely up to you."

Johnny let out a deep sigh. "Okay," he said, finally.

***

The heartache that Lacey felt being in the strange place she found herself in was unimaginable. Without knowing if she was dreaming or awake or worse - dead, Lacey stood in stark fright of her present, unprecedented situation.

"Do you remember what Gabriel told you when you two first met?" the mysterious slithering voice with no source said, becoming considerably louder.

Why was this voice mocking her and asking her questions as if it was awaiting the answers? It knew that she couldn't speak. In fact, it was somehow controlling that aspect of the situation, Lacey thought. She remained five feet above the ground, suspended in fearful silence.

"What was it again? That you are special. Do you know why you are special, my dear? Do you know what makes you special?"

As the voice asked Lacey these chilling questions that grotesquely and cruelly tickled her spine, the figure and source of the sinister voice moved into her frame of vision. She thought her surroundings were the darkest shade of black her eyes had ever seen, but she was wrong. Dead wrong. This figure was at least ten times darker than the jet black expanse of empty nothingness that besieged the endless space. She could clearly make it out. It was tall and skinny -

in a disturbing way and possessed arms and legs and hands and feet just like a human. However, simply by the way it moved, Lacey could tell it was far from being human. Its legs were abnormally long. Joints protruded at every opportunity and its digits - fingers and toes - bent where they weren't supposed to. If it stood up straight, it would probably be close to ten feet tall, but it hunched over and it looked as if something was about to emerge from its back. Unsettling was an understatement.

"Oh you should know by now," the voice angrily embarrassed Lacey. "Aliens? Hmmm...let me think. That is what we have persuaded you we are. Ha! The greatest lie we will ever tell is convincing you that we do not exist."

Untouched and utter fear began to consume Lacey like a plague. She didn't know if paralysis took over because of fear or because the figure was controlling every facet about her condition. She felt like a coward. It drew closer, and the closer it got, the more Lacey's insides burned with sadness. It walked ungainly, knowing that with every inch, Lacey's level of fear skyrocketed. The way in which it moved and the sinister remnant of a smile on its face immediately made the beautiful eighteen year-old worry about her virginity and self-preservation. The closer it got, the uglier it was. Its smell made Lacey want to gag, and although she was unable to, throwing up was all that she desired to do. It reached out its long finger to touch her face, but then abruptly drew back.

"Don't even think about it!" a familiar voice yelled out in a loud command.

For the first time since arriving, Lacey could sense a certain degree of fear in the dark figure. It looked about frantically as if recognizing the voice, but not knowing where the directed command had emanated from. Back and forth, up and down. Up and down, back and forth.

"Gabriel," Lacey said, smiling with her heart. It was the first time she had heard her own voice in a while. And it was a relief.

"It's impossible!" the figure angrily exclaimed.

All of a sudden, a beam of light shone directly behind Lacey, illuminating what was in front of her as she softly returned to the charred ground. Everything still remained black, except the evil figure. It was progressively turning a sickly gray color the more the light shone on it. It got down on all fours and began madly galloping around, making guttural animalistic noises. It was in pain.

"Lacey, you are more powerful than the wallowing figure in front of you. Believe in yourself." An unfamiliar voice spoke inside of Lacey's soul. "Believe."

Lacey considered the unusual notion. As she did so, the figure's skin began to burn. Lacey could hear its skin crackling as the magnificently yellow beam followed it around like a spotlight. She started to believe more strongly and in turn, the figure burned more and more. The light was like fire on its skin, revealing what was underneath - nothing. Lacey smiled and even let an arrogant chuckle escape her lips. Unexpectedly, Gabe appeared to her left. He looked at her with care in his eyes. So focused on the deep peace coming from the angel's eyes, Lacey did not take notice of the different mold Gabe embodied in this different dimension. It wasn't until he began walking toward the figure when she took note. Just like when he appeared to Johnny, the only clothing on Gabe's body was the baggy white pants. His hair still beautifully thick and long and his facial features the same, Gabe's muscles ripped through his skin, which was a strangely glorious transparent white. As he walked, his muscles talked and danced in the free flow of purity in movement.

"Whoa," Lacey mistakenly said out loud.

The figure, who was still in great pain, scurried away from Gabe with immense fear on its face. Gabe briskly continued his walk toward the graying figure with purpose to his strides and anger in his eyes. Lacey watched with delight; however, she still felt cold and wanted to leave the irregular place she had been taken to.

"You're holding her back Gabe!" the figure yelled, evading its pursuer. "You're restraining her power!"

Without hesitation, Gabe swung an abrupt right hook through the air. His fist was more than ten feet from the target, but he still managed to land a direct hit on the figure's face. With the powerful punch, the part of the figure's face began to fall away. If the light was fire, then Gabe's touch was acid, melting the figure on the point of contact. Gabe swung again - this time with a left uppercut. His dirty blonde hair raced over his broad shoulders in uncontrolled dance. The heavy punches were loud, and although she didn't want to, Lacey had to look away. It was disturbing to watch someone so kind and caring like Gabe be so ruthless and angry. It was needed though. This thing - alien, demon, or whatever it preferred to be called - kidnapped her, brought her to a frightening place, messed around with her thoughts to make her deathly afraid, and was about to do unspeakable acts until Gabe showed up and saved the day. No, she was going to watch this beatdown. Gabe walked closer and closer to the figure as it moved slower and slower. The closer the angel approached, the more the demon looked afraid. Next, Gabe let loose a series of jabs, hooks, uppercuts, and haymakers that in the end, left the figure unable to move. As much as it tried to slide away, it was no use. Gabe walked over to it, knelt down and whispered into its mangled, disappearing face.

"I'm not surprised by you," he said, in pity. "Trying to sway what is good to the other side to benefit your cause. Well guess what? It didn't work."

"She doesn't even believe," the figure replied, sharply.

Gabe turned his head back toward Lacey. "She will," he said, confidently.

"She's done so many wrongs. There is badness inside of everyone. You can't erase that."

"Don't you know by now?" Gabe asked, with a slight laugh meant to cause embarrassment. "They are already erased."

"When are you going to tell her, Gabriel?" the figure asked, with disgust.

"When she's ready," Gabe replied. "Lacey, come over here."

The beautiful, but vulnerable brunette moved her feet for the first time in what felt like forever, as she cautiously walked over to Gabe and the incredibly injured figure. As she proceeded, the scenery of the setting took shape with every step. Based on what she saw before - just a big black room - she thought the place was rather simple - but she was wrong. Next to where Gabe knelt beside the figure was an awfully and dangerously high cliff. In fact, she had been standing on an astonishingly high pillar the whole time - its top not possessing a lot of surface area at all. As she looked around the vast open space, Lacey noticed countless identical pillars for a seemingly endless distance. Beneath them at their bases, was fire. The pillars were abnormally tall, thin, and black. It was clear that the figure was trying to slide off the cliff - its desire was to return to the flames beneath. However, Gabe stopped that plan in its tracks.

"Come down here Lacey," Gabe said, calmly and kindly, motioning her to kneel as he was doing.

"You have no power," the figure painfully voiced to Lacey, in an insulting tone.

"I'd re-think that," Gabe corrected. "Lacey, you matter more than you surmise. You are special. This sad excuse will return to the flames, but will not get burned. He will not be in any pain, but you can change that. If you believe. Wish whatever you want to plague him for all eternity. Believe it and it will be done."

Lacey was hyper-focused - a feeling that she had never had the pleasure to experience before. Her eyes breathed. "Make him have a phobia of puking. And have him barf every day, but never get over it," she said, with a sly smile.

Gabe let a smile of his own creep over his face.

Lacey leaned in closer to the figure. "Now you're going to experience hell just like everyone else you helped send there. Have fun being tortured by yourself for all eternity."

The figure began speaking in panicked falderal, which prompted Gabe to stand up, motioning for Lacey to follow.

"Anything else you want to say to him?" Gabe, who was still in true and amazing angelic form, asked Lacey.

Before kicking it off the cliff with a dormant power inside of her, Lacey simply said with a slight smile, "Go where the dead go."

***

"Lacey and I are close. She is a good person, and I was really enjoying my time with her until all of this started to happen," Johnny said, motioning around his immediate area.

After he agreed to tell Victor information about his newfound and exclusive love escape in exchange for his father's safety, Johnny was taken down another dimly lit labyrinth. He imagined the underground super silos had endless mazes, and wondered how many actually existed. After shaking his head, not being able to fully grasp the concept, he gave up. The walls were a dark concrete, and looked as if they had been built for many years. Electric yellow lights hiding behind black metal cages lined each of the walls every sixteen feet. Victor was walking at a fast clip; Johnny followed closely behind. Two rights, five lefts, one right, two lefts, another right, and one sharp hairpin turn later, Victor stopped to place his hand into a seemingly random spot on the cold concrete wall. The opposite side - eight feet behind his back - slowly slid open, bottom to top. No cracks, no hinges, no nothing. The display should have sparked questions from Johnny's mouth, but by this point, he had become accustomed to needing an open mind to accept certain things. Just add it to the long and lengthening list, he thought.

Upon entering another concrete tunnel that was exactly identical to where they had just come from, Victor urged Johnny to continue discussing Lacey.

"What does she have to do with anything, though?" Johnny asked.

"I pride myself in being honest with you, boy, and I will extend my frankness. "We got word that she is different. From whom? You don't need to know. Nonetheless, she is gifted, and these gifts can be used for good, or for other means."

"Your version of good, or the moral version?" Johnny asked, interrupting.

Victor sighed. "When will you ever just accept certain things? We are here to make the world a better place. A more sustainable place. A place where people treat their neighbors well, live healthy lifestyles, and lead lives that promote world peace. Now I ask you, my boy. How is that not good?"

"Ever hear of free will?"

Victor laughed at Johnny's inquiry as if he were presented a computer from the year 2015. "Free will is outdated."

Victor continued leading Johnny through more mind-bending twists and turns. After walking nearly another quarter mile, he spoke up again.

"So Lacey is special. We don't know why or how or what exactly it is that makes her different, but we know that she is gifted. And what is utterly fascinating is that we have been told her gifts come and go. To the untrained eye, it looks as if the coming and going is random. But it is just the opposite. It seems that when she is around certain people, her gifts are enhanced - strengthened, if you will. That is why we must see to it that her whereabouts are monitored at all times. Over the past couple of days, we have watched her every move using top secret surveillance drones no bigger than your hand. Small, but equipped with cameras so beyond your wildest dreams that if I told you what these can pick up, you wouldn't believe me. All we know is that at some point last night, her trail went cold. Our technology is not working properly. We don't know much about her because in the little amount of time she's been on our radar - since she interfered with the development of your kidnapping - she has not been very active."

"Active?" Johnny asked.

"Yes, active. You know - on social media, the Internet, her phone, her television, her purchases - we are unable to gather information about her. But this is where you come in, my boy. You know more about her than we do, so if you'd like to see your dear old dad again, you will tell us everything you know. This may or may may not lead to helping us. But right now, it's the best chance we've got."

Johnny fell into deep thought as he paced behind Victor. He had begun to fall in love with Lacey, and now was he really going to help his captors quell her from possibly fulfilling her potential destiny to protect his father? He sighed. There had to be another way. But he needed time to think. So he stalled.

"You said the drones were small?" he asked, indicating the space between his pinky and his thumb. "When did that happen? I thought they were bigger, like the size of toasters."

"Well since you will never see the light of day again, I guess I can share this information with you. I'm the head of this department, and I can't fire myself. Why would I? Long ago, back in the 1940s, there was a staged event you probably learned from history class or from the history channel. Are you familiar with the Roswell incident?"

Johnny nodded.

"It's reported as a government cover up and there are a plethora of conspiracy theories that surround the incident. Well, as you can probably guess, most of them are wrong. And even the ones that are on the right track fail to come close to touching the truth. Let me shed some light on it for you, just so you understand how powerful an organization we truly are. It was 1947," Victor said, tilting his head back as if looking up at a beautiful blue sky. His silver hair seemed to shine in the pale yellow light that his thin wire framed glasses reflected perfectly. "It was this branch's first mission. Even I don't know what it was called, and the only people who did know are long gone now. Buried, just like the truth. Anyway, newspaper headlines across the country read something along the lines of 'RAAF Captures Flying Saucer.' Soon, everyone and his cousin were demanding answers. Armed Forces maintained, however, that the debris they found at the crash sight was something from an experimental high-altitude balloon

EMERUS: THE WONDER OF WINGS

that we were testing. They were lying to make it seem like a coverup. We found an opportunity that we did not know existed until it was right in front of our eyes. So we were the ones who introduced the extraterrestrial theory. That side of the story came from within. It came from us. It was an opportunity to come up with a fabrication that would live on forever. We planted everything. From the metal flying saucer, to the strange debris, even to the fake alien bodies - those were all constructed about ten floors beneath your shoes.

So there were walkers who passed by and saw what looked like a crashed UFO. They were us. There were quote-unquote secret officials telling them to keep out. They were us. There were other witnesses and reporters who talked to them. They were all us. We created a fake explanation to throw the watchers off the scent. If people began to think that aliens were visiting this planet, then they would begin to blame the government for covering it up. Those people - the first believers demanding answers from government - they were us too. And the senators at the hearings? They were us as well. So we planted ideas in the heads of American citizens - that aliens visited Earth, the government knew about it, and they were covering it up. It took people's focus away from the truth. If aliens are watching you, then I'm sorry, there's not too much you can do about it. But if the government is watching you, taking away your God-given and constitutional rights, then you might become pretty mad, right? Well, no one became mad because they believed aliens had come. They threw their arms up in the air in amazement. We threw everybody off the scent of what was actually happening. So when they saw strange lights in the sky, they would believe the lights were UFOs visiting from another planet. It's a damn good reason for the government to cover it up. So instead of seeing what was right under their noses, they began to think outside of the box, completely dismissing the truth for something greater. Something we made up. A false flag. And it worked. For decades and decades, we tested top secret flying objects - mostly for surveillance purposes over U.S. skies. In fact, to this day, we still test top secret flying objects - they are just much smaller now. You ever wonder why in the last couple of years the frequency of UFO sightings has greatly diminished? Back in the day, we were testing large objects because that was how we built them. It was what the technology of the time allowed. Throughout the decades, some people believed it was the government. But most believed it was aliens. And if living in America has taught you anything, it's taught you that the majority rules. Take for instance the B12 Stealth Bomber. Way before your time. It was built in the early 1970s, tested throughout that decade as well as the 80s, but it wasn't first presented until more than twenty years after it was built. So what were those lights in the sky? They weren't extraterrestrials, my boy. They were computer-operated machines built by us. We had to test them somewhere. That is why most of the sightings happened in the middle of nowhere - the less amount of people seeing them in action the better. The whole alien theory? A complete facade. Area 51? Groom Lake, Nevada? We send people in and out to make it look operational. You know what goes on there? Nothing. Do you honestly think that a top secret place to harbor, test, and store something of that importance would be built above ground, for everyone to see? No, no. Like I said, a complete facade. This is the real Area 51. And it's not called Area 51 either." Victor stopped walking and turned around. "It's called Emerus. And you should get used to it - you'll be here awhile.

Victor again placed an open hand on the gray concrete wall, sliding open the opposite side. Instead of leading to another dimly lit labyrinth, Johnny could immediately tell that the open door led to a vastly different place. Bright lights shining from the progressively rising hidden door illuminated the monolithic tunnel where they were standing so much that both Johnny and Victor squinted in eye pain. Johnny could tell that they had finally arrived at Victor's desired destination. And he was glad. Johnny had come up with a request that would help him in his decision. But he had to ask soon. Something in the back of his mind told him so.

CHAPTER 9

Sunday, 11:53 am

The music, although quietly humming through the minivan's six speakers, mocked Rick Engleheart as he sat in silence, driving. Easton was asleep, Gabe and Lacey were literally off in another world, so Rick Engleheart, doing everything he could to not completely lose his mind, needed some semblance of noise. The radio, however, continued to relentlessly heckle the heartbroken father. His life had turned upside down, and he hadn't the slightest clue as to what the next few days had in store for him. All he knew was that his son was alive, and that he was prepared to do anything to rescue him. Gabe had briefly discussed certain matters pertaining to who had kidnapped Johnny and why, but for the most part, Rick Engleheart was in the dark. Gabe had promised he would reveal more when the appropriate time came, but everyone was still waiting on that.

It had been more than two hours since Lacey was taken. Rick Engleheart wished he had asked Gabe how long it would be until he returned. But that moment was heavily rushed. Before Gabe retired to the back seat, he hastily handed Rick Engleheart a folded road map and said he'd be back. That was it. They had recently entered Indiana - taking the northern route across the state. There was absolutely nothing surrounding them for miles. It was an eerie feeling to say the least. But Rick Engleheart had set the cruise and for the past couple of hours let his elbows rest on his thighs as his cold hands lightly braced five and seven on the steering wheel. He turned his head toward the passenger seat to retrieve the map. Taking his hands off the wheel and letting his knees take over control, he opened up the map out of curiosity and boredom. The combination of the sky being extremely cloudy and the map being written in pencil made it difficult to easily see.

"Ceiling light on."

The small ceiling lights soundlessly obeyed Rick Engleheart's soft spoken commands. He kept his knees on the steering wheel as his eyes traded looks between the black asphalt road and the unfolding oversized map. The crinkling and cracking of the paper dominated the minivan's sound waves as the radio's music took a back seat to the overpowering and resounding rustle. As Rick Engleheart opened up the map, he immediately got the impression that it possessed information which he did not understand. Making a beyond-perplexed face at the gray and white mirage staring back at him, strange and bizarre thoughts began to pass through Rick Engleheart's mind.

"What is this?" he said aloud, as if he would receive an audible answer.

An outline of the United States was clearly visible. However, that was the only aspect of the map that was even remotely recognizable. Countless intersecting lines converging from all directions made up the majority of the United States' interior. Seemingly random circles of all different sizes formed the next prominent image. Their curves intersecting with the myriad of multi-length lines made it almost impossible to see what was beneath the pencilled-in map. That was the next facet that Rick Engleheart discovered. All of it - the lines, the circles, everything was done by hand. Even though it looked as if a machine had completed it, something in the back of his mind told him that this was craftily and carefully done the hard way - by hand with simply a pencil. The strokes were too imperfect, yet flawless at the same time.

Something became eerily evident as the hairs on the back of Rick Engleheart's neck straightened with a shiver. This was obviously a different language - one which no human could comprehend. The simple fact that his eyes were seeing it gave his stomach a tumble as Rick Engleheart's eyes widened in an unexplored emotional combination of horror, amazement, guilt, and reverence. Was he supposed to even set his eyes on this? Was this like looking at the Ark of the Covenant? Were angels of death going to swoop in and suck out his soul? These questions and numerous ones of a similar ilk raced through Rick Engleheart's mind. He shot a quick look in the rear view mirror. He could barely see Gabe, but it was definitely clear he was still motionless. Giving the map another once-around, Rick Engleheart tried to make sense of the peculiarity of it all. There must be thousands of lines, he thought. Hundreds of circles. What do they all mean? It was a good thing Rick Engleheart was driving because he could have tried to study the map for hours on end, only giving exercise to eyes. Continuing to trade looks between the perplexing road map and Interstate 80, Rick Engleheart noticed something in the line and circle chaos. It was extremely difficult to decipher, but he thought he saw a small 'X' in the midst of the map's muddle. It was challenging to tell for sure with the seemingly infinite number of intersections taking place, but Rick Engleheart saw something that looked like an 'X.' He kept the car travelling straight with his knees and peered at the map for a good four seconds before he returned his gaze up to the road. A large seven-point buck stood staring at the minivan, trapped in the oncoming daytime running lights like a tractor beam, merely forty feet away.

Rick Engleheart immediately jerked the van, going 75 miles per hour, to the left by pulling the steering wheel downward with his left arm. An abnormal sound of panic emanated from his mouth as he pulled so hard, he thought the wheel was going to come off of its column. The large and muscular male deer was beautiful - its back a dark gray, almost black in color; its midsection a light vibrant brown; and its neck a powdery white, making its charcoal nose and mouth stand out like a conglomerate of concrete in freshly fallen snow. Black emotionless eyes became larger and larger as the van sped toward the majestically frozen animal. Its antlers stretched up toward the sky like beautiful pieces of artistic driftwood, singing sweet songs to the invisible moon. Probably a warrior out on his daily watch, it stood still in the paralyzing, faint yellow beams, awaiting its inevitable fate with noble and quiet grace. If Rick Engleheart had looked at the map half a second longer, he would have sent the deer warrior to its final resting place, and most likely, totalled the van, endangering his own life and the lives of its slumbering passengers. However, the minivan missed the outstretched antlers by a few inches, and had the deer even leaned to the left, it would have been the end of the its life. Rick Engleheart's animalistic sound of alarm woke Easton up immediately.

"What?! What is it?" Easton exclaimed.

Blood carrying extremely potent amounts of adrenaline was racing through Rick Engleheart's veins like cars at Daytona. It took him a few short and shallow breaths to return to homeostasis. He nonchalantly put on his right turn signal and slowly directed the van to the right lane once again, decreasing the vehicle's speed by four clicks on the cruise control 'minus' button.

"That was too close," he said.

"What was?"

"That deer. We almost hit a deer," he replied, still hot with the adrenaline rush.

"You want me to drive?" Easton asked, offering some help to his affected uncle.

"No, I'm alright. Jeez, that was a close one. Easton, take this map. Do you see an 'X' near the Indiana and Illinois border?" Rick Engleheart asked, handing the map back to his nephew.

"What the heck is this?" Easton asked, trying to evoke a laugh from his uncle, which was only half successful.

"It's the map that Gabe has been looking at. It's obviously in another language or something. Don't you see an 'X' though? It looks like it's marking a spot or something."

Easton was quiet for nearly a minute, after which he replied, "Yes, I see a few Xs."

"You do? Do you know what they're there for? It looks like they would be right along our route, doesn't it?"

Easton nodded his head. "Yeah, it does. I have no idea what they mean though. But we're getting pretty close to the first one."

***

"Okay, where are we, Gabe?" Lacey asked. And how did I get here?"

"We're in another dimension - one of the dark ones. You were taken from the van in a smoke abduction," Gabe nonchalantly replied, as if Lacey had asked for the time of day.

A plethora of questions was clouding Lacey's mind, restricting her focus. So she remained quiet, trying to sort out the extraordinary events she had just experienced. But she had to ask the question that had been burning in her mind.

"Why was I stronger than that thing? What makes me special? I don't understand."

Gabe looked at Lacey with caring and wondrous eyes. After sighing, he responded, "These are questions for another time. But I promise you that they will be answered, and you will be so amazed. Believe me."

"So...how do we get back to reality?" Lacey asked, still affected by her unprecedented circumstance.

"This is the closest thing to reality you have ever experienced, Sleepyhead. The reality that you and all of the other humans have, and still are adjusting to, is just a fraction of a millimeter on an infinitely long line of genuine verity and absoluteness."

Lacey slowly blinked.

"There is so much more to life that human brains are able to understand and human eyes are not programmed to recognize. There are other dimensions all around you, built in circles on top of one another, but humans would have to be so far removed from their universe to see them from the outside-in. But that will all eventually be revealed to humans. Be thankful you know it now, though. It may come in handy someday."

"Okay, you're gonna have to write that crap down for me. I don't know if you know this or not, but human brains aren't computers yet."

Gabe smiled, but his magnificent grin was cut short by an abrupt and eerily frightening sound. It was faint at first, but then grew louder with every second. It was a menacing siren, but unlike regular, run-of-the-mill sirens, this one was deep in tone as if a giant beast was trying to mimic a bigfoot call, while achieving a much higher decibel meter reading.

"We have to go. Now!" Gabe urged.

The pillar they were standing on was its own tower, with no other pillars nearby. And everything else in the entire place was still black; however, as Lacey adjusted to the different reality, she began to make out the other pillars, just as she had before. They looked like dark-red ember skyscrapers, highlighted in the black expanse of surrounding nothingness. Gabe helped as well. There was a certain brightness about him - like an aura of some sort. And Lacey couldn't tell if her eyes were deceiving her or not, but he seemed to be becoming brighter and brighter. The sound began to increase and Lacey covered her ears. The pillar started to rumble and Gabe began to gleam even more. His transparent and beyond-ripped, muscular body gave off a precious yellow light that comforted Lacey's soul just by looking at it.

"Come on!" he yelled, taking Lacey by the hand.

The two began to run at a decently swift clip - turtle slow for Gabe, pretty fast for Lacey. She could see waves of flames starting to form at the base of the pillars. They oscillated like the ocean, and rose like a flood. It was difficult to tell for sure, but Lacey thought she heard a roar from the flames begin to emanate beneath the guttural siren sound.

"Let's pick it up!" Gabe yelled, as he led Lacey racing toward the edge of the pillar.

"Where are we gonna go?" she screamed back, starting to get short of breath.

To help answer her question, Lacey took in the most beautiful sight her eyes had ever seen. Time terminated. Sound ceased. In that moment, Lacey felt as if there was no tomorrow, and if she could only stop and stare at what was in front of her for the remainder of eternity. If only...

It happened in slow motion. And since Lacey was a much slower runner, she had the perfect vantage point being a few strides behind Gabe. They came out of thin air, but when his wings opened up entirely, they were very real. Such a stark contrast to the darkness that surrounded them, the wings' color was the purest of white. The alabaster snow was the whitest color Lacey had seen, but Gabriel's wings were exponentially more pure and immaculate. She did not know such a flawless color even existed. The sheer amount of feathers was unfathomable. Trying to count, Lacey quickly became lost in the beauty of it all. She simply did not wish to look away, and there was something under the surface that was drawing her to them like a magnet. Soon, Gabe began an all out sprint - so much faster than any human could possibly run - and Lacey found herself keeping up with him. Focusing on the beautifully sharp angles of his enormous full wings, Lacey was running at an incredibly fast rate. Realizing this, tingles began to creep up and down her spine, then back up to her neck, raising every small hair along the way. Each of Gabe's wings must have been twelve feet, and as Lacey supernaturally kept up with the angel, she concentrated on the wonder of his wings. Muscles could be seen - ripped muscles cascading through every inch of the achromatic miracles. Pure white feathers did their best to cover them up, but it was no use.

"Hang on!" Gabe yelled, reaching his arm back so Lacey could grab it.

As soon as she had a firm grip on his wrist/forearm area, they gracefully lifted off of the charred ground. Lacey gasped. She no longer heard the guttural siren. In fact, when she thought about it, she had not heard that sound in a long time - it felt like a distant, vague memory. Like a dream that never actually happened. The roaring of the flames ceased as well. This felt odd to Lacey - hearing absolute peace in silence. She could hardly remember the last time she heard something so serene as the peaceful calm surrounding her in every direction. She shook her head in confusion. She was flying. As she looked around, enormous balls of fire were being shot up at them. Pillars were rising up from their unseen foundations. Giant razor-sharp stalactites were raining down out of the black expanse above them. From beneath the pillars, gigantic jaws that looked as though they belonged to a ferocious beast came at them. However, Gabe dodged every fire ball, evaded every pillar, avoided every stalactite, and when it came to the eerily floating fire jaws, Gabe was simply too quick. Lacey hung on for dear life, but something told her that there was an unseen force that was keeping her connected to Gabe. Did he have a gravitational pull? Did gravity even exist in this place, or was it some force that humans have not yet experienced? Whatever it was, it made Lacey feel safe - the safest she had ever felt, which was incredibly ironic given the dangerous setting she currently found herself in.

"We're almost there!" Gabe yelled, although to Lacey, it sounded like a quiet whisper.

Gabe continued to bypass the various deathly obstacles with grace. He sped up. And Lacey could hear the sound of his wings cutting through the air with agile beauty. He dove down, soared, stopped on a dime, as he elegantly flew with delicacy. The sound of his wings was quite possibly the most unique noise Lacey's ears had ever heard. She listened closely, thinking she heard a voice. More intently. Yes. There was definitely a voice coming from the sound of his wings. Full concentration now. There! Lacey could hear it as clear as day. It was the same voice that she had heard inside of her before which said, "Believe." By the time it stopped, tears of feeling true and pure love ran down her face.

"I am your shepherd; you shall not want. I let you lie down in green pastures; I lead you beside peaceful waters. I renew your strength; I guide you along the right paths, bringing honor to My name. Though you walk through the valley of the shadow of death, you will not be afraid: for I am with you; I will protect and comfort you. I prepare a table for you right in front of your enemies; you will be revived; your cup will overflow with blessing. My beauty and love chase after you every day of your life; And you will be home soon. You will be home soon."

Tears that took a leap of faith off of Lacey's cheeks and chin down to the fiery pit beneath hit the flames like enormous water balloons, immediately quelling the whole area of impact.

"I guess gravity does exist in this place," the peace-loving voice inside said.

CHAPTER 10

Since Johnny had arrived to the underground city that had apparently been creating technology with the external help of another world for decades, he had not seen as many strangers as there were now buzzing about in front of him. Even when he arrived and took in the jaw-dropping sight of the centerpiece to the city - the center he had begun to call it in his head - with its foreign and futuristic transparent technology with countless elevators that took off in any and every direction farther than the eye could see. The sheer openness of it all, the astounding sights that produced infinite Kodak moments, the way everything was out in the open but still underground - there was no sense in keeping anything hidden, for everything was concealed by America's vast amount of wasteland.

Even when Johnny was at the center, he did not see the large amount of people before him now. What was eerie about the sight was the fact that the people were creepily quiet. Usually, in a crowd of that number - well over one hundred - a cluster of noise consumed the space. But not here. Not in Emerus. People walked with silent purpose, and the only sound reverberating through the breadth was the quiet hum of supercomputers. Even though their number seemed innumerous, they only whispered softly, but their sound was menacing. The farther Victor led Johnny, the more clustered the space became. Among the quiet assemblage, a thought began to take shape in Johnny's mind. At first, it was just a far-fetched idea. Next, it started to roll to the forefront of his thought process, gaining size and momentum as it did. Then, the snowball effect really started to develop as Johnny's eyes took in more and more of the growing surroundings. Finally, a mere minute after the thought budded in the back of his mind, there was verification as he stepped into a gigantic room much like the center, only bigger with more people and more machines. A towering and thick cylindrical elevator shaft stood in the middle of the immense room. Starting at five stories up, its arms began to spread in every direction. The main shaft continued its climb, but it seemed like every five stories up to the ground and down into the Earth, eight identical arms stretched north, northeast, east, southeast, south, southwest, west, and northwest. It was unlike anything Johnny had ever seen. As Victor led him closer to it, Johnny took a peek up to see if he could spot the top. He couldn't. All his eyes could see was the transparent symmetry of the colossal elevator shaft and its long arms that took passengers to a number of places Johnny's mind could not fathom.

"This way," Victor said, sternly.

He was clearly annoyed with the fact that Johnny had stopped moving his legs. The in-awe eighteen year old had not even noticed his brief curtailment.

"This is another center, isn't it?" he asked Victor, keeping still.

"Another what?" Victor quickly asked, half annoyed and half confused.

"I mean where we were before. This is another one just like it."

Victor nodded his head to entertain his subject. With a smile on his face he replied, "Yes, this is another super silo. Inverted like all the rest, of course."

"How many are there?" Johnny asked, with a slight look of anxious anticipation.

"Oh, more than you could ever imagine, my boy," Victor replied. "Once technology allowed for it, the United States government finally figured out what to do with all of its uninhabitable nothingness. Manifest Destiny did serve a purpose after all."

Johnny was beside himself as he could not help but simply stare at the chrome colored elevator shaft and its numerous arms. The superstructure befuddled him. He had never been close to something so immense and towering. When he first arrived at Emerus, Johnny was told that there were many inverted super silo projects hidden underground, but he figured they were scattered about - one having not much to do with another. What he did not even come close to assuming, however, was a sort of omnium gatherum and interconnectedness of the inverted silos.

"So we just walked to another silo?"

"Yes," Victor replied, very nonchalantly with the inflection of a question.

After silently trading a couple of potential responses in his head, Johnny finally answered, "Why didn't we take one of the elevators?"

Victor considered Johnny's semi-sarcastic inquiry for two seconds and then replied, smiling, "It's more menacing to walk through the labyrinth. Don't you agree?"

"I don't know," Johnny responded. "I think I'm over the whole menacing act. It'd be better to impress me. Don't *you* agree?"

Victor walked away with a little bit of frustration, admitting defeat in that particular short battle of words.

"Come, my boy. We have much to do."

Johnny followed confidently before shaking his head and saying with a smile, "You're slackin', Doc. You're slackin'." As poise built inside of him, Johnny remembered the dream he had had before and smiled.

As they walked, Johnny noticed that their pace had slightly quickened. But he still took time to gaze up toward mother earth's ground and gaze down toward her center to take in a sight similar to the previous super silo. It was very similar. Nearly identical, in fact. Not being able to see the bottom or the top, Johnny noticed countless gigantic circular rooms built on top of one another. With everything transparent, including the walls with all of their tiny fiber optic cables, the sight was dizzying at best.

"So this silo has its own hospital, grocery store, workout gyms, and all?"

"And entertainment sites, and amusement parks, luxurious living quarters, sports teams, television stations, yes. It has it all," Victor replied, over his shoulder, while keeping his quickened pace.

Silence and awe was Johnny's answer. And it more than appropriately sufficed. Victor led Johnny meandering through technology the teenager had never even dreamed of existing.

"So what's this silo do?"

Victor stopped and turned around. "What does it do?"

Johnny nodded with his eyebrows raised, creating wrinkles on his forehead. "Yeah. The first one created technology with help from some other planet or realm or whatever. This one looks pretty important. Actually," Johnny looked around, "More important. So what is this silo's purpose?"

Victor took a long and deep breath. "The first silo dealt with the creation of technology to be used for control of the people. You're correct."

Something about the way he presented the facts was akin to accurately throwing razor sharp daggers at a target.

"The people flocked to the technology like Pavlov's dog. It was more convenient, made lives a whole lot more enjoyable, and made people feel safer. Just a cover up to its real intention and purpose I'm happy to say. Surprise. So what the previous silo created, this silo uses. In a few short minutes, you my boy, get to witness with your own eyes something never before seen by people up there. Prepare to be amazed, Johnny. Now you'll see just how deep the whole spy game goes."

Johnny took a thick swallow, but wished he hadn't because its effect was very noticeable. If there was any ground gained previously in the battle of words, he had just lost most, if not all of it, with one physiological gaffe. Victor took note. And Johnny wanted more than anything to be able to rewind time just ten seconds and redo his reaction so it wasn't so candidly weak. But he couldn't, so he brushed off his blemish as best as he could; however, he felt deflated.

"Come on, we're almost there," Victor said, with a tiny sliver of sympathy in his voice.

After multiple measures of top secret security - facial recognition, fingerprints, handprints, eye scans, and vocal synchronized symmetry - Johnny began to understand the gravity of the situation and where exactly he was. Could this be the epicenter of all of those crazy conspiracy theories Johnny had heard through the years? Just the simple fact that he stood more than half a mile underneath the earth in an underground city of inverted super silos controlled by a secret branch of power told him an unequivocal yes.

The large twelve-foot metallic door that stood threateningly in front of them halted their progress as an identical one that was four feet behind them locked shut. Johnny was now trapped inside a rather small space with the man holding him against his will. For the first time since Gabriel visited Johnny in his sleep, the eighteen year old captive felt scared. However, he tried not to show it. Fifty percent chance his effort was successful, he thought.

"Johnny, my boy," there was a heightened sense of anticipated elation in Victor's voice. "Do you remember twelve years ago when someone named Edward Snowden blew the whistle on the United States government spying on its citizens under the guise of protection?"

Johnny stood still with a quizzical look on his face. He did not remember it happening, but he learned about it in school. From what he could remember being taught, Snowden was a traitor and dangerous to the progress of the modern world.

"Well now, you were what? Only six years old back then, you probably don't recall. Let me enlighten you with something, my boy."

Victor took off his thin wired framed glasses and breathed on both lenses, fogging up the glass, then wiped them clean with sleeves of his tucked-in white button-up collared shirt.

"We were an intrical part of that, as you can probably envision. And the United States government was as well. You see, he was instructed to be the whistleblower on the NSA spying. Mainstream media and history books have it wrong once again, just like they do with many facets of America's past. But that was part of the design as well. The U.S. government figured if they could make a whistleblower out of someone, some but not all of the public would be up in arms. 'How could the government do this? This isn't the America I know.' Two things this accomplished. The citizens who spoke up in protest, social media, and on radio were put on watch. It's like in battle when you're in a stalemate. You take a decoy, show it out in the open, it gets fired upon, and you can consequently see where to direct *your* fire. It works quite splendidly. On the battlefield as well as for domestic means. And it worked for the American government. They saw who their targets were. Who were the biggest threats to their cause. Whom to monitor more closely and whom to sensor. So they did. Why do you think most people were not up in arms with the infringement on their rights by the government? Occam's razor. They simply didn't know about it.

The second accomplishment of creating a whistleblower - truthful deceit. It was true what Snowden had revealed. However, people believed and the government pretended to believe that he blew the lid off of something huge. The truth of the matter was he had only cracked the lid. What he revealed about government spying was only the tip of the iceberg, but the way in which the NSA and the media responded made people believe that he had revealed it all. He didn't. Not even close. But by making United States citizens think he did, the scheme got people to more or less shut up about it. What else was there to dig for if someone had already exposed it all?"

Most of what Johnny heard he cared little about. "So Snowden was told to do what he did?" he asked, skeptically.

"Correct. And he did it well. He's sitting on a pretty nice severance package with his family right about now. Happy as a clam."

"So what's behind the door?" Johnny asked, apathetically.

A proud smile commandeered Victor's face. And just as it did, the large metal door a few feet in front of them slowly started to rise from the ground up. The vibration was so strong that it shook the miniature room's floor. Johnny reached his right hand out to clutch the cold metallic wall for support. Keeping his eyes fixed on the tortoiselike, gradual progression of the rising door, Johnny's anticipation level increased as each stimulating second passed through his intrigued mind. The door was about at waist level, and the six-foot eighteen-year-old could only see the floor on the other side - transparent - just like almost everything else. The metal entryway kept its lackadaisical pace as it crept inch-by-inch toward its revelation. Johnny bent down and squinted at the slowly growing space, trying to see anything that might give a hint to what exactly was on the other side. In his head, he imagined a large room full of supercomputers, countless wires, servers, monitors, and screens. With what Victor had told him, Johnny thought it accurate to guess such a sight. Chest level now. Johnny stood up.

"So what's on the other side?" he asked loudly, over the deep hum that consumed the tiny room. "Come on, Doc. Just a hint. What's over there?"

"Not what," Victor answered. "But who."

As soon as he made his menacing reply, Johnny heard a familiar voice screaming on the other side of the opening.

CHAPTER 11

The look on the eighteen-year-old's face had turned into an ugly and exposed combination of fright, confusion, and gut-wrenching shock. But most of all, anticipation had usurped his eyes. And this was the emotion that showed most. Because as the voice became louder and louder with the door opening becoming larger and larger, Johnny knew that his cousin, one of his best friends, was the source of the chilling screams on the other side. Victor took delight and even a little bit of sick pleasure in the spinning wheel of concerned emotions that had commandeered Johnny's face.

"No! No!"

As soon as Johnny could fit his body through the still-rising metal door, he ducked his way through the opening. A mere ten feet away knelt his cousin, Matthew. A stranger dressed in a black and white suit had his pistol pressed hard into the twenty-five-year-old's temple.

"You bastards!" Matthew yelled.

After an initial frozen shock, Johnny ran to Matthew's side only to be slugged in the side of the face by another man he failed to see. Matthew struggled, but to no avail.

"Don't touch him!" he screamed, in pain.

Victor stepped into the room nonchalantly and in control. However, as soon as he saw Johnny on the ground holding the left side of his face, he shot an angry gaze at the perpetrator, which was followed by a direct and fast long-strided walk.

"Do you have any idea what the boy means to us?" he asked angrily, before abruptly stealing the pistol from the man's side holster and shooting him through the heart.

Johnny heard the gunshot and immediately thought the worst - that his cousin Matthew was dead. Reason and logic were being outweighed by the tragic helplessness of the situation. Tears of despair fueled by confusion and guilt began to well up in Johnny's eyes. It wasn't until he heard sighs of exhaustion - both physically and mentally - from Matthew that he understood what had happened. Victor had come to Johnny's defense, so much so that the Doc killed the man who had punched him. Literally ended a man's life in defense of Johnny. Somewhere between confusion and astonishment, Johnny managed to speak.

"What's going on?"

Victor acted as if shooting a man was a metabolic function. "We're here to get information out of you, boy," he replied casually, as two men in white lab coats dragged away the dead knee-jerk reaction-thinking man.

"Why me? Why…" Johnny stopped his words to prevent tears from forming in his eyes.

"Because! You are the one we have chosen for reasons we cannot explain just yet. Simply trust that they are far more important than you could imagine."

Johnny reached out for Matthew's hand, which his cousin grabbed and held tightly.

"Matthew, what are you doing here?" Johnny asked.

His cousin happened to be one of his best friends, and it pained Johnny to look at his black eyes and beat-up face. He wished there was some way he could help, but the truth of the matter was that there wasn't. And the truth was harsh. Johnny shook his head in frustration and wondered if this was part of the visiting angel's plan.

"I will tell you what he's doing here," Victor addressed the room, as he motioned to two men.

"We need information from you, my boy. And clearly we haven't gotten any yet. So let's see how well you fare while you watch your dear cousin, someone you love and who loves you, get tortured."

The two men lifted Matthew off of the ground and stood him upright, each holding under his armpit, for he was too weak to stand on his own. Another man lifted Johnny up, and sat him in a chair. It was the first opportunity he had to look about the room. It was nothing special compared to what he had seen in his time in Emerus so far. The floor was transparent and revealed something big standing on the level beneath, but all that was visible was its black top, as it expanded over the entire length of the sixteen-by-sixteen foot room's flooring. There was nothing magnificent that differentiated the simplified room from any other room - in the normal world or in Emerus. In fact, it was practically empty. Victor was clearly lying earlier. Johnny understood that.

Immediately after the man forcibly sat Johnny down, he retrieved clasps from his suit jacket's interior pocket, and tilting Johnny's head back, uncomfortably attached the apparatus to Johnny's face. No matter how hard he tried, the eighteen-year-old was physically unable to blink. He clenched his teeth instead. Next, an immobilizer was placed onto Johnny's head to prevent him from turning away. It looked like a hockey helmet, but was much more uncomfortable. He couldn't tell for sure, but it felt like it was attached to the chair. Then after the man was done setting up Johnny, he turned his attention to something behind him. Wheels. He was pushing something along the floor. It didn't sound too heavy. When it came into view, panicked perplexion took over Matthew's face. Its silver color blended in too well with the cold gray walls. Johnny tried to squint, then realized he couldn't. From what he could decipher from twelve feet away, the device looked simple. It was waist high, containing a solitary pole rising from its base, which resembled a shield volcano. Atop the pole, there was a silver basketball-sized sphere with metal straps hanging from its sides. It was wheeled in front of Matthew, whose hands were quickly strapped onto the device. He was too weak to fight it, so he just let it happen. After the man gave the green light to Victor, signalling he was done, Matthew could not move his wrists, hands, or fingers. It was as if he was super-glued to the sphere.

"You bastards!" Johnny yelled. "What are you going to do to him?"

"Well, my boy, for some reason you will not break. We have a special thing we do for people like you. We break them by forcing them to watch a loved one in great pain. When you start talking, we will stop. Simple as that."

"What do you need to know?" Johnny asked, desperately.

"No Johnny. Don't tell them anything. It won't matter anyway. Where are they going to put me if you give in? Back up there? Doesn't make any sense. Don't…"

Matthew could not finish his sentence. Instead, his head reared back and burning pain commandeered his face. After a few seconds, the screams started. Johnny then realized what the torturing device was doing. The sphere was being heated like an electric stove burner, and all Matthew could do was feel the searing pain. He shrieked in short, agonizing breaths, trying to breathe through it, but failing.

"Who is Lacey Hassle?" Victor demanded.

"What do you mean? She's my friend!" Johnny started to panic, not knowing how to help.

"Where is she? What did she tell you about herself?"

"Nothing. I don't know!"

"Tell me!" Victor screamed harshly, over the wails.

Something had changed. It was difficult to tell at first, but Johnny took his attention off of Victor and directed it at Matthew. The twenty-five-year-old was speaking another language. It sounded odd - unlike anything Johnny had heard before. He spoke louder and louder and before long, Matthew was yelling it at the top of his lungs stretching his face toward the ceiling.

"Tell me now!" Victor howled.

"No!" Johnny answered, in defiance.

And just as he did, all of the lights in the room went dead black and everything fell into darkness.

CHAPTER 12

"Security breach! Security breach on B-149. I repeat that's a certified breach on Bravo, one, fo-wer, niner. "

The room turned into a lights out frenzy. Men were yelling out to each other, stumbling under, over, and through multiple machines and devices. Johnny could sense fear in their voices. It was extremely noticeable that matters like the one at hand did not happen very often, or ever. There was a momentary break in the initial noise and cluttered confusion. The men had sent out their signals, per protocol, and simply stood, guns ready, breaths held, waiting. After five seconds of pure silence, a strange sound entered the room. It reverberated like an abrupt gust of wind, like a person pursing their lips and blowing out, hard and short. But it was much louder. And unique. The men in the room could not be sure if they heard it or felt it. For some reason though, the unprecedented sound gave Johnny a heightened awareness and sense of internal peace. He felt that if he exhaled slowly, all of the joy, happiness, peace, and love ever created would follow his ensuing inhale and make a home inside of his heart, mind, and soul. Complete and true peace encompassed his body. It was easily the most harmony he had ever experienced in his eighteen years.

"Whoooo."

The sound again. Sadly and regrettably, the perfect peace that had surrounded Johnny began to slowly drift away. First, it started in his heart. He could feel it leave. Next, it moved to his mind. Pleasant thoughts were being replaced. Then, it finally left his soul. What was once lit with magnificence and pure light and love now felt shrivelled up, alone, and dead. Separated.

"Whoooo." Identical.

The lights flashed on and off in a few half-hearted attempts to come back on all the way. After a couple more tries, they all remained on long enough for the men to notice Matthew missing from the room. Johnny noticed it long before then. And by the time the men were discussing it confusingly, Johnny also understood what had happened. Without knowing why or how, he finally understood why everything was happening. Perhaps the heightened sense of awareness stayed with him and was just being put to use. Whatever it was, Johnny welcomed it as he began to speak silent words in his soul. It was so real, and

Johnny wanted the feeling to last. He wanted it more than anything.

***

It happened in the blink of an eye. All of a sudden, Gabe and Lacey appeared on the back bench seat in the van. It was beautiful weather outside, and the sun's rays streaming through the van's windows forced Lacey to squint. After many questions from Rick Engleheart and Easton about her whereabouts and goings on were answered with honest replies, creating head scratches and perplexion, the four of them simply delighted in nods of recognition and contentment.

"We're just glad you're okay," Easton finally said, as a way of creating a conclusion to the conversation.

Lacey was more than okay. What she had just experienced would stay with her soul forever. Long after she died, Lacey could look back on the abduction ordeal as a turning point in her young adult life. She smiled as tears of joy welled up in preparation to launch. But something stopped her emotions in their tracks.

"Gabe, I don't know what language this map is in, but I know I sure as heck can't read it. I've just been heading west on I-80," Rick Engleheart stated.

"That's good. We need to go west," Gabe replied, with a little bit of fatigue as he wiped the sweat from his forehead.

"One question though, sir," Easton added, with a slice of humor. "What are the X's for?"

Lacey shot a concerned look at Gabe. After a couple of silent seconds, Easton also turned around from the front passenger seat.

"Rick, pull the car over. I'll explain what is going to take place."

Rick Engleheart pressed the cruise control off, but it was evident that he was second guessing his command.

"Come on. We have the time. Trust me, it's okay," Gabe spoke, tenderly.

After a few silent nods, Rick Engleheart pulled the car over the right-side rumble strip, off of the highway, and began meandering through a bumpy ATV path so as to to gain some distance from the highway's fast moving traffic. The minivan came to stop behind some thick brush, sprouting wild blackberries budding from the thorn-entwined green leaves. The vehicle was completely hidden from the highway, as it remained parallel to the moving traffic behind the veil of beautiful overgrowth. To the right stood a marshy and mosquito-ridden pokelogan, bordered by a large strip of meadow containing waist-high silky smooth grass. The meadow seemed to roll on forever. Everyone in the van, including Gabe took almost a minute to take in the peaceful sight. There was no better time for a camera.

Lacey was the first to move. Next, Easton, followed by Rick Engleheart and then Gabe. They had only been sitting in the powered-down car for less than a minute, but the sun, now very high in the sky, beat down on the eight-window minivan, showing its greenhouse effect ability. Lacey lay with her back resting on the minivan's hood; Easton slid open the side door and popped a comfortable squat on the van's floor, with his sneakers matting down the tall grass and crushing the remains of a nearby ant hill. His knees supported the area on his arms between the forearms and elbows. With his back hunched over, he said, squinting, "So what's going on, Gabe?"

"Just be honest with us," added Rick Engleheart, nervously, as he began his second lap around the minivan.

Gabe sat Indian-style among the tall grass. "I have been honest with you. It's just that what I'm about to say might alarm your senses."

Lacey, who was basking in the sun with her tank top pulled up exposing her belly button, opened her eyes to look at Gabe. After seeing him sit Indian-style, she shook her head with a smile. Then, she returned right back to sun bathing.

Gabe closed his eyes. He began a deep breathing exercise. Lacey did all she could to keep from laughing. Both Easton and Rick Engleheart halted their grass picking and pacing respectively and watched a private moment Gabe was having with someone or *something* else. It was evident that he was communicating with his deep breaths. Inhaling through his nose for four seconds, holding it for seven, and then exhaling through the skin of his teeth for eight, Gabe repeated the exercise seven times. Finally, he began to speak.

"What most humans do not realize is that there are angels all around them. They do not look like the angels literature and science fiction have so imperfectly manufactured. They look like you. They look like humans. Have you ever been between a rock and a hard place? Have you ever been down on your luck? Have you ever been having a terrible day and someone randomly comes along and holds a door open for you? Or smiles at you? Or cheers you up with interesting banter? Angels are all around you. Could you imagine if we walked around in our true spiritual form? Lacey, Easton... you've seen me. I'd stick out like a sore thumb. It's the Creator's intention for angels to help humans. It's part of why we were established in the first place. Take last month, for example. There was a sweet, naive college girl named Bethany. She was driving up the highway on her way home for break, and her car's hood came flying up, obviously restricting her sight. Fortunately, she was able to pull over safely. She thought she fixed it, putting it back in place, but as soon as she took off again, the same thing happened. The hood would not stay down unless she was going about thirty miles per hour. Well, driving north on I-87 at that speed is not the safest way to drive. Knowing this, she pulled into the next rest stop, five miles away. She called her father, but he was at work. She called her brother, but he was in the middle of one of his baseball games and never heard the phone ring. Helpless, Bethany began to pray. We angels, we hear prayers. And if it's in the Creator's mysterious plan that we do something about it, guess what? We do. In fact, we only hear the prayers that we are supposed to cover. So I heard this one. And as soon as I did, I transcended to Earth's dimension. I looked like an overweight handyman with a concerned heart and big smile - like someone you know you could trust. The Creator equipped me with a motorcycle and in the crate on the back of it, were three bungee cords. Bethany was vulnerable and she needed help, but you should have seen the light she was giving off. Beautiful. I was wearing a certain kind of lens in my sunglasses that showed me human energy. Every person emits a tiny amount of light. And each individual has their own type of energy, but it goes unseen because, well, there are just certain things that human eyes are not programmed to see. The light that each person emits, from one single photon upwards of five hundred thousand photons, emanates from your souls. Anyway, depending on an individual's spirit, the light is constantly changing. Bethany's light, even though she was in a tight spot, was magnificent. She was easy to find. I simply rode up to her car and asked her if she needed help. She was shy and frightened, but she calmed down soon enough. She told me what happened and how she was still eighty miles from home. I retrieved the bungie cords from my crate, harnessed her car's hood down tightly, said 'God bless you', and then rode away. Situations like the one I just described happen every single day. Sometimes, humans do help out their fellow man, but in all seriousness, it's often an angel that comes along."

The three listeners were silent in dumbfounded gazes.

"So how many angels are there?" Rick Engleheart asked.

"On Earth right now?" Gabe looked as if he was doing some quick math in his head. "Hundreds of thousands. Close to a million."

"Wait a second, wait a second," Lacey announced, interrupting the communal thought process. "If you're so powerful, why couldn't you just touch her hood and voila! It's fixed, right?"

"That wasn't in the plan. I never said any of this was easy to figure out. Maybe she learned something from the whole ordeal, who knows. All I am telling you is that there are angels all around you, and they are going to help us rescue Johnny."

A group of cicadas and other insects started a harmonious chorus that was eerily intense. The buzzing was magnified because upon Gabe's announcement, everyone's mouths fell agape in silence.

"I don't know," Rick Engleheart finally said. "This doesn't seem real."

"Rick," Gabe replied, standing up. "I have not steered you wrong yet, and I don't plan to. I know this sounds crazy, and when people read about it, they might not believe it. But you're here now. You've seen things. You want to believe. And just because you haven't experienced it, that doesn't mean it's not out there. Right, Lacey?"

Lacey thought back to that strange dark dimension she was in until Gabe showed up and heroically saved her. She thought of flying. She thought of the comforting voice inside and the powerful tears it created. She thought of the spiritual changes. Oh, how beautiful.

"Right," she whispered, closing her eyes, attempting to return to the brilliance of spirit. As she progressed in her thoughts, pretty little goosebumps took form on her sun-kissed skin.

"So that is what the X's are," Easton remarked with enlightenment.

"Correct," Gabe replied. There are others coming. And by the time we get there, we are going to have a whole army of angels.

Lacey's goosebumps increased in size; fresh ones showed on Easton's and Rick Engleheart's skin, sending chills up and down spines and back up again.

"And each one of you is individually gifted. That is why you are here with me. Especially you, Lacey.

***

After the authority's embarrassment in the torture chamber, Victor screamed for Johnny to follow him back to his living quarters. In passing the enormous elevator shaft with its plethora of arms stretching to other inverted super silos, Victor dragged Johnny's arm as the eighteen-year-old wished to stop and admire it one more time, for he did not know if he would ever see it again. Ignoring how menacing and diabolical the symbol of it was, Johnny turned as he walked and stared in astonishment at the most awe-inspiring structure he had ever seen. The two of them walked at a much faster pace than whence they came. Even though Johnny had just walked the exact same route a mere fifteen minutes earlier, he was still lost.

"Hey, how come we didn't take the elevator back?"

"Power's down inside of it. A couple hundred people are stuck in there. Each elevator runs in multiple directions close to seventy miles per hour, so to just stop on a dime like that? We have some casualties. Probably in the hundreds. Someone's sick idea of a joke."

"So what are you going to do with me?" Johnny asked, frightened by Victor showing his angry side.

"I don't know," the genius confessed. "I'm bringing you back to your living quarters for now. I've got a lot of rubbish to figure out, and I don't need you precluding my much needed efforts."

Johnny accepted Victor's statement with contentment. He needed down time to be alone just as much as everyone else, and he welcomed the idea with delight. Through the remainder of the labyrinth, neither one spoke. Secretly, Johnny attempted to study the ins and outs of the meandering maze. The eighteen-year-old kept his focus and did his best to learn his way through the intricacy of the underground network. Upon re-entering into familiar territory, a smile crept across Johnny's face. For some reason, maybe it was the angel's message in his dream or the overwhelming sense of peaceful awareness he had just received, Johnny felt safe. For the first time in almost a week, he felt safe. And he knew exactly what he was going to do when he retired to his room. He was going to retrieve the pencil and paper and write down everything his soul had silently learned in the last twenty minutes, just as he had done after his dream. Anticipation built as they neared his quarters. Victor shoved him inside, closed the door, and locked it. Johnny felt a spiritual joy in his mind, heart, and soul -

his strongest perception of that particular emotion ever. Consequently, his atmosphere began to become filled with the pure essence of peace as an awarding smile came over his face, getting wider and wider the more and more he wrote.

"How many?" Victor spoke into his watch.

"Three hundred seventeen, sir," replied a male voice. "No survivors."

Quietly acknowledging to himself with a sly grin creeping across his aging face, Victor declared, "The war has begun."

CHAPTER 13

Sunday, 3:12 pm

Gabe checked his watch, which looked like something from another universe. With multiple hands, mostly different lengths with about half spinning clockwise and the other half countering, the watch could certainly tell more than time. In fact, it had a lot to say; however, its tales were for Gabe's eyes only. As its hands silently spun over seemingly random hash marks, he studied it with impatient eyes. The other three simply waited in silence for him to receive whatever he was looking for. By this time, they were used to their guide's quirks. Whether it was the meditative breathing, the strange way in which he interpreted the jumble of intersecting lines he called a map, or his mathematical stare at the perpetually spinning watch on his wrist, the three humans in the group had learned to accept the fact that they were in the unfortunate position of not having nearly as much knowledge as their chauffeur. They waited.

"Alright," he finally announced. "We have about ten minutes before we have to leave if we want to be at the first checkpoint in time. Go to the bathroom, do whatever you have to do, and we'll be off."

As the captain of the group, Gabe had made these types of announcements before. And when he said ten minutes, he meant ten minutes.

Something had been on Lacey's mind for a while and she figured it better a time than any to satisfy her thoughts. "So you think you'll have time to explain to me what you meant when you said 'Especially you, Lacey," the eighteen-year-old brunette asked, with air quotes held up for sarcasm.

"Hard to say," Gabe replied. "Maybe if you don't interrupt me."

His response was meant to make Lacey laugh, but there was something about his cadence that made it seem like he was serious.

"Okay, then. Shoot."

"I'll tell you in due time, child."

It was the first time Gabe had referred to Lacey as child and chose to address her as such. The fact that he was clearly not going to tell her why she was special after giving her a glimpse of hope took a back seat to the pressing matter at hand.

"Child?" Lacey asked, with a confused and somewhat disgusted look on her face.

Gabe ignored her inquiry with a smile, walked past her, and climbed back into the driver's seat of the forest green minivan. No one had ever called Lacey 'child' before. Not her dad, not her granddad, not even her mom before she succumbed to the cancer raging inside of her. And the unprecedented choice of address stirred latent opposing emotions deep inside of her heart. Half of her wanted to be angry at him, the other half wanted to ask him to always call her that. However, all of her was pleased and touched having known the pleasure of such love.

***

It was after two and a half hours of driving when their minivan reached the first checkpoint. Gabe pushed the vehicle out of cruise control, alerting his three passengers with gradual deceleration - a sensation they had not felt in a long enough time to temporarily forget the feeling.

"Click-click, click-click, click-click..."

The right-side blinking turn signal sang an impatient song of repetition as it ricocheted off of the van's closed windows, dancing around everybody to warn them of the impending enlightenment Gabe had so politely promised. It had been almost an hour since they had passed a sign welcoming them to the Hawkeye state of Iowa. Beneath the broad blue welcome sign, a quote was branded in large white letters, stating, "Our liberties we prize and our rights we will maintain."

Gabe kept his turn signal on as he veered right off of the exit ramp. Using the convoluted map, which lay across the center circle console, as his guide, Gabe quickly found what he was looking for. Unpaved, dirt roads soon supported the van's sixteen- inch alloy wheels. Pebbles, silt, soil, and the sun-baked clay ground were being kicked up from the Earth and spun in the wheel wells, nicking off of the van's metal undercarriage as the vehicle bounced along leaving a trail of brown dust to dissipate in its wake. The sounds of this new excursion forged a wide array of feelings in the van's passengers - excitement, anticipation, nervousness, and discomfiture. Gabe, Rick Engleheart, Lacey, and Easton had grown considerably close to one another during the time spend on the road. And the undeniable and inevitable fact that a number of strangers would be joining them on their quest was slightly disconcerting.

Once again, Gabe began his deep breathing. To the unbeknownst onlooker, such an exercise would cause confused laughter; however, at this point, the three passengers were more than used to it. Four seconds of inhaling, breath being held for seven, then gradually exhaling for eight - it was like a scratched CD repeating itself every nineteen seconds. Slowing the car down to a stop, Gabe's breathing increased in depth. He was completely relaxed and if the word 'peaceful' was looked up in the dictionary, there would be a thumbnail of Gabe's face at this particular moment. In a stark contrast, the humans in the car possessed panicked and anticipated fright on their faces. They were too nervous to speak. Lacey, being repulsed by awkward silence, broke the stillness.

"So," she said.

After ten seconds of heightened expectancy, Gabe finally replied with eyes still peacefully closed, "Calm down Sleepyhead, we're almost there."

Lacey noticed a small dairy farm in the distance. Mesmerized by its simple beauty, she began to take in the classic charm of the setting standing resolute in front of her.

A towering dark blue silo arose from the ground standing at the far corner of the farm, directly across the dirt road from a field of alfalfa. To the silo's right was a barn, housing all of the cows. Its red siding was contrasted by its black overhang roof. A three story haymount stood at the halfway point, intersected by a wide wooden ramp serving as the main entrance to the eighty-yard barn. On the other side of the outbuilding stood another silo soaring toward the sky. Its silver color was dirtied by decades of dust from the dairy farm's focused, hard work. Facing the main entrance of the barn on the opposite side of the circled dirt-road driveway was the farm house. Its beautiful porch jutted out from the house as the resting place for the children's toys, bicycles, basketballs, and wooden baseball bats. The gray house was not much to look at from the outside, but inside, Lacey imagined warmth and beauty combined with the comforting smell of a homemade blueberry pie baking in the oven. It looked like the quintessential farm run by the classically perfect American family. Lacey imagined that in the summer, cousins from all over Iowa came and played on the farm. They would shoot hoops against the wooden backboard, struggling to maintain a consistent dribble on the gravelly stones. They would play hide and seek in the haymount and make up silly games swinging on a long and sturdy rope, falling onto the prickly, but soft fodder. They would go on long walks and adventures with the family's black labs, goofing off in the creek that meandered around their 325 acres. Lacey was looking back in time to simpler circumstances. Back when life was made out of real moments, of things you could touch, of things you could feel, of quiet places you could go and hide to escape the chaos humans called life, and when living consisted of two constants - hard work and freedom. Lacey became entranced by the farm. It was down a long and winding dirt road, but it still looked close enough to reach out and touch. She wished she was part of that family and everything they experienced. Everything.

She kept her eyes fixed on the farm, not being able to look away even if she wanted. Its beauty at the base of a large oak tree-covered hill was captivating the eighteen-year-old suburbanite. On the far end of the dairy farm, stretching all the way to the creek more than two hundred yards away, was a healthy, thriving corn field. In less than a month, the stalks would be over eight feet high, stretching toward the sun-lit sky. Earth's G2V type star was in the process of going down in the west. And it would not come close to the horizon for a few more hours, but when it did, the corn field would appear golden. The sky would be painted a fiery red-orange that only a beautiful summer sunset could produce. The dazzling colors would emanate from the ever-so slowly sinking yellow circle. Trees, normally an emerald green, would morph into black silhouettes, not being able to help themselves on July nights. One particular oak tree stood out to Lacey above all the rest. It looked oddly out of place, in the middle of a rolling meadow on the outskirts of the farm's vast acreage. Lacey imagined it wanted to grow on the hillside with the other oaks, perhaps even on the hill's peak. But its deep roots kept it from its even deeper desires. A thick trunk supported two dozen extremely elongated branches, stretching out in every direction - the longest of which was at the bottom, pointing toward the high hill as if telling the tree which direction its roots wished to go. The sun's rays, like bristles, painted the tops of the corn stalks a rich gold as the field gracefully rolled on. Lacey looked at the undulating farmland and dreamed there was no tomorrow. She was lost in its beautiful artistry. It was the first farm she had ever seen, and it made her not want to ever look at one again. There was nothing on Earth that was more breathtakingly magnificent - the combination of natural creation and human kind's hard work.

Waking up from her silently peaceful daydream, Lacey rubbed her elegantly introvertive eyes and heard a car in the distance. It rumbled over the dirt road on the other side of the farm. Far in the scope of her 20/15 vision, Lacey could see the dust cloud illuminated by the sun, which hovered forty-five degrees above the horizon. There. An old station wagon crossed the small forty-foot bridge near the blue silo. It was a quarter mile away and closing. Difficult to hear over the car's closing route, Lacey thought she saw another dust cloud forming right where the first one had taken shape. Could another car be following the first one? She squinted. With their minivan slightly higher in elevation than the farm and its narrow two-way dirt road leading to and fro, Lacey could clearly make out a second station wagon following behind the first, which was now close enough that the color could be made out. It had a maroon base coat, but its sides were wooden panels. Never before had Lacey seen a car like that in her life.

"You gotta be kidding me," she observed to herself out loud. "Is that real?"

As the second one came closer into view, Lacey noticed it had a similar makeup, except instead of maroon, its paint was baby blue. Similar to the first one, its embarrassing wooden side panels showed its age. What the eighteen-year-old failed to notice, however, was the long line of cars following the first two awkward-looking station wagons. They all ranged in make and varied in model, but all of them were manufactured well before Lacey was born. She looked at the first two like a nine-year-old kid looks at an owl at the zoo. As the first station wagon ascended its way up the hill to the awaiting minivan, Lacey deciphered that it contained four passengers, as did the next car and every vehicle thereafter. In total, thirty-nine vehicles ranging in manufacturing years from 1985 to 1998 ascended up the dirt road. Lacey, Easton, and Rick Engleheart gazed at the long line of compact cars, station wagons, and minivans as they formed a configuration beginning ten feet from their minivan all the way down to the foot of the farm's towering dark blue silo. Gabe looked on with a proud smile.

"Everyone ready to meet the others?" he asked, as he stepped out onto the gravelly dirt.

***

Victor pressed the button labeled *B57* in his private elevator. In Emerus, a small number of privileged individuals enjoyed the luxury of having their own means of transportation throughout the vast, multiple levels. The catch was that the personal elevators were more like pods, containing only enough room for one person to comfortably fit. The goings on in B57 were top secret, even by Emerus measures. The people who worked there stayed there and were restricted from visiting any other level. Victor, being one of half a dozen people given the clearance to come and go as he pleased, arrived with an angry and frustrated gate. He made his way through facial recognition-automated doors without slowing down. Passing countless rows of supercomputers on his left and on his right, he finally entered into the Observation Room. Thousands upon thousands of monitors littered the four hundred-foot-high surrounding walls. Fifty large ellipse-shaped transparent tables were dispersed throughout the enormous room. On top of each table sat a twelve-by-three shapeshifting high-definition, three-dimensional monitor that the user could pull up, stretch out, and control with the wave of his hand. Victor was the lone human in the vast room, and even though he was a certified genius, he was by far and away the least intelligent creation.

Particularly powerful supercomputers, called Q's, acted as voice-command robots, obeying virtually any command the user gave. Users - there were only three of them in Emerus, Victor being one - often used Q's to run detailed intel. on specific people. It was not your run-of-the-mill information though. Starting out by tracking credit card purchases, text messages, voicemails, and phone calls, Q's quickly began tracking more personal information after the Paradigm Shift of 2015. Ten years later, Q's had the ability to tell their users exactly where a person was with up-to-date information by the second. Not only that, but they could predict the future with trend analysis and other information gathered via smart phone microphone audio, text messages, and social media. Using government-installed spy cameras all over public and private property, Q's could zoom in on a person's face, listen to private conversations, and even infiltrate people's homes using super cameras. Reading and subsequently influencing thought process was simply the next step. Enemies of the state would see it as Emerus stripping the God-given right to think freely. Obedient and unknowing citizens would see it as the creation of a better world.

"Q-1, pull up Lacey Hassle," he commanded.

"Hassle, Lacey. Tracking," the eerily human-sounding robotic voice replied.

Victor walked over to the nearest ellipse. There was a small cut out in the framework of the table where the user could stand, giving him control of the three-dimensional screen pulled up by the Q.

"Hassle, Lacey. Last seen heading west in Rhode Island. Sunday 2:33 a.m. Searching for visual."

"No. No, Q-1. I need the most up-to-date info on her."

"I apologize, sir. Unable to detect."

Victor slammed both of his fists down on the table, sending a wave of purple light through the screen. After a second failed attempt - this time to track Johnny's father - Victor was quickly running out of options.

"Q-1, why are you not able to track the subjects?"

Q's could not only obey commands, but they could think for themselves. Weighing options, analyzing the plethora of possibilities, they could operate smarter and faster than any human.

"Subjects are either out of range or they have found an undiscovered stealth mechanism. Only those two possibilities fit in the positive range of probability."

Victor swallowed hard. He knew they were not out of range. The probability of that may have been on the positive side, but it was so minimal. Out of range meant they left Earth's atmosphere. These were normal, everyday human beings. There was really no chance of that. However, Victor wished there was, for that was the better possibility as far as he was concerned. How had they discovered a stealth mechanism? Was it something similar to what happened with Johnny's cousin, Matthew? Victor had commanded his peers to figure that one out, but no word had gotten back to him yet. Clearly, normal humans were receiving some form of support. But from whom? Was this why the new technology, the ability to read minds and influence thought, was only working on part of the population? Questions such as these became a swarm of honeybees surrounding Victor's mind, stinging without relent, and thus creating fear. For the first time ever, Emerus was operating with the unknown. It was a foreign feeling, and Victor hated it. He spoke into his wrist.

"Trail has gone cold," he said. "Whereabouts on Lacey Hassle and Rick Engleheart unknown."

"Affirmative. Same with Matthew Brigham."

Victor breathed a heavy sigh of thought. "Well, looks like we are back to square one, gentlemen. Let's reconvene in one hour. B-47 conference room."

Walking out of the quietly buzzing room, Victor racked his brain trying to figure out a simple answer. "No, it couldn't be," he said out loud. Making his way to his private pod elevator, he commanded it as to where to take him. "Library. And hurry."

***

It took some time for everyone to gather around Gabe and his crew's minivan. Gabe instructed the large group of 160 to split up. Dividing the angels and the humans, it was clear that he needed to address his kind. Thirty-nine men, each well over six-foot with long hair and appearing to be in tip-top shape, followed Gabe toward the farm to a nearby field. The 120 humans patiently milled about among the age-old vehicles. There was something to be said for how they simply accepted their roles. All of them were teenagers of varied ethnicities, and like puzzle pieces, they fit together perfectly, creating an image worthy enough to be viewed in museums for millennia.

"Sleepyhead, come with me," Gabe instructed with a gesture, which was silently obeyed.

Gabe stood atop a grassy knoll and asking for his ilk to form a semicircle around him, he started to speak.

"Hello all and welcome. I am going to make this short and to the point. As all of you know, we are called here today and commissioned by the Creator to complete a rescue mission. We are here to rescue a special someone who is particularly important to the grand arrangement. He is being held captive in Wyoming. Deep underground. It is going to take a lot to not only get him out safely, but also to ensure that we come out with no casualties of our own. It is going to be dangerous. We have reason to believe that forces in the dark world have been directly assisting the captors in motive and intent. Expect them to show up. And expect them to try to lure you over to their side. However, we know the truth. We are more powerful than they are. We are stronger, faster, and are fighting for the purpose of glory. And in a lot of ways, the battle has already been won. But you know how they work. You know their attempts to deceive. Once they are in your head, it is hard to get them out. Hold fast. Stay strong. Even though we cannot see the Creator in this realm, He is here. His Spirit lives in each and every person here," Gabe reassured, pointing back to the crowd of 120. "And, we have our ace in the hole. Lacey Hassle."

At the mention of her name, immediate murmurings and whispering chatters began to buzz about the group.

"Come up here, Sleepyhead," Gabe commanded, with a quiet and loving voice.

"What's going on?" Lacey asked, suddenly embarrassed. "How do they know my name?"

"I told you once and I meant it. You are special. Beyond your wildest dreams."

CHAPTER 14

The rest of the group continued to remain relaxed atop the peacefully warm dirt road overlooking the farm and its proudly innocent fields. Large puffy white cumulus clouds were quickly moving to cover up the radiant sun when each of the 119 teenagers heard a voice speak in their souls. It had a kind, patient, understanding, and loving tone. Exactly what each person heard varied, possessing a personal touch to each individual. The voice clarified for some, encouraged others, and was a breath of peaceful refreshment for all. A weight and burden was lifted off each and every shoulder that evening and redemption songs echoed endlessly throughout their souls. And as they were all about to find out, Lacey was not the only one born with gifts.

The eighteen-year-old brunette stood in front of the gathering with a half smile fueled by a combination of embarrassment and astonishment.

"Gabe, tell me. What's going on?" she asked impatiently, aiming to get an answer to quell her overwhelming sense of ignorance.

It was evident that some of the crowd of thirty-nine were somewhat unaware of all of the details surrounding Lacey Hassle. Some knew everything and their faces showed it as they smiled at the teenager. Others knew only her name, but even that fact threw Lacey for a loop.

"Let me explain some things," Gabe announced to the crowd. "Some of you may be wondering what exactly is going on. We don't have much time, so I'll do my best to explain everything in haste. Lacey Hassle is a direct descendant of the Nephilim. The gene is dominant within her DNA, and the Creator decided long before she was born who she was destined to be. He designed the effects to skip generations, as we all know. For His purpose, Ms. Hassle here has the strongest strand of Nephilim DNA in the history of humanity. George Washington's was close, but not like this. The sequence of bases in Lacey's DNA shows a hybrid genetic code - half human and half angel. It has already started to manifest itself, and her destiny is set out to be beyond great. The Creator has put forward a plan. A plan that takes what the enemy meant for evil and uses it for good. And the start of that plan is rescuing Johnny from his captors in Wyoming. With your help, Lacey, and the others, whom she has in one way or another spiritually influenced and affected, will begin the takedown, and as sure as the sun sets, we will prevail!"

Gabe's inspiring words created much aggressive celebration from the crowd, which the larger gathered group above clearly took notice of. The thirty-nine angels slapped hands with their neighbors like friends in the stands at a football game.

"Gabe?" Lacey asked. "Is that all true? How am I descended from angels and humans? And what is the Nephilim?"

"Look it up on your smartphone, Sleepyhead. And yes, it is true. You are gifted. The Creator is very fond of you, you know. And each one of them," Gabe pointed to the oncoming crowd, "they are here because your spirit has had an effect on their lives. Some smaller than others, but nonetheless, because of you, they are not affected by any thought-inhibiting technology. Neither are you, nor me, nor anybody here. We have a purpose, Lacey. *You* have a purpose. You were created for distinction, and you, Lacey Hassle, are destined for greatness.

In deep and introspective thought, Lacey walked away from Gabe. She knew that he would understand. Everything that had happened to her in the past week - the peculiarity of it all - it was *supposed* to happen. She wrestled with that notion. And every time she thought she might be pinned under the pressure, Lacey thought back to when she was taken, rescued by Gabe, and in hearing that voice of comfort and love safeguard her soul, she remembered watching her tears fall down quelling the flames of agony and hurt. That voice. She longed to hear it again. Even though she was kept in a very dark place - one of the dark dimensions, as Gabe said - when Lacey heard the voice, she had never been at such internal tranquility. Peace was being built around her in every direction, and in her heart, Lacey accepted her destiny. Still unaware of what it was exactly, she nodded in confidence that there was something larger than the life humanity found itself born into. There was something beyond what human eyes can see and what human emotions, bodies, and spirits can experience. Something greater. And her life was intended to somehow in some way act as an integral part to that unseen presence which gives goosebumps and generates tears, grants internal strength, and graciously comforts. Lacey remembered distinctly the wonder of that initial cathexis when Gabe showed up at her doorstep and said, "Lacey I'm prepared to offer you something. A life, a meaningful one." Something inside of her soul pushed her to begin that journey. And she decided that she had come too far and experienced too much to turn back now. She felt aware and ready. Ignoring her perplexity and the questions still circling her mind like vultures, Lacey accepted her fate with an empowering smile.

"Gabriel, there was an issue I think you should know about."

After turning toward the inquiry like someone turns to his brother, Gabe replied, "What's going on, Raphael?"

It was clear that Raphael wanted to get out what was on his mind before the rest of the crowd made their way down to the lower field. His jet black hair was not quite as long as Gabe's, but the two had similar facial features - a defined jaw line, thick cheeks, and anterior symmetry.

"I tried to teleport Johnny out of there."

Gabe responded with an agape mouth.

"I know it's not part of the plan, but I thought there was nothing written against it, so why not?"

Now Gabe gave a look prompting Raphael to continue.

"Well, it didn't work. I came over Johnny, wrapped my arms around his energy, and tried to make the leap, but something was keeping him there. Something was grounding him."

"No one saw you, right?" Gabe warned.

"I killed the grid, correct. But there was someone else in the room with him. Another captive. His spiritual makeup was strikingly similar to Johnny's. He was being tortured, and Johnny was being forced to watch. I think it was one of his family members," he stated, uncomfortably. "So after failing to teleport Johnny out of there, I went over, wrapped my arms around the other's energy and successfully got him the heck out of there."

"Who was he?" Gabe asked, extremely intrigued.

"Matthew!" Easton exclaimed, gravely puzzled.

The gathered group of 119 were walking as one unit, across the dirt road and down into the freshly plowed field where the angels had convened. The comfortable and calming aroma of raw cut grass on a warm summer's evening danced inside everyone's noses, bringing back childhood memories of innocence and bliss that could only be felt during the long, exciting season of summertide.

Easton spotted his older brother through the dense and diverse crowd. The last time he had seen Matthew was at their aunt, Eileen

Engleheart's, wake and funeral, which amassed four times as many people as stood in the field. Easton was surprised he had not noticed his fit and burly brother sooner. Matthew had jet black hair, just like Easton, but it was shorter, accentuating his larger than life smile, which always seemed to show up at the right time. He regularly seemed to somehow run into minor troubles, but just as easily found his way out of them. Recently, he had been on a kayaking trip with his uncle, Oliver, and some friends.

"Wow, you really need a haircut," Easton declared, more seriously than jokingly.

"So do you," Matthew replied, almost before his younger brother finished his sentence.

The two were six years apart, but the best of friends. After initial questions and subsequent answers completed with nods of confusion and agreement, Matthew and Easton felt prepared for what the future had in store for them.

"I've been waiting for something like this my whole life," Matthew asserted.

"What do you mean?"

"Don't you know what's going on here? When we rescue Johnny, it's going to be something that should be written down in history books, but never will," Matthew's eyes gazed at the 325 acre farm standing resolute in the distance. "Taking down the established power structure to get back our God-given liberties. It's going to be fun. Dangerous, but fun."

Easton had never seen such determination in his brother's face. Perhaps it was because of what his captors did to him, what he saw, what he experienced. He was strong, in every aspect of the adjective. And rewarding him for it, Raphael cured his burns. What happened deep inside Matthew's heart that day, however, could not be cured. Human life had its limits. Emotional wounds never heal. Instead, they transform into a new lifeform, going one of two ways - down the path of redemption and making the person a strong overcomer or down the path of loss and making the person bitter, causing he or she to take pleasure in the misfortunes of others. Either way, the rebuilding effort of the soul begins and does not relent until the person comes out the other side amended. Change is inevitable when disaster strikes the soul like a thunderstorm's lightning. It's simply a matter of controlling the change taking place. Matthew had already walked a far distance on the path of redemption, and an overcomer he was going to become, through and through.

The large group of 160 all knew what was individually needed of them. The humans could not explain it, but they felt driven and called to complete the arduous task that lay in front of them. Gabe and the other angels briefly spoke to the gathering as one unit before everyone began to return to their old, beat-up, but serviceable vehicles. Raphael suggested that Matthew go in Gabe's van with Easton and his uncle. The archangel, Raphael, and the young warrior, Matthew, tightly and quickly hugged.

"Thank you for everything."

"It's my pleasure, Matthew. I'll see you in Wyoming," Raphael replied with a serious smile.

It would not be terribly long when the glowing yellow sun would dip below the horizon to take it's circadian trip to the southern hemisphere. Something was peculiar about the sky, however. A star was out. And it was bright. Clouds had been wiped away, revealing a clear and blue sky, and Vega had somehow managed to peek its bright white face against the cerulean backdrop. As its solitary planet invisibly orbited the glittering star, twenty-five light years away from Earth, Vega beautifully sparkled in the summer evening sky. It was noticed by everyone. Thinking in silence was the communal response of Rick Engleheart, Lacey, Easton, and Matthew as they all tilted their heads back, gazing up into the endless space above. Matthew asked Gabe what a star was doing out so early, and Gabe responded with a simple smile, saying, "It's a sign."

"A sign for what?" Lacey asked, with wonder.

"That we're on the right track. That the Creator is blessing all of us on our journey and ensuing mission. That we're doing something right." Gabe, who had stopped to stargaze with his group, continued walking. "You know," he said, looking up as he approached the minivan, "Vega's lifetime is only a tenth of that of your sun. But both stars are going to die out at roughly the same time."

"Will humans still be around when that happens?" Easton asked.

Gabe held his long, fixed stare as he replied. "There are only three things that never come to an end. The Creator and his realm, your souls, and us angels. Everything else eventually finds its demise one way or another. That is true for Earth and it's true for your sun as well. In three and a half billion years, your star will be so hot that Earth's oceans will begin to boil, the ice caps will finally melt, permanently, and snow will become a phenomenon of the past. But humans will never get to experience no snow on their planet. When that happens, no life can exist on Earth's scorched surface."

Matthew opened his mouth to speak, but Gabe continued on before any sound came out.

"Then two and a half billion years after that, your sun will run out of hydrogen in its core, causing it to grow into a red giant, the size of which will absorb the first two planets in the solar system and probably Earth too. Long after that, billions of years later when your sun dies out, no Easton. I'm sorry, but humans will not be around. But the star's core will become a diamond that is over two thousand miles across. Isn't that interesting? Humans will never see it though. Not even close. Your species has not treated your planet with the respect she deserves. But don't worry. The annihilation of the human race is far away by your standards of time. It will come to an end though. Humans, everything they have, and will ever conceive and create will eventually find extinction."

Thinking in cooperative guilt became the new response to Gabe's information, which he in turn, felt guilty for. In an attempt to change the subject, Gabe returned his focus to Vega up above.

"You know, if you were on Vega's planet observing your sun, it would be a faint star in the Columba constellation. Earth would be entirely invisible. It's interesting, isn't it?"

"Not helping, Gabe," Lacey spoke, with a smile.

"So there's really life out there, huh?" Rick Engleheart asked, looking up.

"Not like you guys would think."

"What do you mean?" Matthew asked.

"It's not important. Let's keep our focus. Come on."

The four humans obeyed their captain and climbed up into the emerald minivan. Rick Engleheart rode shotgun and Gabe quickly adjusted and traded out the heavy removable seats, creating a row of three directly behind both Rick Engleheart and him. Lacey behind Gabe, Easton next to her, and Matthew behind his uncle.

"Now let's go rescue Johnny," Gabe said, with a goosebump-giving tone.

CHAPTER 15

Without a doubt, the library was the oldest area of Emerus. Its dusty and chalky smell consumed Victor's sinuses, causing periodic nasally coughs preceded by ugly, abrupt scowls. The floor's green carpet had been there since the 1980s and although it was vacuumed once a month, it showed its age. Not many people ventured to the library. In fact, Victor considered himself lucky as he was old enough to know that one even existed in Emerus. The thin layer of dust that peacefully rested atop every table, shelf, and desk hinted that no one had been there for any reason other than to vacuum in years. Looking around to gather his bearings because he himself had not stepped foot in the lonely room for a few years, Victor felt as though he had fallen through a mirror and time warped forty-three years back to the past. Also showing the room's age, all of the books were still arranged by way of the Dewey Decimal System. However, he walked over to the catalogue drawers, quickly found the correct grouping of call numbers, and began sifting through sandy index cards within the 600 range. It wasn't long before he found what he was desperately searching for. Pulling three separate cards from the neatly abandoned drawer brought Victor's thoughts back to the past, to a simpler but sadder time. His children and wife, forced to stay behind, did not and would never understand. But they tried. Oh, they tried.

Victor snaked around obtrusive bookshelves mindlessly trying to locate the books corresponding to the index cards in his lonely left hand. His body was deep underground in the destitute Emerus library, but his mind was in another place and another time.

"How could you do this to us? We are a family."

"Will I ever see you again, Daddy?"

"But I'm going to miss you too much. Please don't go."

Those three questions circled Victor's mind like vultures as he walked away from a different life. When the scavengers landed, they began grossly picking at his heart and at his soul, and no matter how much Victor yelled and screamed for them to go away and leave him alone, they remained for they knew that they could feast for as long they wanted. It had been more than two decades since he had last seen family, and even though he hated the people who confiscated his old, regular life, he had quickly learned to adjust. It was part of his training.

And now he was prepared to never see his loved ones again. However, many times a month, Victor's dreams would be filled with flashing images of his family, not aged from when he left - young and vibrant, warm and happy. In these dreams, the plot would, for the most part, be symmetrical throughout.

Victor would randomly find himself driving on the same old familiar suburban neighborhood roads in his old little dark blue car. He would pull into his home's driveway to find his son anxiously awaiting his arrival. When he ascended up the three stone porch steps, Victor would pick his son up and hug the little boy in his arms. He wanted to tell him how much he missed him and how he wished circumstances had been different. But no matter how much he tried, Victor could not form words when he attempted to speak. Only silence was emitted from his mouth. But something about the way his son acted led Victor to think that he had never left. It seemed like a normal day back from the office of his commonplace computer programming job.

"Come on, Daddy. Can we please go for a ride in your race car?"

Victor's car, a 1987 Chevy Impala was perhaps the furthest thing from a race car, but his son loved the way it sounded and felt when his hero would push in the clutch and shift into a higher gear, accelerating.

"We will. I promise," Victor thought, but couldn't manage to bring forth from his mouth.

More than anything, he wanted to see his beautiful wife, which was under the realm of normalcy for any routine day back in those times. But dreams are head-scratchers. In the dream, Victor was returning from a mid-week day of work - his old work. But he felt like he was returning from Wyoming, though his car, his boy, and the house had not aged a day. And the strangest part about it was the fact that he knew he was dreaming while in the midst of the dream itself. Something about his life just felt a little too abstract to be real. And even though it wasn't real, he desperately desired to see his wife's face again. However, every time he put his son down to open the door and enter the house, he woke up in a cold sweat, breathing shallow nervous inhales with a rapid heart beat. He had still not seen his wife. Tears would well up in his eyes and Victor would fall back to sleep as the warm salty tears reheated his cold face back to comfort. He lay feeling sorry for himself. It was the only way he could get any sleep.

Abruptly awaking from his daydream, Victor clumsily walked into a thick wooden bookshelf. The sound of his black shoe knocking against the mahogany base startled him enough that he dropped the three index cards. Bending over to pick them up, the bookshelf stared him back in the face. Victor looked more closely at the books tightly stacked on the third shelf up from the bottom. There! A new idea began to take shape in Victor's mind as he excitedly retrieved a handful of books and tossed them onto a nearby table.

"The car!" he exclaimed out loud, in a whisper.

An excited smile came upon his face as he prepared to viciously flip through the first of many heavy books, standing over the messy pile. Initially skimming the book's Table of Contents, next referring to the Index, and finally frustratingly turning over large sections of information meaningless to him with his thumb and index finger, Victor soon fell into a system. After three books with an identical result, much to his disappointment, Victor tiredly tackled the fourth with significantly less gusto than he did the first three. He lazily looked in the Table of Contents, and after not finding what he needed, he flipped back to the Index indifferently and let out a defeated sigh. And just then, he saw it. Excitement abounded in his blood again. He hastily turned to the beginning of the page range the Index provided and began his reading. Ten pages didn't take him long, and upon finishing, he spoke into wristwatch.

"Gather the team and come down to the library. I have a plan."

CHAPTER 16

To the Doc, it was axiomatic that most of the fancily clad group whom he had summoned down to the depths had never stepped foot in Emerus' library. Most of the group of sixteen were at least a decade younger than Victor, with only one aligning with his generation - Michael Willard, a studious and confident man, who looked great for being in his fifties. He and Victor had been good friends for the better part of three decades. In fact, they had been rival computer programmers working for two prominent and competing companies before they were taken. And before that, they each attended Princeton University's graduate program, which is where they met. Two genius minds in the same generation. Both Victor and Michael felt sorry for the other eras that never had the opportunity to be graced by their minds' acumen. Their ability to understand and reason was unmatched by anyone in Emerus, where the world's greatest minds convened. Both of their IQ's narrowly surpassed that of Albert Einstein, and the two men saw eye-to-eye on practically everything. They simply came from different backgrounds.

Michael Willard (he was called Dr. Willard by just about everyone in Emerus except for Victor, who called him Will). By American standards, his family was poor. As tensions quietly grew between the various classes throughout the 2000s and teens and the nonviolent civil war began to change its shape, The Willard family escaped the oncoming violence by the skin of their teeth. The lower and lower-middle classes had had enough, and an uprising was imminent. Nonviolent at first, but quickly turning ugly after Martial law was declared in the summer of 2016, The Willards left the future militarized police-state zone that Spring and moved north, finally finding family in West Virginia. It was there where Michael Willard was able to use his talents and become successful, finally providing his family with what he believed they deserved. However, it wasn't long before his talent, skill, and mind were discovered and consequently recruited, bringing him to Emerus against his will. Just like they did with Victor, they threatened his family and swore that if he refused or attempted to flee, they would find him and slaughter his family in front of his own eyes, all the while telling them that it was his fault. He was left with no other choice but to comply.

When he and Victor reconnected in Emerus, they almost could not believe it, for they had not seen each other since Princeton and the only communication between the two of them since graduate school was via emails. Their back stories, although slightly different, shared a common denominator, and it was that which helped them remain such close, yet distant friends. And now, the matter at hand at least felt more important than wishing circumstances were different. However, every time Victor looked into his friend's eyes, the past roared back like a lion. The case was the same with Will, and even though they desired to, the two men did not make eye contact when Will entered the room.

Victor thanked the men for coming as each of them found a seat at the four tables arranged like the coinciding side of a die. Most of the men contained confused faces; all of them exhibited exhaustion.

"You are probably all wondering why I have asked you down here," Victor stated generally, standing in front of the four tables, his back against a dusty brown book shelf. "I mean think about it. Here we are trying to track down people who are not succumbing to our technology, probably headed here, and who pose a major threat to us and our country. Well gentlemen, I have figured out a possible way to find them."

"Why are we having trouble tracking them?" asked a young man in his late twenties.

Victor silently looked around the room and the silence stared back. "Will?" Victor deferred to his friend because he just happened to head up the department that dealt with investigative tracking.

"We believe they are operating under some form of foreign stealth technology that we have not yet come across in our research. And by foreign, I mean a type of extra-dimensional automated cloaking technology. Most likely coming from the other side. If I had to take an educated guess, I'd say it works something like this: there is at least one person acting as a beacon, most likely a few, who are emitting an unseen type of signal that is an adjutant in not only repelling our technology, but also protecting anyone within a certain radius. This is why when our drones search for known suspects, like Rick Engleheart and Lacey Hassle, no recent data comes up. The GPS locators and microphones in their cell phones have no new data. The trail has gone cold. Drones armed with facial recognition technology can't find them. It is as if they are invisible. And whoever is helping them, well, we honestly know nothing about. But we believe whomever or whatever infiltrated the room and took Matthew has a direct correlation with our suspects. And that was not human. Its capabilities are far beyond that. But Intel cannot bring any information to the surface."

The absence of speech, but abundance of thought filled the room with deafening silence.

"What about the GPS signals in their car?" someone asked, proudly as if a light bulb had suddenly been turned on above his head.

Everyone's eyes moved to Victor.

"This is what I have found," Victor said, his eyes widening throughout his proud declaration. "As you all should know, we started putting hidden surveillance monitors in every car for sale in the United States - micro black boxes, covert cameras, GPS trackers," he emphasized the last item, pointing at the thoughtful man awarding his intellect, "...in 1999. This not only assisted the American government in its spy tactics, but it also allowed us to monitor who was, is, and will be on our side. To this day, it is one of the more successful projects Emerus has completed. Part of the reason why we are having trouble getting at least one hit on where they are is because I believe they are driving a car that was manufactured before 1999."

Low murmurings of enlightenment shot toward the lonely library walls, which enveloped them for a second then spit the inaudible, but telling sounds back to flourish throughout the room.

"At the vehicle surveillance program's investiture," Victor continued, "we knew that eventually cars from that long ago would simply not be prevalent. Surely it would not be common for a car predating the millennium to be driving along American roads. Therefore, it would be a damn good idea if you people got word out to every lowly police officer between Rhode Island and Wyoming. If they see a vehicle that even slightly looks like it belongs before the paradigm shift, they are to pull it over and interrogate the passengers. This is our only hope," Victor grimly concluded, as he turned around to face the undusted book shelves.

Being disgusted by not hearing any movement by his colleagues, Victor turned back around. "Now I don't know if you people have suddenly gone deaf in the past two minutes, but I want some results. And I want them now. Go!"

In startled unison, the group jumped up like frightened forest animals. They scurried out the single door in single file, leaving behind only their ill-fated decisions. One stayed behind and approached

Victor. It was the first time since Michael Willard entered the room that he and the Doc made eye contact.

"Victor?" he asked seriously. "How did you come up with this plan, you brilliant bastard?"

Victor laughed and a proud smile came across his face. Then, he remembered the day dream he had had about his family and his old car. That was the truth. That was how he thought up the grand idea. Perhaps one day he would wish to share his strange and accidental method. But that day was not this one. It had been over a decade since he and Michael Willard were taken from their families, but even if it had been an eternity, Victor would think it too sore a subject to broach.

"Will, you know," he replied with a half serious smile, "Sometimes ideas just hit you like a ton of bricks. You sift through the rubble, picking up one idea, analyzing it, and tossing it to the side until you find the perfect one - the one that will save your ass."

"It takes a genius to see the bricks though, am I right?"

"That you are, Will. That you are."

***

Johnny had become completely content with being in peaceful solitude. He more than learned to adjust to the darkness; he began to thrive in it. He started to grasp the fact that he was caught up in something more important than petty human problems - something larger than life itself. And since the angel, Gabriel, had visited him in that strange dream-like state, Johnny found a calm tranquility in his heart that he could conjure up any time he pleased, satiating his body, his mind, and his soul. It was how he slept the best night sleeps he had ever had and how he learned to focus on the spirit and not the flesh. Let them kill me, he thought. What would be so bad about that? I get called home to join the Creator and Mom in pure happiness where there is nothing that makes you cry, nothing that hurts you, and where there is absolutely nothing to fear, just everything to live for, forever. But he was not resigned to the fact that he would die in Emerus. Quite the contrary. He believed he would get out. He believed that there was more to life, and most important of all, Johnny believed that he played a vital role in one of the most important events in human history. And whatever that role was, he was prepared to play it, to the absolute best of his ability. He had come too far and gone through too much to simply give up. Sure, he almost did plenty of times. But not now. And not ever. He let out a minor chuckle. Being in the therapy office felt like forever ago. How many days had it been? It was so easy to lose track of time underground, not seeing the sunset or a beautifully painted night sky. And he refused to go farther down to the clinic where he could be treated with Emerus' artificial sun. Johnny didn't even know if when he slept, it was even night time. But it didn't matter. All that mattered was his resolve, and he felt it growing stronger and stronger as time pushed on. Everything was coming to a head, and something in his soul told him it would occur sooner rather than later. The situation had taken on a whole new meaning, one with ethereal implications and intangible unearthliness. But Johnny wasn't the least bit afraid, for he saw the line drawn in the sand and knew on which side he stood.

Previous tragedies in his life - some more significant than others but none more cataclysmic than his mother's unexpected and early death - created a sort of delitescent strength concealed deep inside Johnny's soul to spread to both his heart and his mind when needed. He knew that experiencing tragic losses and growing through and from them could create an internal spiritual strength. However, he never knew the consequence on a personal level until this moment. He smiled and became choked up. Tears knocked on the door and kindly asked to be exposed to the outside world. After preventing their entrance for two or three deep breaths, Johnny opened the door and set the warm, salty discharge free. It was the first time in his life that his tears came not because of negative emotions. These tears had a different nature to them. They were called from the depths of his heart by an innate understanding explaining why his dear mother had died. He felt unworthy to know such a truth.

"Why me?" he asked out loud.

The tears that had become a steady flow were washing away his dirtiness and were caused by something beyond happiness. Embracing the joy that was overflowing throughout his entire body, Johnny thanked himself for setting the emotions free. He only hoped that his father had done or would do the same. Healing tears ask for liberation and release from their captors only once and Johnny felt fortunate for the opportunity to listen for them in the peaceful silence that encompassed him. As they rebuilt, rescued, and restored him, he wished everyone who had haunting pasts would experience the healing effect that they freely offered. In fact, he asked for the burden of everyone's souls to be laid upon his heart because the overflowing and peaceful joy overwhelmed him to the point he thought it too much for one person to have. Why was he so favored to experience such beautiful emotions?

"Why me?" he asked again, after understanding it wasn't necessary to take on humanity's burden.

He felt so silly for asking such a thing that his joyful sobs were abruptly interrupted by an unexpected and self-directed chuckle. As pure joy was being manufactured using his tears like a water wheel, converting them into power and peace, Johnny prayed that the feeling would never end. After fifteen minutes of uncontaminated bliss, the placid elation started to subside. He begged for it stay, but started to understand that it must move on to heal someone else. He hung onto it just long enough to say thank you before he saw it calmly disappear like ocean mist kissed by the rising sun. If there was one thing he knew at that moment it was this: life consisted of countless seen material; however, there existed exponentially more unseen material. And it was all around, never to cease.

CHAPTER 17

Sunday, 10:46 pm

The convoy of cars, minivans, and station wagons from a simpler time in the not-so-distant past pushed westward across the Iowa-Nebraska border; the terminus becoming closer and closer with every second, minute, and hour that passed. Forty vehicles took up a considerably long stretch of highway, and to the onlooker, it was a threatening sight. Comfortable and taking solace in the fact that Emerus' technology was not working and therefore would never work on the group, the convoy coasted along in fateful anticipation of what would eventually transpire.

Conversation among the passengers in Gabe's minivan was surprisingly non-topical. This was mainly because of Matthew. He had a way about him that seemed to lighten every human mood. One could be dying of thirst in the desert and Matthew would show up and summon a smile simply by giving one of his own. He talked and talked, mostly grilling Lacey with questions which she could not answer, but that he did for her in his own way. Easton looked at his older brother with admiration in his eyes. Having him in his life lightened it up, and he could not ask for a better brother. Matthew was burly and athletic on the outside with a rebel heart fashioned of gold on the inside. The newcomer in Lacey looked at him with questioning eyes. She had recently met him for the second time and had been attempting to figure him out ever since. The first time they met, she and Matthew briefly spoke at Eileen Engleheart's wake, and it was that connection which Gabe cited as the reason Matthew was not susceptible to Emerus' technology.

"Something Lacey said to you that evening left an unseen spiritual imprint," he asserted.

It did with every person in the convoy, according to Gabe. Whether it was while she was on vacation, communicating through various social media, or ordering a pumpkin chai latte from her favorite coffee house, Lacey unknowingly left imprints on those with whom she conversed. However, it was not every time with everyone.

"Whenever someone speaks," explained Gabe, "He or she gives off their energy in the form of light - not in the visible spectrum -

it's all unseen by human eyes. Angels have the ability to see it, and obviously so does the Creator, but that is it. So when Lacey has spoken to people, some of her energy is transferred, just like when any humans exchange words. Personally, I am not the one in charge of that energy and its implications, so I don't know when, where, or what exactly she said to create that spiritual imprint, but I can tell you this. She has had a spiritual effect on people ever since she was born."

"And why is that again?" Easton asked, slightly confused.

"She is a direct descendant of an ancient race of people. They were very spiritual. And her DNA has their unseen energy, their spirit. It's draped in it."

"So that must mean it's in her family?" Rick Engleheart asked. "How does that work? How come her family members are not spreading their spiritual gifts? And her ancestors. What about them?"

Gabe kept his eyes on the road as he answered. "There is something very peculiar about the specific energy surrounding the DNA. It skips generations, sometimes even whole blood lines. To the untrained eye or distant onlooker, it might seem to be completely random, like there is no rhyme or reason to it. But trust me when I tell you this. It is no accident that Lacey's DNA has it. For this time and for this place, there is an absolute purpose for it. And it is by design."

Everyone kept quiet in thought. Matthew was quiet but was not thinking about what Gabe had just said. He claimed he understood it all. Lacey was not quite there yet; however, her heart and soul smiled every time Gabe spoke on such matters.

The convoy pushed on through the night. With its drivers not needing any sleep, it was rather easy to make up a lot of ground. However, every vehicle was old and beat up so their top speed maxed out at sixty miles per hour, which was fine with them. They knew when they needed to arrive and took comfort in the simple fact that they would. Going sixty miles per hour was just a bonus, turning their ETA to a GTA - guaranteed time of arrival. And even though the humans felt safe and secure under their unseen stealth tactics, Gabe and the other angels knew that they were pushing their luck. Soon enough, they reasoned, the higher-ups at Emerus would figure out the convoy was headed straight for them and maybe do one of two things, but probably both. Send out a massive search party to impede their progress and set up a blockade preventing them from entering Emerus territory. Gabe had a premonition that something was on the horizon, and it wasn't a flat tire. It was something much more detrimental to the mission.

Morning came as the sun effortlessly rose above the crystal-clear horizon in the minvan's rear and side view mirrors. Its rays poked each passenger in the face one by one like a pesky house cat until everyone was awake. Nebraska looked modestly beautiful. As a flyover state, no one in the minivan, not even Gabe who traveled often, had ever been on The Cornhusker State's ground. The landscape kissed by the early morning sunshine glowed in golden, elegant grace. The land was flat and the straight roads seemed to go on forever toward the western horizon. They passed old wooden windmills that sturdily stood adjacent to small pole barns and brick red cottages, making it look like a serene scene out of the movie *Twister*. Thankfully for them, late summer was slightly past peak season for tornadoes.

"How about stopping for some food?" Matthew suggested. "Pretty hungry."

Gabe apologetically explained that there was no time to stop and that it would cause a break in the convoy line lest all forty vehicles stopped at the same place, chancing getting found by local police, which would not end well for the policemen and delay the mission's progress.

"Ohh," the twenty four year-old replied, disappointingly with an embarrassed smile.

"Don't worry, though," Gabe reassured. "We should have some snacks left. Unless Sleepyhead ate them all," he joked, shooting Lacey a grin in the rear view mirror.

"She *does* sleep a lot!" Matthew exclaimed, nodding with his upper body as he looked over at her. "What do we have?"

A sarcastic laugh seeped out of Lacey's mouth, alerting everyone in the minivan that she was more than fine with quips pointed in her direction. She reached behind and underneath her seat, bringing forth a soft-fabric cooler, and after handing it to Easton to pass to his older brother, let out a wide yawn.

Matthew read the visual menu aloud as he discovered the cooler's contents. "Granola bars, pudding, Munchos, more granola bars, Cheese Nips, Cheetos, wow pretty unhealthy Gabe, crackers, Pop-Tarts, ooh I'll take a Pop-Tart. Easton, you want a Pop-Tart?"

Matthew's younger brother laughed through his nose before taking one out of the box. After passing the heavy, ungainly cooler around the minivan, Matthew took it back and placed it under his seat as he enjoyed his breakfast.

Time began to swiftly fly by as everyone started to thoroughly enjoy their time together, Matthew being the catalyst. It was a beautiful summer day in Nebraska. The simple and charming landscapes prompted Matthew to predict moving there in the future to, as he put it, get away from it all. The communal response was silence as everybody, including Gabe, admired Matthew's ability to see beyond the arduous task that lay in front of them like a boulder blocking a one-way road.

Most of the time was passed by talking - Gabe and Matthew filling up nearly all of the space. Matthew told a plethora of mischievous stories in which he found himself in the wrong place at the wrong time. Or tales of doing the right thing and being reprimanded for it - like the time he was in college, living in a two-story apartment in Cranston. He was walking to pick up his Chinese food around the corner when he noticed a man in his upper twenties arguing with a young woman in her early twenties. The two were becoming more and more heated as the argument wore on, and as the argument escalated, Matthew found his pace becoming slower by the second. His inkling proved correct as he saw the man viscously slap the young woman across her face. Hard. In fact, he hit her so hard that she fell down. But that did not stop him from further degrading her with his grotesque mouth. Well, Matthew had seen enough. "I'll be damned if I'm just gonna ignore that," he said, seriously. So he beckoned to justice. Matthew ran across the quiet, tree-lined street and, without words, told the man how he felt. A right hook and a quick, even harder left one later, and the man was on his back, knocked out. To Matthew's amazement, a police car suddenly showed up and the twenty-four-year-old assumed the despicable human who hit a woman would be put in handcuffs and that would be the end of that. Instead, the two overweight cops claimed all they saw was Matthew run across the street and knock a guy's lights out. The young woman had run up the stoop back into her apartment before Matthew could even ask her if she was OK. She chose to remain hidden and thus silent. So rather than put the shameless, beater-wearing man in handcuffs, the policemen began cuffing Matthew. They refused to believe his story and began arresting him for assault. Well, he wouldn't stand for it. He elbowed one policeman in the gut while the other one was preoccupied with the fallen fellow. Running the fastest he had in his life, Matthew sprinted down the block, banked right at the end of it, and seeked safety in his friend's apartment two blocks later. The cops did not pursue him because the young woman shyly descended down the steps and corroborated Matthew's story. She pressed charges against the man, desired to thank Matthew for his heroism and fearlessness, for doing what she did not have the bravery to do - stand up to injustice, but never saw him again. The policeman who received a sharp and heavy elbow to his beer belly vowed that if he ever came across Matthew again, he would teach him a lesson. However, he never saw him again either. Matthew, energized and hungry, kindly told his friend, John Sandorn, to pick up his Chinese food, which he did after ordering some of his own. The two enjoyed a feast, skipped class, and spent the afternoon watching episodes of Seinfeld.

Gabe told stories as well. One that stood out in everyone's mind was a miraculous one, happening in the early 1990s. Gabe had been commissioned to speak to two men needing a ride back to Queens from Brooklyn. In the blink of an eye, he found himself driving a taxi cab. Noticing his two targets standing on a corner under a thick birch tree, trying to stay out of the cold April rain, Gabe pulled the cab over and picked them up. It was two o'clock in the morning and it did not take a genius to notice that they had had a rough night.

Under the canopy of small trees that lined the lonely Williamsburg sidewalks, Gabe drove along Kent Avenue. After taking a right onto North Seventh and passing Wythe, Berry, Bedford, and Driggs, Gabe took another right onto Roebling Street and hooked up with Metropolitan Avenue. Not knowing what exactly he was supposed to say to the two good looking men in their late-twenties, Gabe spoke quietly to the Creator. He tried to be inconspicuous about it, but his efforts came up slightly short. The better looking of the men, who confidently and kindly introduced himself as Tim, asked Gabe what language he was speaking, for it wasn't English nor any other known language. Gabe did not know what to answer with so he tried to make conversation with them by changing the subject. He asked what they did and after answering they, in turn, asked him what he did besides drive a cab.

"I do the Father's work," Gabe replied.

The two men contorted their faces in confusion.

"Did you look weird?" Lacey asked. "Like when you showed

up to my door that night I was watching Disney movies?"

Gabe laughed heartily. "Not yet," he explained. "I wore blue jeans, a black windbreaker, and my hair was short."

"I envy them," Lacey quipped.

Again attempting to change the subject so the two men would not get completely freaked out, Gabe gave them words of encouragement. He told them not to worry about impressing women and that the harder they tried, the more epically they would fail. He also said that love comes in a variety of ways, but that romantic love in particular usually comes when it is least expected. His message really seemed to scratch the men right where they itched, and was not the only reason an angel was sent to them. According to Gabe, if he had not picked them up right at that moment, they would have been shot and killed by a gang initiation right where they stood waiting to spot a cab.

After taking a left onto Sixty-Ninth Street in Middle Village, the two friends directed Gabe when to turn down their block. Upon doing that, they looked at the meter. It read '$19.87' so they scrounged up the cash in their pockets to make twenty two dollars, preparing to give it to the strange, albeit friendly, sage-like cab driver.

"No, no," Gabe insisted. "Keep it. Your money means nothing to me."

The two men urged their driver to take it, but he kept on insisting that in the grand of scheme of life, temporary treasures mean nothing and the almighty dollar had absolutely zero value to him. The men in their late-twenties thanked him with sincerity and closed the door. Upon doing that, they witnessed a miracle. The triangular advertisement that ran along the cab's roof changed right before their eyes. It transformed from an ad for a small construction company to a spectacular golden display with the text, 'Trinity 3.' Tim shot his gaze back to their driver and surprisingly noticed that he had changed as well. He had transfigured from an everyday New Yorker to a majestic angel glowing in gold with long and flowing white hair. The cab remained for three seconds as if presenting a visual gift to the two friends before it pulled away. Before entering their respective houses, the two men wept tears of miraculous joy together, because there was nothing else to do.

Gabe told many other stories in that vein, a stranger helping someone out, never to be seen again. They captivated everyone in the van, but Matthew, a self-proclaimed history buff, relished in Gabe's story of the distant past. Whether it was angels paving the way for the Enlightenment, or being instrumental alongside the young colonies' success in the American Revolution, Gabe explained that angels have helped shape the world for centuries. And, as he pointed out, the current mission was simply another one of those examples.

"Humanity is very imperfect. What your species has done to its own planet, to its own people, ignoring compassion and approving greed, has honestly been a travesty. You are all one people. Why can't you set aside your petty disagreements and differences and just love one another? That is what you were designed to do. But humanity quickly became corrupt with selfishness and war, indulgence and hate. Having things, meaningless things! Do you know that when you die, you do not take any of what you acquire here on Earth with you? Do you realize that? Not your cars, not your money, not your clothes or jewelry, not your sports, not your music, movies, television shows, or video games. Nothing. What you take with you to the by and by is your spirit and your soul. That is what is most important in life," Gabe reasoned, with a mournful and pleading tone. "How you love, how you forgive, how you're forgiven. Those are things with true value. Everything else, all of the material world, it will wither and die. It's all temporary. But your soul and your spirit? Those are eternal. And they mean everything."

The overall mood inside the minivan had turned from enchanted to somber with silence.

"So how does this secret branch of power kidnapping and keeping my son captive fit into all of this?" Rick Engleheart asked.

It took Gabe a few seconds to answer. "Something happened back in the early 1990s. The people in Emerus made first contact with what they believed to be extraterrestrials. It is for this reason…"

"Wait a second. What do you mean with what they believed to be? What were they?" Matthew questioned, quickly and suspiciously.

"They were dark forces," answered Gabe. "From the depths of the darkest realm. Shadow people."

Lacey swallowed hard. It was too easy to remember when she was taken from the van and brought to that dark place. She recalled the sinister way it moved, the evil in its tongue. She shuddered.

"Their specialty is deception. Always has been. So they were thought to be aliens, imparting their knowledge and technology on humanity. Wrong. But humans, as usual, went along with it, thinking that any progress is good progress while completely ignoring the potential consequences. Technology started to evolve at a rapid and record pace. Soon, it got out of control and because of the vast array of individuals' use of the technology, people began to lose their liberties and freedoms, one by one. It's 2025. Do you know how easy it would be for the government with the assistance of Emerus to delve into your personal life? It's been that way for quite a while. You think you're having a private conversation with somebody? Think again. Lately, they have been experimenting with taking away one of the last freedoms humans have - the freedom of thought. Like I have said before, Johnny was the first successful pilot study in this endeavor. I can't tell you why the higher ups at Emerus chose Johnny as their next subject, but boy, did they choose wrong. He's protected and they cannot figure out why.

Lacey stopped shuddering.

"And just for the record," Gabe continued, "I cannot wait to see the surprised look on their faces when they find out. Because no matter what they do, they can't win.

CHAPTER 18

Victor awoke in a panicked sweat. The cold beads of excretion danced on his skin to the beat of his racing heart. It was clear that seeing his old friend, Will, made the per usual nightmares ten times worse.

"Maybe that is why we avoid each other," Victor surmised, severely frightened by what he recently saw in his sleep.

Talking to himself was something Victor frequently did, often weirding out his peers; however, most geniuses are not what the general public considers to be normal. At the inexperienced age of eight, Victor invented his own language. It was an uncomplicated task for him. After learning the alphabets of the German, Spanish, and French languages, he simply combined them with English to construct his own method of speaking. With 105 letters in his language's alphabet, when spoken, it sounded quite strange, even to Victor. He would combine vowels, making sounds unlike anything ever spoken before. As he learned it in greater depths, Victor would combine whole words. For example, he would couple Spanish and English to spell the word 'dog' as 'pogorred,' which joined in a jumbled fashion 'perro' and 'dog.' However, he would say it with a German accent and use a French inflection. The language became his only friend, besides his loving parents. He called it the Amestec language, which is Romanian for 'to blend.'

With a father from Cardiff, Wales, Europe's oldest capital and a mother from Baia Mare in northwestern Romania, Victor did not need another reason to be an outcast in school. However, the discrimination against his "dirty blood," as the other children called it, ran rampant throughout Victor's young life. He remembers having to eat the lunch his loving mother had made for him in the secondary school's dirty bathroom stall. He would search for the quietest, least trafficked restroom so he could at least eat in peace, but everything came with a price, as the muted laboratories were usually the dirtiest, hence the reason students rarely frequented them. However, Victor was content with cleaning a little bit of filth so he could enjoy his lunch in peace and quiet, without being ridiculed and bullied. It was a welcome tradeoff to getting harassed by the popular kids, and growing up, Victor was too shy to ask other students if he could sit at the end of their table given the off chance a seat would even be available in the crowded cafeteria. So, he would leave class, walk down hushed hallways and into his bathroom, pray he would find it empty, and eat his fancily prepared meal behind the stall's locked door. He felt safe there because for the only time each day, he was invisible. He didn't need to put on a fake smile or be forced to discuss Shakespeare with people who hated him before knowing him. It was just him and his language. He would ask a question in English and then answer it in Amestec. Even though he was speaking to himself, it felt like he had an imaginary friend who could talk back. So when he would find daily messages from his mother written on index cards, Victor would read them aloud in English (even though they were written in Romanian). Then, in Amestec, he would say, "Deinetu mere liebtvouste aime," which combined German, Spanish, and French to say, "Your mother loves you." As if responding to a friend, Victor would reply in English, "I know," with a smile on his face.

After he was done with his sandwich and snacks, Victor would read his weekly book. This was an arduous task for some, but Victor easily finished a book every week, regardless of the length. For the enduring ones, he would take the weekend to complete it. But for the most part, the book started and finished in his bathroom stall. Victor would read everything, from historical non-fiction, to plays, to all kinds of fiction. Often times, he would read one page in English, the next in Romanian, and then the next in Amestec, looping back to English, repeating the language carousel for the duration of the piece. Tasks such as this one made the boring and mundane routine of school more interesting for him. Every test he took, he finished in half the time it took the teacher; every paper he wrote, he wrote in English, Romanian, and Amestec just for fun; and for every exam - whether it was standardized or in history, science, or mathematics - he never studied an ounce of content. Victor found it easier to learn by listening and reading, teaching himself in a way. In fact, it wasn't long into secondary school when Victor started to teach the teachers. This was especially true in math and physics. He would stay after school once a week and hold sessions where teachers would come from various departments, mostly the mathematics and science administrations, pay him five Euros each, and sit and learn whatever Victor decided to teach on that week. It was very much against the rules, but all involved kept it under wraps and the student genius kept his earnings under the table. It began a long life of rule breaking for Victor; however, even back then he viewed it as enlightening the uninformed and the misled.

Whether expanding upon Albert Einstein's Theory of Relativity, developing complex derivatives before even taking a calculus class, or coming up with new rules regarding Planck's Law in quantum mechanics, Victor would have his audience beyond captivated for an hour a week. His locker and Volkswagen were an absolute mess, but he always knew where everything was and his car always seemed to have a full tank of gas.

Gasoline cars appeared as relics of ancient history in Victor's mind. At the University of Oxford, which Victor began to attend at the age of seventeen, he developed the first plans for a hydrogen-powered car. In fact, he helped build the first electrolysis machine and was instrumental in making them available at energy stations in Norway. He was the first to suggest the construction of Hynor, the Hydrogen Highway of Norway, which provided drivers multiple stops to refill their hydrogen-powered vehicles. In 2006, he saw the first hydrogen refueling station was built. Later, when Victor first got recruited to Emerus, he started work on placing mini high-powered electrolysis machines in vehicles. America was too vast to build multiple hydrogen highways, the stations for which were too expensive to keep up. Plus, with the United States' government in bed with the fuel companies, Victor knew that it would take an impossible effort to completely switch outdated gasoline stations to updated hydrogen stations. So, he conceived a car with the all-important electrolysis machine manufactured in it. This way, there wouldn't need to be an expensive hydrogen highway. In fact, there wouldn't need to be many hydrogen refueling stations at all, making a car that ran on water a near-future certainty instead of a far-fetched pipe dream. The only catch was that because of supply and demand, hydrogen-powered cars equipped with electrolysis machines were incredibly costly, with only two percent of Americans being able to afford them. Unfortunately, this minute portion of the population was also in bed with not only the oil companies, but with the government as well. So it was a beyond burdensome assignment to find a feasible marketability. Nearly impossible, but Victor was not going to give up. He envisioned a future where driving was virtually free, as long as the driver had access to tap water, and the only emission from the vehicles was simply drinkable water. It was not far off, but the project at hand in 2025 delayed

Victor's efforts. However, his vision was still there, and on his free time, he worked and worked hard.

Commanding his coffee machine to go to work, Victor walked about his spacious and lonely room, thinking. Rarely could he think hard about something and be still. Whether it was flipping a pencil end-over-end and catching it with his fingertips or slowly rubbing his head - his hands starting at eyebrow level and gradually going back and stopping at the posterior of his head, Victor would think in motion. The simplest problems would be resolved while he sat down and rapidly tapped his right foot on the floor like a drummer trained in the 'heel-up' method. Other issues, a little more complicated, would find their solution with the pencil or head-rubbing routines. Larger dilemmas, like the one currently in Victor's mind, would be worked out by walking around in elongated ellipses, mimicking a comet's path around a star.

He thought of his family, wondering if and how he would ever see them again.

"If only they understood," he said aloud, exhausted.

It had been slightly over a decade since the powers that be at Emerus recruited him for his genius mind. He wished he wasn't so smart, then felt dumb for even having such a thought. He yearned for his family, and was so close to completing the project that would ultimately set him free. However, in the back of his mind, something told him that the higher-ups did not plan on keeping their promise. Sure, they might let him drive away, but somewhere down the road, his car would explode, or live high voltage power lines would come crashing down onto his car, or there would be an earthquake, or he would painlessly be the target of a drone strike. Any and all of those calamitous endings were well within Emerus' power to construct.

"They're not going to let me just walk," he said, aloud again. "How could they? With what we've done here - changing thought processes, even if it created a better world - they're not going to let someone have that information. No," Victor surmised. "This comes at a price."

He slammed his hands down on the bare countertop upon reaching the bitter, irrevocable conclusion. The price was his life. If he stayed, Victor was absolutely sure he would be safe. Heck, he would be praised for his efforts and probably be given even more luxurious living quarters. Everything a single man would ever want would be at his fingertips. But men change. Once they marry and start a family, new priorities begin to take shape, placing the old ones on eternal back burners. And Victor waved goodbye to those old concerns long ago when he and his wife had their first child. Even though he had been immersed in Emerus for over a decade, everything but his heart had adjusted to the drastic change. His heart still longed to live its previous life - waking up, jogging with his wife, going to work, coming home right at five o'clock every day, eating dinner, spending quality time with family, and going to bed only to wake up and do it all over again. How he desired to do that just once more!

"Ding!" The coffee machine brought Victor back from his intense thought.

Vines from his old life deeply rooted in acquisitive wishes entangled the fifty-eight-year-old, attempting to keep him in the wistful headspace. His heart was there, always had been and always would be. It cried out for him to remain.

"No," Victor said, sadly. His heart cried louder. "No!" he screamed, in an angered reply.

Afraid that his yearning would negatively impact his work, Victor fought back against the vines' grip, cutting and wriggling himself free from their grasp. He ran across the uncrowded quarters and hastily opened a cabinet. After finding a wrinkled ziplock bag with a medicine drop applicator suspended in a liquid that existed only in Emerus, Victor filled up the applicator, tilted his head to the side and dropped two beads of the elixir in each ear, which was excessive because he usually only needed two total. Within a few minutes, he forgot about his previous thought processes and began to focus on how alive, energetic, and at peace he felt. Just in time, too, as his wrist began to vibrate.

"Yes?" he answered.

"We have a possible hit on Rick Engleheart and Lacey Hassle. You should come to the deck."

"Be there in ten," Victor replied.

The immense elevator system had been up and running long enough for its recent crashes to go unnoticed by the Doc. And even though they operated at high speeds, it still took Victor nearly five minutes to arrive at his destination. The deck, which it had become known as, was a sinful place. In fact, Victor disliked ever needing to frequent its cylindrical, colossal room, illuminated by countless high-definition monitors. During the extensive, fast-paced elevator ride, he hoped he would not have to be there for too long. The stories he heard made his fifty-eight-year-old face frown in disgust. He started to silently tell himself that it was for the greater good, to keep the people safe. One half of his mind discredited that thought process, though. He began to wordlessly argue with it as if he were speaking to another person telepathically. A step up from his lonely days in secondary school, except this time, he reasoned and soundlessly quarreled in English.

"It's for the safety of the country," one half of his mind contended.

"But it's against everything this country was founded upon in the first place," the other half reasoned.

"That doesn't matter. Circumstances change. People, culture, laws - they evolve. It's for the people's safety. Don't they want to be safe?"

"That's the problem. Your misology. While you are keeping the people safe, you are stripping them of their liberty."

"What they don't know will not hurt them."

"Imagine if they knew. There would be a second civil war."

"That's why we are down here."

"Ding! The elevator bell rang, alerting Victor that he had arrived. "Welcome to the observation deck," a female robotic voice greeted.

Victor stepped off, siding with the half of his mind that spoke last. He breathed a sigh of determination.

"Let's get to work."

CHAPTER 19

Upon seeing Victor, busied men in lab coats moved out of his way - a perspicuous display of their respect. Although not everybody in Emerus and the neighboring inverted super silos knew Victor, they all knew of him through rumors and stories. The fifty-eight-year-old greeted them as best he could - with smiles and nods of recognition - looking left, then right, back left again, and so on and so forth. The bridge on the way to the observation deck stood high above other overpasses, allowing pedestrians to see extremely far down the main transportation shaft. Looking up, one could see endless floors as well - everything transparent because there was no need to keep anything hidden. It already was. The main transportation shaft was like a monstrous dumbwaiter; however, when George Cannon invented that system in the 1880s, he could never in his wildest dreams have imagined something so immense existing not even a century and a half later - a mere fraction of time on the grand age of the human era. Victor stopped to look down. Every few floors, the main transportation shaft's arms stretched out ad infinitum. It really was a beautiful sight and Victor took it in with a deep and quenched inhale. Satisfied, he continued his champion-like pace with smiles and nods at the strangers admiring his genius.

The deck loomed straight ahead. It was one of the many super structures in Emerus as it took up over thirty floors, from its base to the top of its gigantic alabaster dome. It looked so peaceful and pure, untainted and chaste, but it was the epitome of the old saying, 'Don't judge a book by its cover.' After multiple facial and optical recognition security protocols, Victor entered the imposing, cold dome. Entry doors were located about halfway up the thirty-eight story structure. What was quite monumental about the observation deck was the fact that it was just as wide as it was tall. The exterior as well as the interior were built by smart machines, which was strikingly noticeable. Humans simply were unable to construct something so extraordinarily perfect. If a layperson saw what was inside the observation deck, he or she would think that they had been transported at least a hundred years into the future - and that was just at the superficial sight of it. It was partly because of this that the higher-ups at Emerus refused to introduce smart machines into society. They did not even budge on the issue.

The first smart machine was invented in Emerus in 2004, and would most likely not see the light of day until sometime around 2050. Built by super computers, smart machines could think, analyze, and compute impossible equations in mere seconds. Upon doing that, they would assess how many smart machines it would take to build what was needed in the shortest time. The observation deck was built by ten smart machines and was fully functional within eight hours. Experts at Emerus estimated that if smart machines had built the Freedom Tower in New York City, the entire project would have been completed within days. Convenient, yes; but dangerous, too. The machines thought for themselves and were downright massive. If a smart machine felt threatened in any way, it would destroy its target without a second thought. With too many people existing on Earth's surface, introducing smart machines to mainstream society would pose too great a risk. They were much better off in Emerus under constant monitoring. When they were not in use, they were in sleep mode and lockdown in an isolated steel-constructed room. Ranging in sizes, the smallest smart machine looked like a chrome-colored basketball hoop, and the largest was the size of a middle class house. There were dozens of various sized smart machines in Emerus, and they were one of the super silos' largest dangers.

"When humans build machines that in turn construct other machines," Victor would say, "the human race is walking on thin ice."

They were handy, though, and saved literally years of time since their inception in 2004. Nothing like the observation deck could have been built so perfectly in such little time, especially for no compensation.

The final steel door of security slowly ascended from the floor. Its deep and menacing sound imposed anticipatory guilt in whoever heard it, even in Victor, and he had a hand in what the deck was used for. It took a full seven seconds for the door to complete its ascent, enough for someone of Victor's height - 6 foot 1 - to walk under. However, the time lapse was just long enough to second guess one's decision to enter, twice. Victor walked in ducking before the steel door had finished its vertical climb. The gigantic dome-shaped room was significantly colder than the bridge. That was the first thing newcomers noticed. The supercomputers needed cold, dry air to operate at a high frequency, and there were thousands of them. Each supercomputer was a three-dimensional monitor ranging in size from a square foot to an IMAX movie theater screen. Each one had the same mind-bending ability, but the larger ones were more convenient for the user and assisted in their own diabolical way, allowing the user to access certain areas by "eclipsing" as it had come to be called. Eclipsing gave the user an opportunity to infiltrate a subject's area as if he or she were actually there. Predominantly, it was used in drug busts and kidnappings and other situations of that ilk. This is how it would work: the user would track the subject by typing their name into a database. The supercomputer database innately knew each United States citizen better than their closest friends did, so it was not too difficult to find whom exactly the subject was. Tracking the subject was a simple task, too. After the leap in smart phone global positioning technology, it was easier than ever. There was a time back in the 1980s and 90s that the higher-ups at Emerus were working on GPS tracking chips to be placed in humans. However, in the year 2022 the American government supplied free smart phones to any remaining citizen who did not have one - even the homeless. This enabled the crazed conception of tracking chips to be thrown out the window because they were not needed. Emerus could track anybody no matter where they were simply by typing their cell phone number into one of the many databases. It was a simple way to control the masses, since over ninety percent of Americans now owned smart phones. And once again, for the most part, people either did not care or did not know. Either way, it worked in Emerus' and the American government's favor.

After the database found where exactly the subject was, the larger monitors would be called up to the plate. Perfectly hidden surveillance cameras and drones were able to construct a detailed three-dimensional map of the subject's location - this is what came up on the large monitors. The user then transcended into the scene, stepping into the holographic map. They were able to walk around in a virtual reality and locate what they needed, whether it was a kidnap victim, stolen goods, drugs, or anything they wanted. It violated the Constitution tenfold, but for the most part, it was used for good.

At times, people in Emerus used the deck to their own, sick advantage. Whether it was spying on a beautiful woman and sharing her most private and personal moments or simply and sickly watching people who assumed they had privacy, people in Emerus carried out these acts and were never held accountable. It was a silently accepted practice. It made people like Victor sick to even think about it. Still, the temptation was there and it was strong.

Even if users did not go down the dark road of virtual pornography, sometimes they simply had a little fun. When one can see and hear anything and everything about everybody and anyone, the human mind begins to explore. Victor was guilty of this, as was every user in Emerus. And it was not a difficult task to become a user. Simply by passing a hands-on test using the technology on the observation deck and successfully finding multiple targets in a given time span, the learner became a user, and there was a plethora of them. Having some fun to quell the boredom, users would type a name into the database. Sometimes it would be someone they once knew; sometimes it would be a totally random person; but most times it would be someone famous. Wherever the targeted subject was at a given moment, the supercomputer-laden observation deck took the user there. Listening in on live conversations, watching what the target was doing - cooking, cleaning, walking, shopping, sleeping, working, and everything between and beyond - no United States citizen could conceal their identity and privacy because there was no place to hide. Users could even watch people who lived off the grid. If a person lived in the United States, then they were under constant surveillance. Thousands upon thousands of supercomputers saw to that.

The smaller monitors, equipped with a tiny supercomputer each, stored citizens' data on a last name basis. Citizens with last names 'A-F' were stored on one supercomputer, 'G-L' on another, and so on and so forth. The user would call up a name, the supercomputers would run it through their database, and the designated monitor would bring up their pinpointed location. It wasn't just an 'X' on a map, though. Drones, security cameras, hidden and microscopic government cameras, and smart phone microphones gave the user all the information they needed to get an ultra-detailed live look at the targeted subject. The government cameras constructed in cars and houses were built in Emerus and most of them were equipped with microphones as well. The recently constructed drones were built with long range microphones to pick up conversations, too. It was a new kind of technology that Emerus proliferated in 2022 that was being used more and more frequently. Just as the user could zoom in on a target with the camera, the new technology, called, Telewave, had the capability to zoom in its microphone from as long a range as twenty-five miles. All the user had to do was program the drone where to fly, put it in hover mode miles and miles above the target, and anything personally heard and privately seen was at the user's fingertips. Different angles, a plethora of zoom-in options, and beyond state-of-the-art technology not known to the outside world provided the user with everything he or she needed to spy on the target.

Victor used to have fun with the freedom to take it away from others. This time though, his visit was strictly business.

CHAPTER 20

Since neither Lacey Hassle's nor Rick Engleheart's names could be found in the database search - something Victor anticipated - the Doc called upon the use of multiple new Telewave-equipped drones. He was briefed by a robotic female voice about a potential hit on an old minivan traveling west. When a user used technology on the deck, it was one of the few laws in Emerus that he or she needed to be alone. It was a desperate attempt to keep humanity's evil on the outside of the observation deck. However, like most similar pursuits it was an unsuccessful pipe dream. Victor did not know why more than one person was disallowed. He surmised that it was meant to simply cut down the evil that was already necessary - better to only have one person at a time using the deck than two people. Just that simple one-number subtraction cuts the amount of inevitable evil in half. With the single user law though, being on the observation deck felt more like business. Even though there were some users who still abused their power, the law significantly decreased the frequency of such abuse.

"Hello, Victor. Potential hit on a 1995 forest-green Chevy Lumina traveling west on I-80 in central Nebraska."

"Bloody hell." Victor's candid response showed his frightful surprise that they might be that close.

"Bring up drone number 3275 on monitor six."

Each state in the union had hundreds of surveillance drones flying about a mile above the troposphere. Number 3275, in particular, was currently stationed over Interstate 80 in central Nebraska. Upon calling up its camera and microphone on monitor six, Victor immediately noticed that the minivan was in fact built before the government-mandated tracking devices were unknowingly placed in vehicles in the form of a small black box.

"Bloody hell," he said again, aloud to himself. Victor stood atop a narrow bridge constructed halfway up the towering superstructure. His view was worthy of a picture. All around and from every direction, countless high definition and three-dimensional monitors waited patiently against the curved walls, floor, and ceiling. Their LED lights dimly illuminated the immense room. The only thing on the narrow and thin transparent bridge besides the user was his or her station, which consisted of a simple-looking twelve-by-sixteen inch flatscreen monitor built into the deck's railing. Looks were deceiving, though. The little screen had three supercomputers running its operating system and with the users' fingertips, it controlled the thousands of monitors lined up side-by-side throughout the room's walls, floor, and ceiling. One particular function of the user's station was one that Victor especially enjoyed operating. It allowed users to override a drone's OS and fly it themselves, directing it to go anywhere within its designated flying zone, gaining intel on any targeted subject.

"Bring close-up on monitor six." A close-up was when monitors came off of their resting place on the wall, floor, or ceiling, stopping twenty-four inches from the user's face, which allowed him or her to gain a better look at whatever the drone was picking up.

It was an eerily quiet sound. Monitor six was on the far left wall, about ten stories down from Victor's nine o'clock. Each monitor was attached to its situated place along the interior walls by an ultra-thin, steel-like wire that coiled up into the wall. The wire was so strong that it could easily support the monitor's weight, and it was steel-like only because steel was the closest metal to it. This particular compound was made by the smart machines, and the people in Emerus had not thought of a name for it. They probably never would, either. The wires were so thin that they were, for all practical intents and purposes, invisible. So when a user called for a monitor to come for a close-up, the wires, which had mysterious intelligent qualities themselves, obeyed the user's command and began to uncoil. Victor loved this part of the job, and when the observation deck was first built, he would spend hours simply calling monitors in for a close-up. The sight and creepy, quiet sound never aged. He stood mesmerized and watched with his mouth slightly agape in admiration and awe. Holding his breath so as not to disturb or obstruct the tiniest melody of the uncoil, Victor could only hear the rhythmic beating of his heart and the wire's slight intonation. What was unusual about it was that users could not decipher if they heard the wire uncoiling or felt it. The modulation reverberated throughout the immense room, making it difficult to cite its source. It sounded like the softest whistling wind, impossible for humans to mimic. Victor liked the sound, though, and wished he was a mile away from the monitor, only so his heart could feel the vibration for a while longer.

The oscillating sound of the uncoil made Victor feel like closing his eyes, and normally he would like nothing more, but he did not want to miss the awe-inspiring sight of the flatscreen monitor floating through the air as gently as a feather glides through Earth's invisible wind currents. The sight and sound blended together in elegant harmony, slowly coming closer to the user, inch-by-inch and foot-by-foot, enveloping him or her in two of the five senses' most pleasing moments. Victor swore there was something more to the wires and their uncoil than met the eyes and ears. He stood watching monitor six drift effortlessly toward him, forgetting every care in the world. That was, until the female robotic voice notified him that the green Chevy Lumina in question was stopping.

**

Monday, 4:16 pm

Gabe had been listening to both Matthew and Easton complain about their need to go to the bathroom for too long. Matthew, who said multiple times that he would just go in an empty iced tea bottle, would in fact do that if need be without batting an eye, but Gabe did not know it. Easton, on the other hand, was a little more shy than his bold and adventurous older brother, and refused to urinate in front of a girl, especially one as stunningly beautiful as Lacey. She, also on the other hand, called Easton a baby and said that if she had to go badly enough, then all she would need is Matthew's iced tea bottle and a funnel. Always willing, unabashed, and unafraid, Lacey was unique - in every sense of the word.

Matthew was more than ready to simply start going into the blue-tinted glass bottle, but his uncle stopped him with a howl. Rick Engleheart loved Matthew like a son, and usually laughed at his antics, but he also had gained a respect for Lacey that only he and Gabe knew. A guilty smile commandeered Matthew's face as he looked at his uncle, whom he also loved, looking back at him. Rick Engleheart returned the smile and with his eyes, comforted his nephew's uneasiness. Lacey let out a half-chuckle, half-snort at the situation she saw unfold a few feet to her right. Gabe assured that he would pull the van over, but told both Matthew and Easton to act with haste.

"Do it quickly," he instructed.

"Why don't we all take a go," Rick Engleheart said to himself, opening his door.

Gabe looked at Lacey in the van's rear view mirror.

"I'm good," she answered, with an ounce of delight in her voice.

***

"Drone number 3275, which state is the Lumina's license plate registered to?" Now that the monitor was two feet from his face, Victor could clearly make out the stopped green minivan. He saw people get out of the vehicle, but could not make out any defining characteristics other than the fact that they were human.

"View to license plate obstructed. Gaining better vantage point."

A sigh of frustration seeped out of Victor's nose and mouth. If the drone wasn't looking for the license plate, he could override it and zoom in on the faces of those who had gotten out of the van. He kept his eyes on them. They were simply standing on the other side of the guard rail, looking off in the distance.

"A little faster, please," Victor commanded, with urgency in his tone.

Even though the drones did not have the ability to see two different elements at once, Victor remembered that they had recently been equipped with Telewave, so he decided to put the relatively new technology to work. "Drone 3275, give me Telewave audio inside the minivan." Surveillance on sight and listening in on sound were two functions that could be completed simultaneously.

"Initiating Telewave. Complete. Commencing audio feed."

Victor was anxious to hear how clearly the Telewave technology brought the audio to the observation deck. It seemed to come from out of nowhere, but all of a sudden, the massive room filled with a crystal-clear quality conversation.

"Brilliant," Victor said to himself. He heard two clear and distinct voices - one male and one female.

***

"So Gabe?" Lacey asked.

"Yes, Sleepyhead?"

"There's something I don't understand. I mean, if you're an

angel and this is all like good versus evil stuff, what does that mean? Like when I was taken, where was I? Was that hell?"

Gabe hesitated for a few seconds and then turned around to answer. "No, that was not hell, but it was one of the few dark dimensions. Do you remember when we were flying away and your tears put out all of those flames? I told you that you are special. And right then and there, you started to believe. As for what it all means? This is just another example of angels stepping in to help humanity. Like I said before, if we had not interceded," Gabe stopped to shake his head, "then the human race would have killed itself off long ago. And this is just another time where angels need to assist. And the timing is perfect. We have you."

"Yeah, I'm still trying to figure all that out."

"In time, in time."

"But here's the other thing I don't get," Lacey stated, confounded. "If you guys are so powerful, then why don't you intercede all the time? Stop wars, end hunger, end poverty, prevent crime - you know, stuff like that?"

Again, Gabe hesitated, but with pain and sadness in his voice, he finally answered, "Because humans have something called free will. And my goodness, have you guys screwed up. This isn't how it was meant to be. But hate and greed spread like wildfire, and the human race is beyond lost. Mother Earth is hurting. You treat your planet like you treat others - sucking them dry, only taking and never giving. Only when it's necessary, do people live generously. Humanity has free will, and it is a beautiful thing, but for the most part, the human race has dug its own grave and does not have the capability to rescue itself. That is where we come in."

Gabe's convicting words regarding how adrift humanity had become had a way of silencing his listeners. Lacey reflected on what he said and decided that she was ready to make a difference and stand for something. Looking south out the wide window over the vast Great Plains, she stoically said, "Whatever you need from me, I'm ready."

Gabe smiled and said, "I know."

***

It didn't take long for Victor to realize that the two people in the minivan were speaking a different language, one in which he knew extremely little about.

"Do we have anyone available that knows Japanese?" he asked into his wrist.

"Negative," a voice replied ten seconds later.

Smart machines could translate any language, even extinct ones, but there was no time to summon them up from the depths. Victor, keeping an eye on the minivan and the three people milling about outside of it, began to think. Brushing both of his hands through his thick, silver hair, he thought it too much of a coincidence that an old minivan would be on I-80, heading west with a male - presumably Rick Engleheart - and a female - presumably Lacey Hassle - riding in it. As for the other people, Victor did not know nor did he care. He thought it prudent to eclipse, but was still unsure. However, what happened next pushed him off the fence.

"License plate MLK 4087. Connecticut."

Victor nodded with haste. He knew the Englehearts and Lacey Hassle were from Rhode Island, but assumed they placed Connecticut's plate on their minivan. He didn't think Lacey knew Japanese, but believed that whoever or whatever was assisting them in their travels was obscuring Emerus' surveillance. An old vehicle from the northeast traveling west with a male and female inside of it. Those are good odds. This was Victor's best chance, and he knew he had to act, and act quickly because the people who had gotten out of the minivan began to assemble back into it.

"Drone 3275, stay on that plate. Bring up monitor number 1865. Prepare to eclipse."

One of the large, three-dimensional movie theatre-sized screens began to calmly float toward Victor. The transparent floor opened up next to his right foot. A toolbox-sized compartment held a specialized suit for eclipsing. Victor bent down, took it out, and the floor closed back up. As monitor 1865 continued to glide smoothly through the air, Victor had no time to listen to the sweet melody of its uncoil. He took off his lab coat and stepped into the meshy-type material made by the smart machines. Its fabric resembled a window screen, but its shape was a one-piece jumpsuit. And even though it looked like a screen, its surface could not feel more different. It was soft to the touch, feeling like the smoothest skin imaginable. It was an eerie sensation putting the suit on because as Victor clothed himself in it, the material tightened up and stuck to his body, which created a great and uncomfortable pressure. After a few seconds, though, the tension ceased and Victor was covered with the most comfortable material he had ever worn. The material was cool and refreshing and literally breathed. It had a life of its own, and now it and Victor were one.

"Monitor 1865, bring up the video feed from drone number 3275." The three-dimensional monitor obeyed its user's command.

"Drone 3275, give me eclipsing angles." The drone obeyed. With a single high voltage vibration, a hologram of the minivan appeared right in front of Victor's face. Now Victor could clearly see the back of the minivan in front of him from the vantage point of the road. All he had to do now was step off of the observation deck bridge and into the three-dimensional display.

"Prepared to eclipse," the robotic female voice announced.

The monitor hovered ten feet away and five feet above. Its four edges lit up a deep and bright blue. Victor could feel its three-dimensional display slowly sucking him in as if he were the north pole of a magnet and it, the south. He was sure that this was his chance to finally gain the information he had been looking for this whole time. So taking a deep breath, he stepped through.

CHAPTER 21

It was a strange sensation - eclipsing. The only other time Victor had needed to execute such a task was to infiltrate underground tunnels of a Mexican drug cartel in southern Arizona. An important assignment to say the least - but nowhere near as significant as the task at hand. That was back two years ago, when he first eclipsed into live action, and it was his first time feeling the ethereal effects of a virtual, but actual reality. Victor did not know if he had completely forgotten what the sensation felt like or if it was different every time, but he didn't remember it feeling like this. He looked down at his body breathing underneath the full head-to-toe body suit and noticed that the material took on a different nature upon its wearer stepping through the portal.

"Maybe that's why," surmised Victor, out loud to himself.

After thinking hard for a few seconds, he arrived at the conclusion that the smart suit impacted its wearer's perception of feeling. The suit still remained its charcoal color, but no longer had a meshy appearance. The numerous tiny holes making up its surface had all closed up, forming a slowly moving, viscous material. The longer Victor looked at it, the more blended it became, finally stopping to become a celestial blend of milky obsidian somewhere between a liquid and a solid. The first time he eclipsed, the setting was very dark, and Victor was very nervous - his superiors watching his every step to confirm his acumen on becoming a certified user. Thinking back on it, Victor realized that he never even got a look at the smart suit on the other side. He had no idea it became something else - something allowing its wearer to eclipse into a live virtual space and gain information as if he or she were there, while being invisible the entire time. Even though users could see and hear as if they were there, they were not physically present underneath a stealth cloaking mechanism; they were only existent in technological spirit, invading unknowing citizens' privacy.

It was true and apparent to Victor that his bodily sensations were unprecedented. It felt as if his skin had flipped inside out and could finally breathe. He felt weightless. He felt like if he even ever-so-slightly jumped off of the ground, he would soar through the air and never come back down to land. Breathing was no longer just an involuntary reflex. On the contrary, it felt like never before, and Victor could take as deep a breath as he wanted. Each breath was instantaneous medicine for the mind, body, and soul, reaching every part of him, polishing it with delight. And the deeper the breath, the better it felt. Realizing this, Victor inhaled for twenty seconds before letting it escape to gallop down to his toes, purifying every inch along the way. It was a great approach to waiting for the setting to appear. It calmed Victor's nerves and brought him to a place of inner peace that he never even knew existed. There was about a two minute time gap between stepping through and seeing the desired coordinates appear.

During that two minutes, the bodysuit was analyzed in preparation for eclipsing. For some users, that two minute stretch was an eternity. In fact, this was where many potential users would break. Being suspended in a virtual space surrounded by nothing, desperately awaiting for some semblance of a landscape to appear had an effect on some people, but they never became users. The only thing that could be seen during those two minutes was the user's own body. The time in suspension was coming to a close because the smart suit began to give off a strange blue-green aura. The majestic light came to a dead stop three inches away from the body, though. If it wasn't inside the blue-green neon light, it was blacker than space itself.

Victor focused on the euphoric feeling running through his body a mile a minute, which was so intense, he thought he might effloresce into a new lifeform. He kept his eyes open and breathed deep inhalations of delight. Being suspended in virtual nothingness, there was no direction - no up or down - no side to side - no north, south, east, or west. With seeing no direction and with the exuberant feelings raging inside of him, Victor felt like something marginally more than a human. He was calm, breathing and focusing on feeling, but something in the back of his mind planted a thought. A thought from the shadows. And the thought created a slight sense of panic, which combated the deeply embedded blissful sensation. The two streams of consciousness wrestled. The phantom-created frightening idea of becoming trapped in virtual nothingness and the smart suit-instilled enchanted sense of peace grappled for the remaining countdown. There was nothing Victor could do. So he watched his thoughts and feelings like a spectator, suspended in the endless void.

***

"No more stops. We'll be too late," Gabe announced, as Matthew, Easton, and Rick Engleheart climbed back in the minivan. "Now or later, Sleepyhead. It's life or death."

"Hey, like I said, I'll go out the window if I have to. Don't have to go now, though. Press on, Gabe," Lacey responded, evoking smiles from everybody else.

Gabe started the van back up, lightly stepping on the gas pedal with his big toe as the engine turned over. The long caravan of old, rickety vehicles slowly pulled away from the dry, sandy shoulder of Interstate 80, following suit. It had been a long trek, especially for Gabe, Lacey, Easton, and Rick Engleheart, but they were nearing the last leg of their odyssey; however, common sense told them that the intriguingly dangerous part of their journey was just beginning. And everyone besides Gabe still felt very far from their terminus.

"Gabe, I'm just curious. You said that it's a matter of life and death. So what will we be too late for?" Rick Engleheart asked, as if only half-heartedly wanting to know the answer.

"Your son is alive, Rick. Alive and well, actually. But something is going to happen on Wednesday morning. Something big. And we need to be there before then."

***

An unearthly high-pitched rumbling sound became progressively louder starting from far off in the distance and began rolling its way closer to Victor. Every time the desired coordinates were about to appear, the bizarre modulation acted as its signal flare.

"Target moving," the robotic voice announced.

"Place me inside minivan plate number MLK 4087."

Very slowly, colors started to appear as if gigantic invisible hands were placing honeycomb-shaped puzzle pieces in a sphere around Victor. First, a gray honeycomb came into sight directly in front of him. Next, a skin-colored one to his left. Then, a blue sky-colored one behind him. Every time a new honeycomb appeared in seemingly random places, an external and unfamiliar sound accompanied it. This was not Victor's first time eclipsing, so he had heard the noise before, and even though the tone stayed identical for every honeycomb that appeared, it still rattled his bones. His neck hair stood up straight and his spine shook and shivered. As new honeycomb-shaped colors came into view and the modulation was heard more and more, Victor tried to put a finger on the noise, desperately trying to figure out what it sounded like. It was not necessarily high-pitched - a lot less high-pitched than the signal sound, which had stopped the second the first honeycomb appeared - but it was not low in pitch either. No matter how hard he tried, Victor could not think of anything that he heard in his fifty-eight years of life that sounded even remotely like the noise his ears were picking up in the virtual reality. If he had to think of what would make the sound, there was only one thought that came to mind. If rays from the sun could generate their own sound as they appeared in the sky, hitting objects on the Earth, it would come close to this noise. A two-second pretty revelation sound. That was the only way Victor could describe it to someone whose ears had not had the pleasure of hearing it. Clearly, it was a sound that human ears were not meant to perceive.

Visually, the virtual destination was marginally recognizable, becoming more and more like a vehicle's interior every two seconds. After all of the honeycomb-shaped pieces had been placed, the audio kicked in, and eureka, a live virtual reality became actuality, invisibly placing the user in the midst of unsuspecting privacy. It wouldn't be long until the simulation was complete, and Victor was ready to finally have the wool, even if slightly so, pulled from his eyes.

$$***$$

The most excited person in the van was Matthew. He had always lived his life as a rebel. Even as a child, he had a disobedient spirit. One time when he was ten- years-old, Matthew and his multiple cousins asked their grandmother, a lovely, generous, and amazing woman, to film a movie of them. This was nothing new. In fact, every summer when the cousins would get together, they created their own versions of their collective favorite movies. Whether it was for these reenactments or filming a family summer picnic, 'Grammy' always had an old video recorder on her shoulder, preserving memories of the good old days - a thankless job, but one upon which the grandkids could look back and smile with their hearts and with their souls.

One summer, the cousins decided to remake the famed mystery classic, *Clue*, citing 'Grammy's' house as a perfect setting to film it. At a dinner scene, Matthew and his cohort cousins convinced their parents and grandparents to allow them to use of real red wine.

"It won't be authentic if we don't use it," they argued.

Giving in, the parents reluctantly agreed. "You can pour it. Just don't drink it," they sternly instructed.

Whether the point was to not waste the wine or to not put it in front of pre-adolescent children, it didn't matter. The directions were simple. "Just pour it."

So it was poured. Each wine glass was filled about halfway until the bottle of red wine from the Finger Lakes was empty. Almost all of the child actors gazed at it as if it were the Ark of the Covenant, and only one dared to test the forbidding rule. Matthew, calm as a cradled child, gracefully picked up his wine glass, looked directly at the camera across the table, and downed the whole thing in three gulps. Setting the empty glass down, he shot the camera a smirk, knowing that all hell would break loose if the scene were to be interrupted.

Now, many years later, Matthew still possessed a recalcitrant spirit, as he allowed it to grow with age. And he was ready to use it; for the matter at hand was exponentially more important than disobeying family elders.

"So tell me," Matthew addressed Gabe, "Lacey. She's like a hybrid? Part human and part angel?"

Lacey was more than fine with an open discussion about her. Gabe knew this, and that is why he answered so casually.

"Well, there's a lot to it. It's like an algebraic equation, you know? When you simplify it and find 'X', you're correct. She is a hybrid." Gabe was responding to Matthew, but speaking to all of his passengers as well.

Gabe looked at Lacey's flawless face in his rear view and smiled proudly. "Right now, her spiritual touch on others is her most prominent gift. She has made each person in this whole convoy temporarily more than human, which will become a vital part of our mission."

"And how have I done that again?" Lacey asked, with sarcastic unbelief to incite Gabe.

The group leader saw through Lacey's fabricated skepticism and shot her a look showing his clairvoyance. He knew that after all Lacey had been through in the past couple of days that the eighteen-year-old bore self-efficacy and was fully on board with the situation. Keeping a hardened exterior was just Lacey's thing. So Gabe ignored her tone.

"Well everything you've done up to this point has been on a nonconscious level, which should come as no surprise. Almost all important battles take place on that level. Your mind fights its own unconscious wars every day, not always good against evil, but it was in your case. And good won. So, unknowingly, your spirit, energy, and life-force began to stretch its wings for the very first time. This happens to a lot of people," Gabe now addressed the group. "Sometimes, they finally figure out their purpose in life, or eventually break through in discovering something significant about themselves, or something as simple as remembering that the coffee pot was left on. The nonconscious is always hard at work. In Lacey's case, she began to spiritually impact others after the death of her mother. And if she did not have a hybrid DNA, her gift would never have come to fruition in the first place. Her life would be a lot darker. These types of things happen incredibly often, but humans don't know it because they can't see it. And just because you can't see it, touch it, or feel it, doesn't mean it's not real. The nonconscious is on the front lines of the battlefield of the mind, and I'm telling you an absolute truth when I say that tragedies, failures, imperfections - they're all meant for a purpose, an invisible rebuilding objective that gives sufferers the opportunity to become something greater than they were before.

"In Lacey's circumstance, she came out the other side of her family tragedy a new and unique entity, although she didn't know it. She was remade nonconsciously, and for the first time in her life, she began to use the gift that had laced her DNA since the day she was conceived."

"And now she'll use to it help get Johnny back and take down a massive control center. You seem pretty important over there," Matthew teased, admirably.

Lacey smiled and looked the other way out the window and tenderly said, "I know."

Gabe didn't have to look in the rear view mirror to recognize the value underlying the meaning of Lacey's response. For the first time during the trip, she started to take her gift seriously, and if angels could cry, Gabe would have wept tears of prideful joy. Instead, he simply smiled.

***

The sphere surrounding Victor was almost all the way full with honeycomb-shaped puzzle pieces. It was obvious to him that he was going to be placed in the back of a minivan, as he saw the back of heads and the rearward side of seats. The audio was about to come in, right after the last honeycomb appeared, and it was also at that moment when Victor was able to move around. He could sit anywhere he liked. Heck, he could lay across the dashboard if he wanted. Victor felt as if he might burst with excitement.

He was finally prepared to get some intel on who was assisting Rick Engleheart and Lacey Hassle, both of whom were supposed to be dead. Why weren't they? And why did they feel it even possible to take Emerus by storm? These questions, along with a plethora of others, like New York City marathon runners to a stationary spectator, raced by Victor's mind.

The last eerie sun-ray sound acted as the harbinger, signalling the simulation's completion. And there it was. The minivan, the passengers, the driver - Victor looked around his space like a desert coyote searching for food.

"Commencing audio," the robotic voice notified.

Victor simply could not wait. He saw five people - all male except one teenage-looking girl with dark hair.

"That must be her," he whispered, even though if he screamed it they wouldn't hear.

"Translating language…"

Victor felt his stomach do a somersault. "No, no no!"

He quickly moved from the back of minivan to the middle row of seats, accidentally bumping into one of the passengers, which breached a general guideline. However, the only effect was a chill up the unsuspecting person's spine.

"Blast!" Victor screamed this time. His guess was wrong. All of the passengers were, in fact, Japanese. He had known they were speaking it, but surmised that it was part of the stealth technology they might have been using. The last thought he had was that he would actually stumble upon a traveling Japanese family, but that is just what he did. He swore some more as he stomped his heels on the minivan's floor like a child having a tantrum. One of the many computer-like functions of the smart-suit was the ability to translate foreign tongues into English instantaneously, as the words were being spoken. Victor didn't want to listen, but he didn't want to return to Emerus either. He could have disabled the translation function, but with his energy drained, he didn't feel like going through the necessary, yet simple steps. So he crawled to the back seat, again bumping into the same passenger, making them shiver, and sat down. Feeling utterly defeated, he listened. There was nothing else to do.

"No, sweetheart. I'm sorry, but I have to take umbrage. There is no way that they're controlling the weather. It's just a crazy conspiracy theory."

"It's not necessarily controlling the weather, it's more like manipulating it. Weather manipulation is a more accurate term. Cloud seeding has been done since the 1960s. Can you imagine what they're capable of now, sixty years later? They can wield hurricane paths; they can facilitate conditions for tornadoes; they can even cause earthquakes. Not to mention the cosmic events they can expedite."

The father, who was driving the van, shook his head. "Who do you mean when you say "they," he asked his teenage daughter.

"I mean HAARP. The first one was built in Alaska, completed in 2007," she replied, pointing to a book in her left hand. "And now, there are others. One in Russia, one in England, one in Antarctica, and one in South America."

The husband laughed lovingly. "If I read the book, can we stop talking about it? Let's play Twenty Questions or something."

The nineteen-year-old young woman finally concluded that her father's offer was fair. "Thank you, Otoosan," she said, genuinely, smiling at her dad, to which he tenderly smiled back.

Victor shook his head and smiled, for he knew the truth. HAARP was simply a research facility and a front to distract conspiracy theorists from what was really going on. Similar to the faked UFO crash in Roswell, it was just a false flag meant to mislead people. It seemed to be working. It had been a while since Victor had heard conspiracies talked about, especially above the crust of the Earth. If the family only knew the real treason behind the invisible curtain, under the Earth. The truth was almost comical - top secret technology had transported a user to covertly sit amongst them. If the teenage boy had only known that the two shivers up and down his spine were the accidental effect of Victor eclipsing. If they had only known that Emerus had the capability to do everything they were discussing, and more. If they had only known. Victor wanted to shout out the truth that had been kept secret behind his lips for so long. He wanted to blow the whistle to be heard around the world. Not caring if he would be killed, he wanted to pull the curtain aside, finally revealing the cold, hard truth. He wanted all of those things, but most of all, he wanted his family. The higher-ups at Emerus put up a firewall preventing users from visiting anyone from their previous lives before Emerus. Victor became enraged at their control as tears of despair began to flow from his tired eyes. Hopelessness started to sink in until it was all around him like quicksand. He didn't care. Maybe he would follow this interesting family around. There was no hindrance regarding the time limit of eclipsing. At least Victor had never heard of such a thing. What would happen if he decided to stay in live virtual reality, on the run? Perhaps he gave his freedom too much credit because without any effort of his own, he heard the robotic female voice say that the simulation was ending.

"No. Please, no," Victor pleaded as he stretched out his hand to touch what he most desperately missed and desired. The last sight he saw before being unwillingly pulled out was a smile on the mother's face as she handed her children a bag of their favorite snacks.

It happened in the blink of an eye. Soundlessly, he was back inside the observation deck. Painful tears of misery stung his skin with embarrassment and exposure as he looked side-to-side to see his fellow co-workers and colleagues making up a small semicircle around him.

"Victor," Michael Willard said.

"Will."

"Are you ready to be briefed on the Lacey Hassle case?"

"I already have been. What do you think I've been doing for the past few months?" he asked, defensively.

"Trust me, old buddy, you haven't. Come on," Michael Willard motioned with his hand for Victor to follow him.

CHAPTER 22

Johnny was thankful to not have seen Victor in a while; he had gotten tired of the Doc's boring and grandiose soliloquies, not to mention the elaborate and gratuitous forms of interrogation. The truth was Johnny felt almost completely adjusted to the darkness - the evolutionary ability of humans to adapt at its finest. After everything he had been through in the past three months - extremely taxing for an eighteen year-old - he oddly felt at peace.

Dealing with the unexpected and tragic death of his mother, the eerie dreams that haunted his sleep, getting kidnapped and brought beneath the Earth to learn every mind-bending fact about what Emerus was commissioned to do, only to feel complete tranquility? Johnny was altogether perplexed, and even though he was alone, the eighteen-year-old felt the opposite. Something in his heart told him so, and he believed it. Perhaps it was the revelation of what Emerus could do, the unbelievable aspect of it all, that gave Johnny a new sense of acceptance in the unseen. Whatever the source, Johnny welcomed the unprecedented feelings with open arms. That had become the story of his life recently, and in Johnny's mind, it wasn't a bad life at all. He was inhabiting a zone that he had never been in before, like the angel told him in his dream: "This is how humans are meant to live."

Johnny felt released from the shackle-laden reality humanity had become adjusted to, and something, something unseen, but invigorating and full of love, had taken him to a new reality, a new realm. In it, he felt invincible. No longer did nightmares haunt his unconscious mind. No longer did fear have a grip on his soul. And no longer did he even feel part of this world. He felt anew - a mess transformed into a masterpiece. An integral part of his instauration was the rest and relaxation he was able to get. Unlike normal sleep, which was usually difficult to fall into for the teenager, ever since the strangely beautiful dream, Johnny was able to fall fast asleep at will. Upon the closing of his eyes, he was in dreamland, which contradicted what he had learned in psychology class as a junior. Emerus, however, contradicted everything he had learned throughout his life, so he simply accepted that sometimes science and history could not explain everything.

It was that thought that relaxed his mind, causing him to lie down on the twin-size bed in the corner of his quarters. "What else have I been taught that is wrong?" he asked out loud, as if someone or something would audibly answer him back.

Silence responded to his question. However, Johnny surmised that the answer failed to carry any weight anyway. He didn't know what time it was, and regardless, he didn't care. Rest was on the horizon. He felt it begin to envelop him like a much needed monsoon hovers over the desert after a long stage of drought. He had been getting an inordinate amount of sleep lately, but always felt that it was essential. Whenever he awoke, he felt more indomitable and mentally tougher, just another step along the way of an uncanny transformation. Johnny closed and his eyes, and he was sound asleep.

This dream felt different than the others. Instead of flying from tree to tree across infinitely high cliffs or walking through walls with Lacey, Johnny quickly understood that he was not the main character this time. Something about it just made him feel like a spectator, and this differentiation caused him to sharpen his focus. He was sitting cross-legged in a totally white room, the whitest ivory he had ever seen was encapsulating the square chamber. As his eyes adjusted to the shade, he understood that he wasn't in a cubicle. In fact, the expanse seemed to go on forever, but if he squinted deep into the distance, he thought he could see an endpoint. However, something in the back of his mind told him that it was an infinite distance from where he sat.

At peace, Johnny stayed motionless, gathering his surroundings. All of a sudden, the utter silence was beautifully broken by a twelve second tune. It was very far off in the distance, but Johnny could clearly hear something. After the twelve seconds, it repeated, and kept repeating as it grew louder and louder each time. Johnny could sense the tune was a message in a missile, and he sat motionless, as its target. He focused his hearing. Words. The tune had words. He couldn't make them out, but there were definitely words being sung in the form of the most elegantly perfect tune his ears had ever heard. He let the exquisite notes melt over him in comforting love. Each twelve second streak carried endless amounts of warmth that soothed his soul. Johnny closed his eyes and remained seated, fearing that if he moved a muscle, he might accidentally escape the beam of amenity he found himself in. The tune became louder still, repeating itself after each twelve-second cycle. Soon, Johnny could hear that countless voices were behind the noise. Its only source was the a capella singing of a seemingly infinite chorus. Louder. Louder still. He could nearly make out the words. Johnny had meditated before, done breathing exercises, even sat in an isolation tank for a full hour, but all of his past peaceful experiences paled in comparison to what he felt at this moment. Just when he thought the euphoria could not get any stronger, he heard the words that were being sung. All at once, every word of the tune was heard as the singing exponentially picked up its amplification.

At the dawn of it all, we will come and rescue you.

A relaxed jubilation commandeered Johnny's heart, mind, and soul. In the blink of an eye at the end of the tune, they appeared in front of him. An endless army of angels as long and as wide as the eye could see stood in rank and file, repeating the words in perfect harmony. They were tall, most standing around eight-foot. Each angel was dressed in majestic combat garb and stood upright with their arms outstretched in front of them as if they were holding an invisible lamp. Their shields and armor were a magnificent silver, shining like diamonds. Their hair was long and flowing in the unseen air currents. Everything seemed to be happening in slow motion, except the celestial sound, which the chorus kept on repeating every twelve seconds.

It was difficult to discern what the angels were like underneath their battle gear because of the sheer amount of their armor and the way it shined, which caused Johnny to squint. The more his eyes became adjusted to the luster, though, the clearer his view became. As the picture sharpened, Johnny noticed that the angels were not wearing anything underneath their diamond-like armor. Their bodies were translucent, but with explicitly-defined muscles. Perhaps the most mesmerizing spectacle was the radiating waves of energy emanating from each angel's body. Like seeing the effect of heat coming off of car roofs on an early August afternoon, the angels were exuding a similar type of wavy activity. Something about it looked as if their bodies were generating a soundless power by simply existing. The waves were thicker than the effect of heat, and they retained a strangely beautiful color that Johnny's eyes had never had the pleasure of seeing before. Something no human eye had seen before, Johnny surmised. It looked like a lighter shade of ultramarine, but had an intangible quality to it that was difficult to put a finger on. The color had an ethereal presence and the longer Johnny gazed at its grandeur, the more he questioned whether or not he was seeing it or feeling it, or perhaps a marvelous combination of both.

Being so focused on the radiating waves of brilliance coming forth from the army of supernatural beings, it took Johnny a guilty amount of time to notice their wings. Comfortably tucked back behind their straps of armor, the angels' wings were a brilliant white. The shade was so pure that it stood out as considerably whiter than the alabaster room. Their wings were extremely large; the tips peaked at near-head level and the lowermost feathers pointed downward about a foot from the ground. Definition of healthy muscles could even be seen in the wings, and soon the wonder of it all forced Johnny to stand up and raise his hands to the heavens thanking creation for such magnificent beings.

He knew he was dreaming and could not remain in the extraordinary setting forever, but if he could, Johnny would give anything to be able to linger for a little while longer. He closed his eyes and listened to the flawless sound.

At the dawn of it all, we will come and rescue you.
At the dawn of it all, we will come and rescue you.
At the dawn of it all, we will come and rescue you.

Inherently knowing that his time was running out, Johnny fixed his eyes to take in the unbelievably astonishing sight. Normally, he thought he might be frightened by such a scene - an army of angels prepared for battle all singing in unison. However, it was a peaceful display of hope on Johnny's heart, and he couldn't help but be completely captivated by the beauty of it all. He shook his head in wide-eyed amazement. The longer he looked and listened, the more the energy inside him became awakened. He forgot to breathe; he forgot to blink, but it didn't matter. In this place, there was no obligation for involuntary reflexes. So Johnny just gazed in awe, with his senses of sight and of hearing in paradise.

At the dawn of it all, we will come and rescue you.
At the dawn of it all, we will come and rescue you.

Anticipating he only had one more chorus left, Johnny inhaled for the first time. He didn't know why he did it - perhaps to empower and fortify his spiritual energy - but when he deeply inhaled the angels' last sweet song of hope, he felt overwhelmingly refreshed, renewed, but most of all, redesigned.

At the dawn of it all, we will come and rescue you.

After his long inhale, Johnny began to hastily evaluate the new predominant sense of awareness. The only way he could describe the feeling was an unprecedented sensation of being redesigned. A plethora of questions stormed Johnny's mind like protesters at a pep rally. But he never had time to answer them. Before they had a chance to embed themselves, Johnny awoke from his dream. With a quick inhale combined with a simultaneous opening of his eyes, he was back in his bed. Immediately after recognizing where he was, Johnny reached for the small nightstand and opened the drawer to retrieve the crumpled up piece of paper and dull-pointed pencil. Just as he had written down pertinent information from the previous dreams, he found a small amount of space to write down exactly what the angels had sung. After reading what he had scribbled on the worn and about-to-tatter paper, Johnny knew that something was on the horizon, something big.

***

During the brisk walk to a secure conference room a few levels beneath the observation deck, Victor was silent in thought. Embarrassed that his dear friend, Will, had watched his thoughts flash across the monitor inside the deck, Victor was not ready to speak. It was an odd feeling - being in such a strange place, virtually, going to where he was now. It was a mere minute ago that he was invisibly inside a minivan amongst a happy family. A lot can change in a minute, he thought.

Workers in lab coats dodged out of the group's way. Besides Victor and Will, there were eight others - a minute percentage of Emerus' work force. For the first time in years, Victor was in the dark about something. What was going on? Why the urgency? Questions such as these circled his mind. To the best of his knowledge, he was heading up the operation, and the instructions were simple. After the pilot study's initial success in Johnny Engleheart, it was paramount to keep the boy in Emerus for further monitoring. Dealing with the elimination of the freedom of thought had its risks. When Emerus had tried before, without a successful test pilot to study, monitor, and, if needed, modify, the results were disastrous. Foreign disorders misdiagnosed as multiple personality, paranoid delusions, schizophrenia, and others of that ilk became the by-products. This time, however, with a successful test subject, the odds greatly increased that the mission could be completed. Part of the United States was already being inoculated, or so Victor had been told. So now, the goal was to keep anyone attempting to rescue Johnny Engleheart as far away from Emerus as possible, especially Lacey Hassle, whom the American government had classified as intellectually dangerous. However, Victor was now seriously questioning the goings-on surrounding the mission.

"Will, I..."

"Shh. Not out here," Michael Willard replied. "Inside."

Victor kept quiet for the remaining fifty-seven paces. After multiple levels of clearance and security, the ten men finally entered a small conference room. Victor had been inside of it before. It was one of a handful of secret chambers in the depths of Emerus. Built into the wall, it could only be accessed by a select and privileged few by way of a hand print, a primitive science on Emerus' spectrum of technology. The person high enough on the hierarchy had to know where exactly to place their open hand, spreading their fingertips as wide as possible. There was a one-inch margin of error on each of the hidden rectangular panel's four sides, and the comrade only had one chance to get it right. If he or she failed, the chamber would remain locked for an unknown amount of time, and not even the smart machine builders knew for how long. Victor had always succeeded at finding the right spot; he had never heard of someone failing to do so, and this time was no different.

Chamber 2 was the room's designated name - the people at Emerus threw creativity to the wind when naming rooms, buildings, and bridges. This particular secret enclosure happened to be the smallest one of them all. And Chamber 2's interior, much like the rest of the secret alcoves, was uncommonly simple. It was a circular room, similar in shape and size to the Gravitron carnival ride. The ceiling was low and the walls bulged out at their sides, making newcomers feel as though they were inside a flattened disc or flying saucer type of object. Lighting inside was dim. The only luminescence was a soft orange glow that originated from a singular point on the bare ceiling and spread its beams out like tentacles. The glow was faint and silent and gave off an overwhelming reticent ambience. On the floor directly beneath the orange light's center point was a table bearing the same shape as the room, with ten chairs connected to it. That was it. Nothing more. Nothing less.

As the ten men found their seats, Michael Willard, who sat next to his old friend, spoke up.

"Alright, as you all know, Victor has done amazing work for us. Heck, if he hadn't, none of what we have, are, and will accomplish would even be a possibility. So for that, Victor, I thank you."

Victor smiled and nodded his head. "Thank you, Will." He couldn't think of anything else to say.

So Michael Willard continued. "But something has been brought to our attention recently. You were slightly in the shadows, but still, you knew that she was different."

"Lacey Hassle," Victor stated, as if finally arriving at the answer to an impossible algebraic equation.

"Exactly," Michael Willard replied. "There is something peculiar about her, about her makeup. As you know, since the Paradigm Shift, there are sometimes certain people they tell us to watch out for?"

Victor nodded in knowledge. "That's why I've been trying to make sure she stays away from us."

"Well, things have changed. Supercomputers are still collecting puzzle pieces on her, but it seems that she has the innate ability to connect to people's energy. No one, not even The Source can explain it, but the ability is there, and it is strong."

"Okay," Victor replied, with an inflection implying he wanted Will to continue.

But Michael Willard was silent for almost an uncomfortable amount of time. "Her ability, unmatched by any other person on Earth? Boy," he said, insatiably, "That would be a great addition to our work down here."

"So you're saying…"

"I'm saying we use Johnny Engleheart as bait. Intel says that Lacey Hassle is on her way here. So let her come, but don't let her leave. Can you imagine what we could accomplish? It would blow the Freedom Wave Operation out of the water."

Victor had never seen his friend like this, even back in the old days. "But she's receiving help. Somebody or something is with her," he said.

"Well that may be, but I'll be damned if it's more powerful than what we have here in our arsenal," one of the men, a burly fellow with a red neck replied.

After thinking for a few seconds, Victor nodded and told everyone that he was on board. Will patted him on the back. "Let's get to work."

CHAPTER 23

Johnny did not know how much time had passed since his most recent dream. Ever since he awoke in that sharp, liberating inhale, he was desperately trying to relive what had abruptly turned into a memory. His efforts, despite their valiancy, were to no avail. Johnny gave it everything he had, though, trying harder than ever before for anything. However, he came up short. He closed his eyes and wanted to see them again. He held his breath and wanted to hear them again. But all he saw was nothing. And all he heard was silence. And then, it hit him. In the lull and quiet calm of his simple, yet cozy living quarters, Johnny realized that once was all it took. The personal revelation he began realizing seemed to come out of nowhere, but it had vitality to it. It was like something was whispering to his mind and convincing his heart. It was then that he understood what was happening. At least, he thought he understood. A little far-fetched perhaps, but if the past had taught him anything, it was to question everything. Doubt the experts; believe your eyes, but know that there are worlds we cannot see; trust your soul's instincts; and be ready for your calling because it comes only once. Having learned all these lessons and more, Johnny relaxed his body on his bed. Interlocking his fingers, he put his hands behind his head, his six-foot body laying flat atop his bed. His brown hair stuck out through the spaces between his fingers like overgrowth pushes its way through lost cities in the jungle.

Johnny deeply inhaled a sigh of beautiful relief. He thought of his final sensation before waking up from the dream. Closing his eyes, he swore he could see the thought gently fluttering about like a butterfly across his line of mis-vision, disappearing only to re-enter from the right, slowly and peacefully flying across to exit on the left. Reappearing again, the little butterfly-shaped concept continued its dance three more times before Johnny finally had it within his grasp. He pictured, when it disappeared out of view, that it carried on its orbit around his head and he could only see it when it crossed in front of his mind again. Without overworking his brain on how he could see color with his eyes closed, Johnny simply awaited for the shape to once again cross his line of mis-vision. There it was. Innocently floating by. Its bright, brilliant blues left a dazzling trail of intense orange speckles as it flapped about, showing off its resplendency. How small it was. But something about its appearance and its movement told Johnny that even though its size was modest, whatever it was, it held power within.

Waiting until the opportune moment when it was right between his eyes in the center of his sight, the eighteen-year-old showed patience. Five seconds. Two seconds. There! Johnny captured the notion with his mind. It was the epitome of the old idiom 'Big things come in small packages' and Johnny knew exactly what it was. It was more than a thought, more than a strong concept. The last sensation he had right before he awoke had manifested itself in the butterfly-shaped abstraction. And now that Johnny had caught it, the celestial intellection began to manifest itself within his being. Keeping his eyes peacefully closed, he focused on what it meant. After realizing full-well, he smiled. Redesign.

***

It was a sight to see when Victor, Michael Willard, and the other geniuses of the world put their heads together to come up with a plan. The act belonged in a zoo or traveling circus so all other humans below an IQ level of 160 could watch in awe. Just for fun, the group of ten superior men spoke in different languages. One would ask a question in French and another would answer in Chinese, then someone would comment in German and somebody else would make a remark in Portuguese. At one point, Victor made a wisecrack in Amestec and all at once, his peers looked at him, confused. After awkwardly explaining how and why he had created his own language while in secondary school, the others were all for it, trying to learn it on their own.

Completely ignoring what they were previously working on like they had forgotten about Lacey Hassle, the nine men learned Amestec under Victor's tutelage. The greatest part about Amestec, as Victor would say, was that it was a constantly changing language. For example, one could switch out words at will, but the sentence and its meaning would remain the same. 'My wife has an ear infection' can be said any number of ways as the speaker enjoyed the option of which word to say in each language. Sometimes they even combined languages within each word. The same meaning would be obtained no matter which way the sentence was spoken. So because of the constant fluidity of Amestec, speakers had to fluently communicate and understand each of its four languages. Fortunately for Victor and his peers, they all did. So it was rather simple once everybody got the hang of it, which took no longer than five minutes. The rest of the two-hour-long meeting was spoken entirely in Amestec, and Victor loved every second of it, feeling as if his education, effort, and giftedness had finally come to fruition. It had made a complete circle, and it warmed Victor's heart in a very sentimental way.

The plan, at its foundation and substance, was quite straightforward. The people at Emerus will gladly welcome in Lacey Hassle and Rick Engleheart, even whoever the person is that is helping them out. It would probably take a lot of convincing for them not to be hostile, but there was something about the situation that made the men confident Lacey Hassle, Rick Engleheart, and whoever was with them would not mind coming down to the depths. And, if they were hostile, Michael Willard was prepared to unveil a top-secret weapon that he was not at all hesitant to use if the situation called for it. It was a new technology built by the smart machines that suspends gravity for a short amount of time, forcing anyone within its sights to relent control of their bodily movement and levitate off the ground at a height of the user's choice. Similar to the science fiction-created tractor beam, Emerus' new gravity gun quickly became more and more of a desired option, especially for Michael Willard, who had been testing its capabilities every day for the past two months. The gravity gun was finally field-ready, and they were all looking forward to seeing it in action.

Once the subjects were secured in Emerus, whether it be by convincing or through force, the truth would be explained to them, just as it was to Johnny Engleheart. There was no chance of escape, so leveling with detainees was something that was widely practiced in Emerus. Lacey Hassle would be the key to future plans, which Michael Willard already said he had gotten a head start on.

"Imagine. The ability to impact thought without use of radio waves or smart phones, or needing to access the ionosphere. How can the public uncover what they don't even believe exists in the first place?"

He was adamant that harnessing Lacey's abilities was going to change the world. The excitement that Will possessed toward the new project cascaded toward the other nine and instilled in each of them a fresh, raw desire to accomplish the most recent scheme.

"Can you even imagine what they'll give us then?" they all asked in wonder.

After the meeting, the ten men dispersed from the secret room, spreading out like water droplets being dried on a windshield after a car wash - some to their quarters to put their ear drops in again, others to the cafeteria. They each took different routes. That was something about Emerus that Victor and other men of his genius enjoyed. With a plethora of secret passages, hidden hallways, unseen doors, and unrevealed tunnels, the higher ups at Emerus knew about all of them and were given free rein for twenty-four-seven use at their leisurely pleasure.

Often times for fun, Victor would try out a new route for an everyday destination. Punctuality rarely mattered; so frequently, he would take the intricate elevator system to a whole different inverted super silo. Sometimes, he would travel the absolute farthest he could, then meander his way back blindly, trying to find the best possible route all to do it differently the next time. It was not only extremely enjoyable for the genius mind, but it also allowed for a collection of knowledge of the elaborate labyrinth system. If some unforeseen circumstance called for it, Victor and the other higher-ups would have an unrivaled understanding of the entangled tunnel structure. If he had to guess, Victor would place the number of hallways and tunnels - including the hidden ones - at somewhere in the tens of thousands, which made for almost infinite possibilities when it came to navigating through the hundreds of underground super silos. It was always fun for Victor and his colleagues to acquire new knowledge, and this was an entertainingly satisfying way to go about it.

It had been some time since Victor had last visited Johnny, and in an odd way, he missed the eighteen-year-old to some degree. Now that the original successful pilot study subject was just going to be utilized as bait for something even greater, Victor thought he should visit the once-heralded hero. To some extent, he felt bad for him. He had such potential, and now, not long after his capture, Johnny Engleheart was just a worm on a hook.

Victor was considerably giddy to share the latest news with his old project. Of course, he couldn't reveal the whole truth and would end up lying to preserve the peace, but nevertheless he was excited to see Johnny's reaction upon learning that his dear old dad and little girlfriend were safely on their way. He assumed Johnny would be ecstatic. A luxurious life in underground interconnected cities with the two people he perhaps loved the most? There was no way the boy would pass that up, Victor thought, especially with everyone's safety guaranteed. Lacey would be used in one way or another by the system Will was cooking up, and that was it. Not much of a sacrifice, in Victor's eyes.

He took the most direct route to Johnny's living quarters, excited to share the good news with his subject. A fast-paced lateral elevator ride, two tunnels, and a left turn later, Victor arrived at Johnny's door. He walked in confidently and quietly. Expecting to see the teenager distraught and depressed, the Doc was greatly taken aback when his self-assured entrance was welcomed with an even more confident smile from the teenager.

***

Wednesday, 2:23 am

Gabe's troop was leading the way, and the caravan was just hours from their destination in Wyoming. Rick Engleheart was becoming more and more excited and nervous, hopeful and scared as time wore on. Easton was brave and positive. Lacey was sure of her own salvation, but unsure of everything else. Matthew was as upbeat as ever. And Gabe, supplying enough positive energy for thousands, was courageous and convinced, exuding fearlessness - the likes of which no one else in the minivan had ever seen.

Rick Engleheart had not asked any questions regarding the exact location of his son, the details of the mission, or the 'how' questions that floated about his mind in constant fashion in over an hour, which was the longest he had gone since the trip's inception back in Rhode Island. It was a relief to Gabe. For he had something to tell everybody before he could even begin to broach the subject of the operation's structure. It was something foreboding, but necessary. However, it had to be done. A roguish smile came across his face.

"Rick, I have something to confess," he stated, matter of factly.

At the time, Matthew and Easton were in a discussion with their uncle about the Mets and their last championship season, nine years prior in 2016. The three of them were perhaps the biggest Mets fans on the face of the Earth, at least, according to them. Lacey could not have been more disinterested. Swiping away on her smartphone, lost in the world of digital communication and information, if asked, Lacey could not have so much as ventured a guess as to what the three men to her right were deliberating over. But Gabe's tone was ominous. Lacey even stopped her finger movement and looked up at him. Silence among Rick Engleheart and his nephews told Gabe to continue.

"I don't know how to say this," he said, stopping his sentence abruptly. The roguish smile was still tattooed on his face.

"Well just say it," Lacey spoke up, clearly concerned.

"What is it?" Rick Engleheart asked, in the form of a nervous demand.

"Rick," Gabe declared. "Do you remember when your son was in the hospital?"

Everyone held their breath.

"Did he ever tell you about any strange dreams he had during the observation night?"

Johnny was very discreet about his chilling nightmare in the hospital, but his father remembered the horrifying tale. The strange beings, what they did to Johnny, their cold skin and their painful experiment - it was beyond eerie. What bothered Rick Engleheart the most was how convinced his son was that what he experienced may not have been a dream at all. Johnny thought it may have actually happened. That was all his father knew, though. He had actually disclosed more about his frightening situation with Lacey. She knew of the hospital, and of the multiple three-in-the-morning bedroom visits, and how creepily similar they were.

"What are you talking about, Gabe?" Lacey asked, angrily.

Gabe looked to his right at Rick Engleheart, and said, "I was one of the two visitors in the hospital. And in the middle of the night in his bedroom, and in the living room, and in the guest room, and at Lacey's house. That was me. I was the the one who haunted his quote-unquote dreams."

CHAPTER 24

It was something about the way Johnny looked at Victor and the teenager's demeanor that perturbed the Doc. Victor could not put his finger on it, but there was definitely something different about him - something unspecifically strange. Johnny no longer looked like someone being held captive, someone very far toward the bottom of a situation's totem pole of power. Instead of evading eye contact, Johnny seeked it. And instead of appearing vulnerable, Johnny's gaze, in turn, made Victor feel jeopardized. It had only been a little over a day since the Doc had last seen the eighteen-year-old, so he was trying to comprehend what had changed.

"A lot can change within a day, Victor," Johnny declared, as if the Doc had been thinking out loud.

Victor was careful to react. He had gone through months upon months of training in the interrogative arts after arriving at Emerus more than a decade prior. He was confused by Johnny's turnaround in disposition. However, he knew not to show it.

"Well, my boy," Victor uttered with a smile, "You seem happier. You must have received the news."

Johnny had no idea what Victor was talking about, and knew that he had been lied to multiple times, so Victor's words meant less than nothing to him. He laughed through his nose and hummed with his mouth.

"Why, what on Earth do you mean?" Johnny asked, sarcastically.

Without two seconds passing, Victor shot back a straightforward, no-nonsense answer. "Your father and Lacey are en route. Just like I had promised. You should start trusting me." Immediately after Victor had finished his sentence, he turned around and walked out of the room, gently shutting the door behind him. Knowing that Johnny could no longer see him, Victor's face wrinkled in confusion. He shook his head in frustration, not being able to come up with even so much as a guess as to what could have possibly changed in a day. Angrily, he walked away with purpose in his stride.

Johnny, on the other hand and on the other side of the door, knew that his poise had confounded his captor. He was pleased with his performance, and was once again ready to read through his personal notes on the crumpled looseleaf paper. Dream descriptions, exact quotes, intimate revelations, and future plans made up the mess on both sides of the rumpled sheet. To the naked, untrained eye, it was a bunch of nearly illegible scribble. But to Johnny, it was a masterpiece and his most prized and sacred possession. Retrieving it from its hiding place, he read through every word once more. It was as if he was seeing it for the first time. Butterflies fluttered in his stomach, hitting the walls in rapid fashion. Chills ran up and down his spine. The hairs on the back of his neck became erect, stretching for the sky. Goosebumps formed on his forearms. And a long-lasting smile came upon his face. He focused on the words written and believed with all of his strength that they were coming to fruition. Then, something happened. Something that changed Johnny and his future from that day forth.

Victor knew something was amiss. His genius and his training sensed it. Without stopping to think, he took a fifty-mile-per-hour elevator ride to his old friend Michael Willard's current location. There was a plethora of technology in Emerus that the outside world would not see for decades. This had always been the case - from military weaponry to household appliances - new technology was always first tested below Earth's surface. Emerus saw the inception of the B2 Stealth Bomber in the 1970s; however, it was not first used until the early 2000s. The digital video recorder function, known as DVR and built into every television starting in 2017, had been part of Emerus residents' lives since 1995. Around that same period of time, citizens of Emerus began to enjoy personal use of smart phones and tablets as well. The most recent example of technology that the mainstream world had not yet seen was a type of social GPS, which Victor began to use.

While everyday smart phones contained GPS tracking systems, this personal social GPS technology was only seen in Emerus with its implementation for the outside world set for the year 2029. Part of the Emerus protocol, workers were implanted with microscopic GPS tracking chips in their wrist area. Not only was the person's location transmitted to the main server, but just like social networking, people had the ability to pick and choose their "friends." Their location would then be transmitted from the individual's chip to their brain, essentially giving the person an innate knowledge of his or her friends' location. With this technology's proliferation, phone calls, text messages, and other forms of communication would become outdated and were immediately cut in half, giving people the ingrained ability to push the boundaries of human normalcy. Victor had had the chip in him for years, and having that capability had become so ordinary and commonplace, he sometimes forgot to use it, even when it was convenient to do so. He smiled to himself when he remembered the old quote, "What one generation tolerates, the next generation will embrace."

Finding people within one's GPS network was quite simple. Victor pushed his thumbprint into the injection spot on his right wrist and said aloud, "Michael Willard." Almost instantaneously, his old friend's exact location was projected into Victor's mind. The Doc stopped walking toward the elevator harbor and turned around. According to his social GPS chip, Will was closer than he thought. Much closer. Victor stood puzzled, wondering what his old friend would be doing in this part of Emerus. As far as he knew, Will was doing his own work in a neighboring super silo. This particular silo was Victor's jurisdiction, containing all of the pieces of his current project.

Part of the implementation of the social GPS was a timed location option, which gave people the preference to choose how long their friends' position was projected into their minds. This was notably convenient when a friend was moving, as was the case with Victor and Will. So the Doc once again held his thumb print on the injection point and quietly said, "Fifteen seconds." His eyes widened when the realization struck him like a bolt of lightning. Michael Willard, who had never even met Johnny Engleheart was heading for his room.

Johnny could not believe his eyes. He even pinched himself just to make sure that he wasn't still in the midst of one of his otherworldly illusions. No change. He blinked slowly, hoping in the back of his mind that when he reopened his eyes, the letters would stop moving. But again, his effort was to no avail. Had he lost his mind? Was he going insane? Reality, as it once was, had been becoming something entirely different for quite some time, but this was a whole new level of distinctness. He was not dreaming; he was fully awake. But was it all in his mind? Questions of this kind once again circled his mind like vultures, waiting for Johnny's faith in himself to die so they could pick and eat at the remains until his self-certitude became a dry, rotting carcass. However, something inside of him infinitely more capable than the vultures was telling him to take a leap of faith. Johnny had always been self-assured and grounded, but the recent events in his life caused him to question himself like never before. He couldn't deny what he had seen in his visions and dreams. And instead of acting on how he felt and focusing on his feelings, which were so fleeting anyway, Johnny fastened himself to his spirit. For he knew it could not and would not be broken down by man, principality, or even death. He fastened and held tight.

Collectedly inhaling through his nose and calmly exhaling through his mouth, Johnny returned his focus to the paper. He shook his head in amazement. Everything he had written down with the dull pencil was being rearranged right before his eyes. Letters disbanded from their words and effortlessly lifted off of the paper. Suspended an inch in the air directly above their previously perpetual resting spot, the letters remained hovering for three seconds, just long enough to impress Johnny. Then, they gently floated to different spots on the paper, each going its separate way. First, it was one cluster of words. Next, a different cluster. Then, another, and so on and so forth. This pattern repeated itself so many times that Johnny lost count. He was not one hundred percent sure, but he thought he saw letters that had originally drifted to one spot on the paper gently glide through the air to another spot after all of the letters had been reshuffled. They moved slowly enough to stimulate Johnny's senses and make the hair on the back of his neck stand up, but also swiftly enough to prevent him from knowing where exactly they fell back onto the paper.

At first, he just thought that they were being randomly jumbled around because their positions made no sense. 'Rpujbiel' was not a word. He knew that for sure. At least, not in any known human language. The letters stopped moving and all at once, soundlessly fell an inch to the paper. The letters were all still jumbled and bore no significance at all. Johnny was confounded. He looked closer, picking up the piece of paper off the cold tile ground, and bringing it just inches from his eyes, he bit-by-bit read it out loud, pronouncing the words to the best of his ability. As soon as he declared the final syllable, every single word on the page simultaneously changed. It was too rapid of a transformation for Johnny to notice if the newly created words contained the same letters as their jumbled ancestors. It was as if the old words disappeared and fresh ones instantly took their place. Still in his handwriting, this time the words were in English, and taking up the whole front side of the paper, they built a message. Something told Johnny that if he had not read the previous strange language aloud, the words on the page would not have changed, and upon reading the first few words, his inclination was proven correct.

"Now you have read the language of the angels. On Wednesday they will come, and on Wednesday you will rise. Not hidden, not captured. You will break free out of the snare and escape. The snare will be broken and you will have escaped."

Johnny read the message aloud three more times, and as he ended each one, a broad smile came across his face. There was something significant about the words - how they touched Johnny's heart. For the first time since his capture back in Rhode Island, there was a direct hope stirring inside of him. This was so, wholly because he was given an exact day when he would depart from the depths of Emerus.

"They're gonna flip," he said out loud to himself, anticipating Victor's and the other higher-ups' reactions. He figured it best to act normal - not expectant, nor excited, just reasonable and not so well-adjusted. Looking back on how he had just acted in front of Victor, Johnny mentally kicked himself. He was afraid Victor would think something was up, and maybe take him to another facility, one that was impossible to escape from. Perhaps next time the Doc stopped in for a visit, he could act ultimately crazy, quelling any suspicion in Victor's mind as he might write off Johnny's demeanor changes as normal side effects of the life they had brought him into. But what about the message? It was displayed after Johnny had spoken with Victor. So was it simply fate that had preordained Johnny as an escapee? A plethora of emotions and difficult-to-answer questions were swirling around his mind. He looked again at his paper.

> *Now you have read the language of the angels. On Wednesday they will come, and on Wednesday you will rise. Not hidden, not captured. You will break free out of the snare and escape. The snare will be broken and you will have escaped.*

Silently reading it to his soul, Johnny started to understand that it *was* predestined. He closed his eyes. Desperately trying to remember what day it was, Johnny became frustrated at his own inability. He wished he had marked the wall or something like that every time he had fallen asleep or something to that degree. It was too late now. He shook his head in regret.

"Damn!"

He looked at the paper, wondering if the words would ever return to what he had originally written. On cue, the letters rose from the page once again. Still mesmerized, Johnny anticipated a reversal of events. However, he was wrong. Instead of returning to what what they were previously, the letters remained in place with the words and moved toward him. Maybe it was supernatural shock or maybe it was fright, but Johnny didn't move a muscle. The words moved one behind the other, staying in order, the sight of which reminded Johnny of a train. He watched as the word acting as the caboose stretched all the way to the wall four feet from where he was sitting. The engine of the word train moved closer and closer to him, aimed an inch below his heart. When the first word entered, it felt warm, almost hot. But he was used to it by the third one. Paralyzed, he simply let what was happening happen. There was nothing else to do, and the way he felt when the words made a comfortable home in his soul was unlike anything he had sensed before. It was an empowering feeling, but also loving and fearless - a strange mix to say the least.

Immediately after the words disappeared, Johnny began to recite them perfectly. It was something beyond memorization, something beyond having an eidetic memory. It was as if the words were speaking for themselves and Johnny's mouth was the medium which they were using, but at the same time, he was in control of when to say them and when to think them. He looked at the sheet of paper again, hoping to see his former work take shape, but he was too late to see the change. And now something else was being created. It had started when Johnny was focused on the train of words and was almost finished. Immediately, he knew what it was.

A countdown clock. Its numbers were disappearing and then reappearing without sound. Still in the darkened gray color of his dull pencil, the countdown took up the paper's whole horizontal front side. '3:57:04, 3:57:03, 3:57:02, 3:57:01.' Inherently, Johnny knew that when the clock expired, it was then time to flee. He didn't know who was coming to assist, but with full and complete confidence, he knew that when the clock struck zero, he was walking out the door.

Satisfied at what had just taken place, Johnny picked up the piece of paper, and upon folding it, he placed it back in its hiding place, lodged between the back of the drawer and the inside wall of the nightstand. A little less than four hours, and it begins, he thought.

Johnny breathed a huge sigh of relief at the grand timing of it all as the door handle to his room began to turn.

CHAPTER 25

"Will! What are you doing?" Victor bellowed.

Michael Willard rarely showed emotion; however, in this instance, his face was covered in an overabundance of it. Surprise was the first one to show in his eyes. Next came confusion. It showed in the fifty-six-year-old's wrinkles. Then, a minor sense of culpability commandeered Michael Willard as he lowered his head and raised his hand. The whole display of mixed sentiment lasted less than two seconds, but Victor had seen it develop in slow motion. His old friend was clearly rattled.

"Victor, umm, hi," he awkwardly stammered. Gathering himself, he continued. "You are probably wondering what I am doing here," Michael Willard conceded, logically with a nod of his head and a close of his eyes.

"Why, yes Will. I am. What business do you have with Johnny Engleheart?"

Michael Willard did not want to tell Victor what he was doing in his old friend's jurisdiction. However, he wasn't one for deception. So, he attempted to improvise.

"It's not the boy I'm looking for, Victor," he said, through a bewildered laugh. "It's you." It was not a complete lie, but it wasn't the exact truth either.

"Me?"

"Yes, the social GPS guided me to Johnny Engleheart's room when I tried to locate you. It said you were there."

Now Victor's face was the one possessing confusion. "I was trying to locate you!" he stated, emphasizing the last word. "We need to talk seriously about something."

Michael Willard let out a two-tiered laugh. "Gotta love technology. We were both looking for each other at the same time. Waves must have crossed. When did you try to locate me?"

"Right after I left the boy's room," Victor replied.

"That must be it then. I was locating you concurrently and the last place you were probably became locked in for some reason. Even down here," Michael Willard said, as he shook his head in sarcastic amazement and disappointment.

Victor's old friend had a very convincing way about him.

Perhaps it was the honesty in his eyes, but the Doc did not question Will whatsoever. He shook his head as well, in awe of the imperfections that existed even in Emerus' technology.

"I just spoke with the boy, and I sense there is something amiss. That's why I was looking for you. But why were you looking for me?"

Michael Willard did not have an immediate answer waiting for Victor's request. But he knew that his old friend believed what he had just said. So he continued with his half-true story.

"Frankly I wanted to grab a bite to eat with you and discuss our plan. I'm not surprised that you think something is amiss. I, too, sense some potential weak points. It almost seems too easy, and as we know, if it's too easy, there's usually something fallible with it."

Victor bought it. "I'm glad you think that way, Will. Come to think of it, I could go for a bite. The cafeteria in this silo has some amazing Pakistani food. Let's go to work."

The two friends had said more to each other in the past couple of hours than they had in the past decade. It felt good.

"Great minds think alike, Victor. Great minds think alike," Michael Willard said, slapping his old friend on the shoulder as they took up a casual stride.

The doors in Emerus were not quite sound-proof, at least, not in the living quarters. If someone on the inside had exceptional hearing and held his or her strong ear up to the composite material, a low, but clear conversation could be potentially perceptible. Johnny fit the bill, and his right ear was flat against the door. He heard every word.

***

Wednesday, 3:40 am

Rick Engleheart's mouth had dropped to the floor in both disgust and fright. Hair on the back of everyone else's necks lifted up as goosebumps began to take shape. Beginning at the neck, they made their way down both arms like a whale of a wave crashing to the sand and racing up the shore, but not receding back to the depths. No, these goosebumps kept advancing, in an unprecedented manner. In addition to being aghast and frozen by Gabe's words, everyone also became unnerved by the way their goosebumps were eerily speeding forward. It was an amazingly unique horripilation. And those experiencing it became entranced by its sensation. After it hit the hands, the wave jumped to the midsection and began its descent down to the legs and feet. Instead of a frightening feeling, an overwhelming sense of wonder came over everyone in the minivan. Even Rick Engleheart felt it. Emotions of anger and confusion put up a good fight, but ultimately lost, forcing him to succumb to the fascination and reverence of what was happening to his body and spirit. It was as if coming forth from Gabe's words was a spirit that simultaneously touched everyone and instilled a sense of astonishment and peace that did not recede. It was a tidal wave of awe that crashed on their shore and progressed forward, lifting hairs and forming bumps, consuming and consoling. Its casualties were drowned in a strange sense of reassurance.

Lacey was the first to speak. Her voice calm and in wonder. "Gabe, what the heck are you talking about?"

Everyone else was either too relaxed to talk or too in shock to think.

"I know what you all are thinking. But trust me when I tell you that my intentions were nothing but for the best. There was an opportunity to sabotage the enemy's plans. Just one shot. And I took it."

The overall consensus of silence that consumed the minivan's space told Gabe two things - they were listening and to keep going.

"As you all know, Johnny served as a test dummy for a top-secret government-sponsored Emerus project whose main objective was to take away the freedom of thought. With a sort of utopia in mind, the future goal was to create a species of humanity that thought and acted just as those in power would decree. Dangerous is an understatement. Johnny was the first successful test. He did not develop severe mental disorders and he did not die. After he was taken to Emerus, they began to send out the authorization codes, using radio waves, invisible light technology, and smart phones against the public. By manipulating the ionosphere, they found a way to impact thought. Radio waves impacting the brain processes, state-of-the-art light technology affecting what is seen, and smart phones influencing decisions with suggestive science. Some of the population is already being controlled. We, and the rest of the convoy, though, are not. And there are others. But it is our job to rescue Johnny. His fate is so much more than what you may think. That is why I did what I did. If I hadn't, then they would have won."

"Gabe, I don't understand," Rick Engleheart confessed and pleaded. "Why did you torment him in the hospital and in his dreams...or whatever they were?"

"The enemy had their plans," Gabe continued. "The plan was to implant in Johnny a device that would alter his thoughts. The device, built years ago, has recently been broken down far enough to the subatomic level to use invisibly in radio waves. But before that happened, Emerus had to test the technology. And that was where I came in.

"I received word about the enemy's plans with Emerus. So, I disguised myself as one of the shadow beings. Lacey, you know what I'm talking about. It was an arduous process, and all of it none of you would understand. But I sabotaged the plan by infiltrating the dark domain and personally placing the device behind Johnny's eyes. Little did they know, I switched devices. The shadow that was with me knew nothing, and was quite clueless to begin with. It was easy. The device I put behind his eyes was something that was much more powerful. Something that could go undetected because it would influence thought, but everything else as well. In visiting Johnny in the middle of the night, I checked on him and watched over him, making sure the plan would still go forth. And Rick, I'm sorry, but sometimes, humans have to go through hard times to get to the good ones. That's just life. Pretty much summing up human existence, it's like wandering through the desert to find an oasis. Rick, there was no other way. "

Lacey, Easton, and Matthew sat in silence respectfully waiting for Rick Engleheart to respond. He let out a sigh of relief. "So he was in good hands all along." His voice remained steady and did not crack, but a single tear drop of alleviation fell from his tired eyes.

"I assure you, Rick. Your boy has been free from harm the whole time he's been in the hands of the enemy."

"So let me ask you a question," Matthew announced, addressing Gabe. "You switched out devices and put your own behind Johnny's eyes. So there is something influencing his thoughts. What is it?"

Gabe spoke as if it was a communal question and he was answering it for everybody. "It would be difficult for me to describe what exactly it is or where it came from. But I can tell you that it was not of this world. It is from another realm, my realm. That is why it is undetected by the people at Emerus. Even the enemy working with them does not recognize it. As far as they know, everything is going to plan. But what is influencing Johnny's thoughts will have the opposite result of their scheme."

"What is it?" both Easton and Rick Engleheart asked, almost simultaneously.

"It's nothing ruinous, trust me. Quite the opposite, actually. What it basically is doing is making him realize his full potential - who and what he really is." Before the four passengers began to speak up, Gabe stopped them in their tracks. "And that is something that is beyond exceptionally rare, but something that I cannot reveal at this time. But he's one of a kind, and his fate is extraordinarily unique."

None of the passengers, not even Lacey, attempted to contend with Gabe. Learning from past attempts, it was pointless and exhausting trying to pull information from him if he was not ready to disclose it. All he did was promise that it would all be unveiled in due time, and soon enough, they would know. That was not good enough for Matthew, however. He wanted to know when they would find out.

"Before the sun rises," Gabe stated, prophetically.

***

Victor showed his old friend around Super Silo Two. It was the second one built by the smart machines when the ISSP (Inverted Super Silo Project) began fifty years prior. The structure itself was half a century old, but newfangled technology inhabited it. Elevators, doors, supercomputer voice-commanded televisions, living quarters, even the walls were all being constantly updated with the ebb and flow of new and unique technology pouring forth from the depths of Emerus' epicenter.

The change was difficult to notice for the silos' residents and workers, for they were much too close to perceive any steady innovative changes. Similar to how beach-goers drift bit-by-bit in the surf, the change was immensely gradual and almost impossible to realize. One minute they are in the water with their belongings thirty yards directly behind them. Riding waves, treading water, going over, going under for fifteen minutes, and they have imperceptibly strayed from their starting point. It was the same in Emerus. Before workers and residents could realize it, no-touch-screen monitors had been placed in walls, elevators moved more rapidly, food was made faster, and buildings were erected at a perplexingly fast rate. Emerus inhabitants simply succumbed to the undulating current of new technology. It was just the way it worked.

Michael Willard told Victor he had never been in Super Silo Two, so the Doc was more than happy to show him around. It was not all that different from the other silos, though. The smart machines had been programmed to build numerous inverted super silos and used the same programming code for each. So since the machine-made virtual reality was uniform throughout, the only real differences distinguishing the massive structures from each other existed in the man-made matter. However, these topped the boring list with the likes of tables, chairs, beds, and other simple and elementary furniture. For the most part, Michael Willard saw nothing he had not seen before.

"So where's this Pakistani place? I'm famished," he told Victor.

The cafeteria was perhaps the one attraction in Emerus that did not deviate from the outside world, at least not in design, only in size. It looked like a large high school lunch room combined with the Mall of America's vast food court. Long rectangular tables with swivel chairs connected to them grazed the floor like a great herd of buffalo. There were other workers gathered at the table to the far left, and a handful of lonely men contently eating by themselves. The room was so massive, though, that it felt as if Victor and Will had the whole place to themselves.

The design was simple. Tables in the middle of the long rectangular room with an immense variety of food vendors lining all four of the outside walls. It was exactly how high school and college cafeterias looked in 2025 and probably would not change anytime soon. There was only one difference between them and their counterparts in Emerus, but it was stark. Instead of people preparing and serving the food, machines did. Built by machines themselves, these particular apparatuses were extremely adept at making the food that they were programmed to. So, after Victor and Will chose their entrees from the touch screen menu, they were each enjoying their fare less than five minutes later. Victor ordered his old standby - Chicken Vindaloo. Will was more adventurous and went with something he had never ordered before - Chana Masala.

During their meal, they conferred on what they had come to discuss - Johnny Engleheart. Michael Willard was concerned that the plan of luring Lacey Hassle in seemed too easy and was convinced that they would run into problems.

"Whatever or whoever is helping Johnny's father and Lacey get here is not going to go down without a fight," he surmised. "I mean, we are prepared for anything, but I don't see it going very smoothly. The last thing we need is a slew of casualties on our hands. That won't please you know who."

Victor nodded in serious agreement. "So what do you propose?"

"I think it might be prudent to plan an attempt to take Lacey before they get here. We do it quietly and quickly, under the cover of night."

"What about the boy's father?" Victor asked.

Will half-nodded his head for a few seconds before answering. "We'll take him too."

Victor liked the idea, but told his old friend that the plan would have to be airtight to work.

"That's why I'm here," Michael Willard replied, confidently.

"Let's stay in contact about that," Victor said. "Something about the boy has been brought to my attention, though, Will. Something I've never seen before."

"What is it?" he asked, very interested.

"It's the way he's acting. Especially recently. It's the exact opposite of how someone in his shoes should be acting. Very peculiar. It's as though he knows something that we don't. He's confident, self-assured, even bold. Something has changed in him, and I don't know what it is or even how to find out. But I'm serious when I tell you this. I think he's cognizant. In some way, the boy is aware of the goings- on, and what's more, he's not afraid. Something is happening, Will. I don't know what it is, but something is definitely happening."

Michael Willard was staring through his old friend's eyes in silent thought. Finally, right before Victor planned to ask if he was listening, Will spoke up. "I wouldn't worry, Victor. I really wouldn't. I mean, the boy is locked in a room. What could he possibly do?" Will asked, with a laugh that exuded power.

"You may be right. Maybe I've spent too long on this whole thing, I'm a little paranoid. I still think it might be a good idea to put a reinforced steel door behind his current one, though."

"If you think it's a good idea, then it is. I trust your instincts,"

Michael Willard replied. "We'll get the machines on it right away."

CHAPTER 26

Will and Victor went their separate ways - Will to his archives and Victor to his quarters. Will began to work on the various elements of his kidnapping plan - when to do it, where to do it, and who would see to it that it was done. There were only a few hours left until sunrise, so whatever the cost, Michael Willard knew that it had to be done with haste and in the dark. He quickly retrieved a pencil from the long horizontal slide-out drawer sitting above his knees in his large and heavy mahogany desk. An abundance of scrap paper already lay deserted and thus ready on top of the dark brown escritoire. Spread out like clouds on a warm summer's day, Will gathered the blank white pieces and organized them into one pile. He shuffled them in his hands, clicked them twice on solid surface, and let out a heavy sigh as he gently laid them flat on his desk.

Without knowing where exactly Rick Engleheart and Lacey Hassle were, it was an arduous task to formulate a plan involving their kidnapping, especially so quickly. However, Michael Willard was a super-genius, and he was up for the challenge. The first marking his sharpened pencil made was the word 'tranquilizers.' The last thing he wanted to do was murder in cold blood. In twenty minutes' time, only one lonely piece of paper remained blank. The others were covered in gray diagrams and words, no longer innocent and pure. A couple droplets of sweat had formed on Michael Willard's dark-complexioned forehead, but they dried and returned to their place of origin instead of leaping to their deaths. In his mind, he had come up with the airtight plan Victor had desired. Now, it was just a question of who was going to carry it out. Victor, a man who had connections to the outside world, as it was part of his job description, would be the ideal person to contact someone who would do the job. Michael Willard spoke into his wrist.

"So what's the Doc been doing since we last spoke?"

There were a few seconds of silence before Victor responded. "Digesting," he replied with a joking tone.

"What say you digest down here in my archives? They told me the air is good for that down here."

"You have a plan?"

"Yeah, but I need your help. Should be airtight though. I've looked at it through all possible lenses and from all possible directions."

"Alright, I'll be there in ten. You have a virtual chess board down there?"

Michael Willard looked around the small room with his eyes. "Negative," he responded.

"I'll bring mine," Victor stated, casually.

"Don't feel too much like working?"

"This was your thing, Will. And it works."

Michael Willard laughed. "I know," he said. "Thanks for thinking of it. See you soon."

For years, whenever a plan was being drawn up or whenever a project needed to be sifted through for holes or potential problems, Michael Willard would play a game of chess. This, he contended, opened the mind and allowed the person to view the issue from all different angles, greatly enhancing their problem solving skills. It was not scientifically tested, but both he and Victor wholeheartedly believed that disruptions found in previous plans would not have been discovered if they had not played a quick game of chess before analyzing them. The two old friends had played chess by themselves, against the computer, but this time they would be playing each other for the first time ever. Although, for the pressing matter at hand, they planned to play what they called speed chess, which allowed only ten seconds of time to think before a move. The game was over with much more quickly, but it still provided both players with ample opportunities to think outside the box and analyze from a variety of angles.

Victor showed up carrying a clipboard in his hand and a V-square in his pocket. Almost anything could be downloaded to V-squares. Creating a virtual, augmented reality, the V-square projected the desired downloaded material onto a flat surface and allowed the users to go about their business as if whatever they were doing was actually there. The V-square itself was no larger than a nine-volt battery, but just like many elements of Emerus, it held up the old adage 'Don't judge a book by its cover.' Victor set it down on the destitute low-to-the-ground coffee table taking up five feet of Michael Willard's archives' limited real estate.

The two friends sat at opposite sides of the chestnut-colored coffee table. Both men, although well into their upper fifties, were flexible and lithe, so they comfortably sat cross-legged at their respective posts.

"V-square. Can you synthesize a chess board please?"

The little gray cube spoke back in a polite female robotic voice and obliged. Without warning, a regulation-sized chess board appeared at the end of a thin beam of light escaping the V-square's northern face. Very methodically, Michael Willard closed his eyes and Victor silently picked up a black pawn and hid it in the palm of his hand with a clenched fist. It was a strange sensation - holding light. And it was difficult to describe, but Victor rather nonchalantly claimed that it felt like holding energy.

"Alright, Will. Black or white?"

Michael Willard guessed the color correctly, so he went first. Victor placed the pawn back in its appropriate spot and spun the board around so the white chess pieces were in front of his friend. The board and the pieces themselves subsumed a blue glow that mesmerized the eyes. And even though the pieces shared the same internal glow, they somehow also managed to turn out black and white, respectively.

Michael Willard moved out his pawn to E4, and the game was underway. Sticking to their rules of speed chess, the two men moved their pieces in less than ten seconds each turn. The rule forced both of them to think ahead, and think ahead swiftly. Through castling, en passants, and e-pawn advances, the whole game took less than five minutes. If Victor and Michael Willard played one hundred times, each of them would probably win fifty games. In this particular instance, Michael Willard came out on top.

"Good game, Will. Using the old destroying the defender move, eh?"

"Well you know, even in speed chess I need to have some tactic. Thought I'd catch you by surprise."

"That you did, that you did. V-square, return the chess board."

Just as instantly as it appeared, the board and the pieces got sucked back into the device by the beam of light. If they blinked, they would have missed it.

"Alright, let's take a look at what you've come up with, Will."

Michael Willard gracefully rose to his feet and retrieved the papers from his desk behind him. Sitting back down across from his old friend, he laid the papers down on the coffee table like a father shows off his 'Employee of the Month' certificate to his family before dinner. Victor could immediately tell that his friend had worked hard. The papers all had that worn-out look that could only be the byproduct of determined diligence.

The plan was simple. Multiple surveillance drones would be commissioned to survey the area above ground in Wyoming. Within a twenty-five mile radius of the only entry point to Emerus, the drones would scope out any vehicles on the road and in scanning their license plates and using facial recognition technology, the drones would be able to see exactly who was coming. Once Rick Engleheart and Lacey Hassle were located, there would be enough time to get boots on the ground and this was where the plan got tricky. Michael Willard had planned on employing multiple men to carry out this particular part, but Victor disagreed.

"Something tells me that they would see it coming. We need to surprise them, similar to how you just beat me in chess. Maybe hire a contractor and have him disguised as a lowly town police officer. Someone they would not view as a threat."

"That makes sense. Someone who would make them feel comfortable. Maybe at a routine traffic stop?" Michael Willard stopped to think. "DWI check?"

Victor nodded in agreement. "That's good stuff, Will," he said, after a few seconds of thoughtful nods.

"Now it's just a matter of deciding on the man. Have anyone in mind, Victor?"

Victor held his breath in abrupt thought. He looked past Will's face at the desk against the wall.

"What is it?"

A proud smile crept across Victor's face. "I know what will give us that extra ounce of trust." He paused to allow his old friend time to figure it out. A few seconds of silence later, Will spoke up.

"A woman. She will be the police officer," he stated matter-of-factly.

"Exactly," Victor replied.

"That's perfect," Will said in wonderment. "Do you have someone in mind already?"

"No," Victor replied. "But I know someone on the outside who could find the perfect candidate."

Michael Willard nodded in contentment. Getting back to the plan, the two friends made a few more minor tweaks and adjustments.

The woman posing as a police officer would ask Rick Engleheart to step out of the car and walk around to the back, and as he did so, she would stick a sedative needle in his leg. Catching his fall so as to not alarm the others, she would then walk around and stick a second sedative into the driver's neck. At this point, both Victor and Will assumed Lacey Hassle would be in shock and with nowhere to go, it would be a rather elementary task to stick the third needle either into her neck or her leg. The driver, whoever he was, would be safely left in the car, waiting to wake up three hours later. But by then, Lacey and Rick Engleheart would be long gone, and the hope of finding them all but lost. The woman would have placed Johnny's father and the gifted teenage girl in her car and driven them to the operation's given coordinates where someone would meet her, give her the promised money, and take the sedated prisoners down to Emerus. Victor and Will were proudly pleased with what they had come up with.

"Let's get those drones programmed, shall we? Let them circle the skies while we wait?"

"Sounds good to me. I'll get in touch with my contact."

<u>CHAPTER 27</u>

Johnny had been hearing the machines on the other side of the door to his quarters for about thirty seconds. It sounded like they rolled in, leaned something very thick, metallic, and extremely heavy against the door, and drilling into it, bolted it into the sides of the wall covering the entry way's width. The whole operation lasted less than two minutes. In a sense, it worried Johnny that his captors were on to him, and were so to such an extent that they reinforced the only way into and out of his quarters with an impenetrable guard door. However, on the other hand, the more and more he thought about it, Johnny felt inspired because the people at Emerus were threatened, and to him, that was a positive sign. It was as if they were trying to instill fear close to his inner being. But little did they know, something else was much closer to his soul. And if they knew what exactly it was that was so near to Johnny's inner self, they would run as fast as their hypocritical legs could carry them. In the opposite direction, they would scurry.

***

Gerald Green, who had taken a few days off of work since his last operation, was still hesitant to go back to work. His orders were to shoot and kill the driver. He shot him in the head with his trusty McMillan Tac-50, twice. And the man remained standing as if a child blew air into his face. Something was afoot; Green's training clearly told him that. He and a woman whom he had only met a few times before were en route to Wyoming, under strict orders from an authority somewhere above the United States government. Green was not a religious man, but still he prayed that the current mission had nothing to do with what he had witnessed a few days prior.

This one, at least on his part, was simpler. He was only told to sit in a police car and act as if he were an officer presiding over a routine DWI stop. Backup. That was his role - to only get out of the car if the plan went amiss. Extremely more straightforward than his last mission, he welcomed this new one with open and appreciative arms. Nonetheless, Green was nervous. He had failed at his last assignment, and not gotten paid. His wife, a beautiful and picturesque stay-at-home-mom had recently given birth to their first born daughter and the two new parents could seriously use the money.

"Five minutes out," the pilot's voice spoke over the intercom. Supersonic top-secret military jets were fast, flying high above the troposphere. It had only taken off from Pennsylvania a little over an hour prior.

"You alright?" Faye Koehler asked her new partner. A twenty-nine year old slim and fit woman from Maryland, she was more than prepared for the task. In fact, she had been waiting for an opportunity such as this for years, holding tightly to the old adage 'Patience is a virtue.' This opportunity paid off, both figuratively and literally. Faye Koehler would receive a healthy compensation as well as a promotion if she carried out the mission successfully. Her defined cheekbones, flawless skin, and beautiful deep red hair would make a dishonest man question his commitment. However, Gerald Green was an honest man. And Faye Koehler was all business.

"Green, are you ready? We're five minutes out."

Lost in a sea of thought, Green apologized and replied with a stern voice. "Yes, I am," he lied. Angry at himself for letting something rattle him so extremely, Green turned his blindfolded thoughts around and faced them toward focus. "My role is pretty simple. I should be asking you if *you're* ready."

Faye Koehler let out a soft chuckle. It was as far as she would go. "I'm always ready," she replied.

Green nodded with calm confidence, after which he thanked his emotions for retreating from their advance. Shooting someone in the head usually yielded the opposite result of what he witnessed. Green forced the bewildering thoughts that scared the wits out of him out of his mind. The remaining minutes went by with silence that was only broken by breathing and by the pilot's voice announcing deployment at one minute intervals. Green and Koehler sat across from each other in their wide leather seats in the small cabin. They had already gotten dressed in their respective police officer uniforms.

"One minute."

They were ready.

***

Victor was sitting at his desk in his luxurious living quarters. He looked around, seeing everything that many people would view as signs of an amazing life. However, he had never felt more empty and alone. He was missing something. After soul-searching for a few minutes, he discovered what it was. Love. Instinctively, he stood up and began to make his way over to the closet where his hoard of ear drops were. He stopped, though, in his tracks, as if he had just spotted a sasquatch. Something was holding him back. It was a feeling deep inside of him - a sense of indifference and apathy that existed beneath the surface. Coupled with them was an overwhelming sensation of sadness and self-pity. Victor felt like he had nothing, not even himself anymore. He had never before prayed. But for the first time in his life, he began to internally talk to someone, something that he felt was there.

Turning to the tablet built into his desk, he decided to send his old friend, Michael Willard an email. One of the convenient implementations of technology in Emerus that was about to make its way out to the masses above was instant email. It was rather invasive, though, requiring a tiny computer chip to be inserted into the wrist area. The injection was painless, however. And once in, convenience came rushing like the wind. Connecting to the person's brain using magnetic waves, the chip instantly notified its host when an email, text message, or any other mode of communication was being transmitted. To the onlooker, it was telepathy. Victor and other inhabitants of Emerus had had the chips in their wrists for five years and they were more than used to it. So when Victor decided to send Michael Willard an email, he knew that his friend would immediately read it, like he was recalling something he once saw written in a book. It would be as if Victor was telling him himself, except instead of his voice speaking it, Will's own thoughts would be delivering the message. It was the next step in human evolution - over-stimulation would become hyper-focusing on multiple levels, and Victor and Will had already easily adapted to it.

Tears welled up in his eyes after the email was typed, and after he read it over, the tears were slowly sliding down his face. He knew that as soon he pressed it to be sent, Michael Willard would read it instantly. Feeling ashamed at his recent release of emotion, Victor shook his head in embarrassment, glad that he was alone. He thought it ironic, though, that he wept because he was alone, for when he did, he was happy and thankful for the seclusion. Hesitating at first, Victor hovered over the tablet for a few seconds and finally pressed 'Send.'

Will, I know you'll receive this instantly, but don't try to save me. It'll be too late. This most recent project has stretched me too thin. I feel helpless. When they recruited us more than a decade ago, they told us that we'd be making a positive difference in the world. I'm not so sure about that anymore. The Engleheart boy is no longer needed. My tenured undertaking has turned into less than a cockroach. He's just a worm on a hook. And in this, I too am no longer needed. All I desire is to see my beautiful wife smile at me and to watch my children grow up. Oh, how proud of them I would be. What a good father I could have been. But those are nothing more than pipe dreams. And in turn, I have become nothing. You know how it works here. As soon as they don't you need anymore, execution soon follows. I see the writing on the wall, and I don't need to light a candle to see the sun. Hiding would only worsen my fate. So consider this goodbye, old friend. I have always cherished our time together. Thank you for your companionship. My only wish is that we were able to share more moments. Goodbye, Will.

Michael Willard burst into Victor's living quarters in a desperate rampage. The door was locked, but the very much in-shape man had no problem whatsoever breaking it down in an explosion of energy and force. He called out his friend's name in a panic and then stopped. He stood still as if he were thinking extremely hard, like he needed complete silence to complete his thought. A few seconds later, he turned to his left and looked into Victor's bedroom. With a sure and accelerated stride, Michael Willard paced into the room and slid the large closet door open. He shouted a gasp with wide eyes and then quickly lifted up his dangling friend. Victor had a black tie around his neck, the other end of which was attached to the closet's steel crossbar. Michael Willard acted quickly after seeing his neck was not broken. He swiftly loosened the tie from Victor's neck and after undoing it, laid his friend on the short, beige carpet. He put his right ear on Victor's chest, desperately hoping he would hear the low thump of a heartbeat. After a few seconds of nothing, Will's own heart began to sink. And then, a tiny thud. It was barely audible, but Michael Willard felt it. Immediately, he started mouth-to-mouth resuscitation, and although he was not CPR certified, he was acting like a professional. All of a sudden, Victor started to cough and inhale deeply. A couple tears of joy began to stream down Michael Willard's face as a smile of unbelief came over him.

"Victor. Victor, speak!"

The Doc kept his eyes closed out of embarrassment. "I'm sorry, Will. I'm so sorry." It hurt to talk, and his voice was raspy. "It felt like I had my eyes closed for two seconds, and then you were hovering over me. How'd you get here so quickly?"

"I don't know how long you've been in your closet, but I can assure you it was longer than two seconds, a lot longer, I think. I got your email and ran here as fast as I could. Victor, I won't let anything happen to you. That's a promise, okay?"

Victor felt what he could not feel before. He felt loved. Repeatedly, he thanked his old friend, and continued to feel what he was so desperately searching for. Unworthy, but loved nonetheless. The two men remained in their spots on the floor. Michael Willard threw the tie in the closet and slid it shut as a way to shut the door in the face of the depression that had crept into his friend's mind.

"You're on board with me now, Victor. Your beautiful mind is going to be used for so much good, you cannot even conceive it. Trust me. We're going to do amazing work."

"So you save me and take me under your wing? How can I repay you?"

"That's not needed. Just look me in the eye and promise that you will never, ever do anything like this again. No matter how tough it gets, no matter how much things don't go the way you thought they would, no matter how bad a day can get, there is always an end. There is always a light waiting. We just need to be aware of it. Time will get us there. You just have to push."

Victor felt like a teenager at a juvenile detention facility. But it warmed him, and Will's words touched his heart in a way that he never thought words were capable. "Thank you, Will. I don't know what to say. But I give you my solemn word that I won't let myself do something like this ever again. How stupid."

"That's more like it, Victor." Michael Willard said, with a smile. He would have held it for longer, but the expression was interrupted by another instant email. He read it and looked at his friend. "We've got 'em. Two drones have found the license plate and the facial recognition has checked out. Two passengers and the driver cannot be identified. Probably something in the way to get a full analysis. They're working on it, but Rick Engleheart and Lacey Hassle are in the vehicle. Your contact is on the ground. They're heading straight for her. Two miles out. Let's go watch."

Victor rose up and stretched out his sore neck. "Will, this is very embarrassing for me. Please don't mention it to anyone."

"You have my word," Michael Willard replied. "You don't even have a mark," he lied, as he reached out and touched his friend's neck.

"Thank goodness," Victor stated, still ashamed. He looked in the mirror. Will was right. There was no mark. "I'm ready. Let's do this."

"I just hope your contact is as good as people say she is. Come on, let's head to the deck. Lacey Hassle is our cash cow. Let's go watch her capture."

CHAPTER 28

Wednesday, 5:07 am

"We'll be there in less than an hour. Hope you all are rested," Gabe announced to his passengers, like a city tour guide.

Everyone in the minivan, everyone except Gabe, had gotten tranquil shut-eye. And by this time in the long journey, they were all running on pure adrenaline. And that, coupled with excitement and nervousness, gave each of them a very sharp and heightened sense of focus. Matthew was being very inquisitive, pleading for Gabe to discuss the details and the parameters of the plan. The angel was resolute, however, and would not share any specific design of his plan.

"Just follow me," he would say. "And listen to what I tell you. This isn't a time to go in with guns blazing. Matthew, I'm talking about you." Gabe smiled in the rearview mirror, but there was an overwhelming presence of seriousness in his eyes. "Just stay with me, do what I say, and you'll be safe. I'll give you cues to go one way or another, or to shoot in that direction or this direction. Act quickly and don't even give a second thought to my instruction. Our mission will be successful if you do these things."

"Gabe?" Lacey asked. "You're an angel, or an extra-dimensional or whatever, right?"

"I've been called both those things, yes."

"I don't really know the rules and everything, but I saw you kill one human already, back at the Engleheart's. We're going to do more of that, at least it sure sounds like it. Doesn't that somewhat go against the whole angelic, heavenly thing?"

Gabe hesitated before responding, but the resounding silence in the car screamed that everyone, not just Lacey, was anxiously awaiting his reply. He paused the way a parent ponders before explaining something major to their children. After a deep inhale and relaxing exhale, he spoke. "The man that I killed at the Engleheart house was not a man at all. It was an extra-dimensional. It just looked like a man. And I know what I'm about to tell you may be difficult to believe, but the truth often is. Many, in fact most, but not all of the men in Emerus are extra-dimensionals. As shape-shifters, they can take the form of almost anything. And in this case, they have taken the form of men in power. That is why the current climate surrounding all of this is so dangerous."

Rick Engleheart, Lacey, Matthew, and Easton contemplated, then accepted what Gabe told them. After some thought, though, Matthew asked a question to which everyone else longed for the answer.

"But how are we gonna kill them? I mean, it's one thing to kill a human. It's probably another to kill a demon or extra-dimensional, or whatever the hell the things are."

"Well, that's the thing," Gabe replied. "You can't kill them in that sense of the word. But you can send them back to where they came from."

"Go where the dead go," Lacey said, quietly, looking out the window.

"Once they're back there, they're unable to transcend back to this dimension. So it would be like killing them. But they won't be afraid of your guns."

"Why's that?" Easton asked.

"Because normal bullets won't do the job. And they don't know we have these." Gabe motioned for Rick Engleheart to open the oversized glove compartment. There was a black case that held what looked like an organized assemblage of semi-jacketed nine millimeter bullets. Rick Engleheart lifted up the main display, and like stairs, other displays stacked themselves and came forth from their hiding place.

"Each of you will have your own. This is what we'll be arming ourselves with."

"What are they?" Matthew asked.

"To the naked eye, they're just bullets. But they came from my dimension, and they're the only thing we have that can send the shape-shifting demons back to where they came from. They don't know we have these, and they won't find out either."

"And now why is that?" asked Rick Engleheart, as if he was very close to grasping the whole concept.

"There's something about the bullets' makeup," Gabe responded. "Once they send one back, even if another sees it happen, it somehow makes them believe they're being transported to another place on Earth. They'll still think the bullets are powerless. Some kind of deception...technology, if you will."

"Giving them a taste of their own medicine?" Lacey asked, with a smile.

"Exactly," Gabe said.

"So we'll each have our own gun, our own bullets. We follow you and obey your commands. Seems easy enough," Matthew claimed, with confidence.

"Well, it's not that simple," Gabe said, correcting. "They'll be firing at us. And humans are fragile. We're going to do try to do this without any casualties. But that's something I can't promise. It's a risk, but trust me when I tell you this. I, and the other angels, are going to do everything we can to ensure that that doesn't happen. Just please listen to me and my commands. No one needs to be a hero. You'll all be heroes if you adhere to my instructions."

Rick Engleheart, Lacey, Matthew, and Easton all nodded in compliance. They felt safe under Gabe's direction. They trusted him, and felt prepared to handle whatever was to come their way.

"What's this?" Gabe asked himself.

"What?" Rick Engleheart questioned, as if his eyes were closed.

"Up there," motioned Gabe. "Police lights. It looks like some sort of a blockade."

"Maybe it's just a routine traffic stop," Matthew surmised. "Like a DWI check or something."

"Perhaps," Gabe said. "I guess we'll find out." He retrieved his pistol from the inner breast pocket of his jacket and loaded it like he had done a thousand times before. "No matter what happens, everyone stay in their seats."

***

Faye Koehler was in direct contact with two people whom she had never met. All she knew was that they came from a very high authority. She asked for their names, but it was the policy of Emerus for any worker or inhabitant to never identify themselves to anyone in the outside world. Strict rules such as this one helped keep Emerus' clandestine practices in the background, beneath the surface. Things would get done - technology would work, a specified president would get elected, a regime overseas would be replaced - all the while in a hidden manner so no one could discover who or what exactly was pulling the strings. This was simply another one of those cases. So Victor and Michael, although excited, viewed the operation at hand as

BENJAMIN DEER

rather routine.

"I see a few vehicles approaching," Faye Koehler spoke into her wrist.

"First one should be a green minivan. That's your target. Just wave on the drivers of the other vehicles," instructed Michael Willard.

The confident and lithe agent stepped off the sandy gravel that made up the shoulder and onto the road's black pavement. A westerly wind blew the loose strands of hair that had escaped from underneath her uniform's hat sideways across her face. Her eyes sharpened with focus. There was something innocent about the way the wind blew the hair across her face. She looked vulnerable, but strong at the same time as she walked out onto the road. Faye Koehler was prepared, but just as a duck on a pond gracefully glides atop the still water while its feet are going a mile a minute, similarly the twenty-nine-year-old's heartbeat was racing.

Gabe had slowed the minivan's cruising speed down to fifty miles per hour to give himself time to think. After a few seconds, he spoke out loud. "Raphael, fall back. Let's not make this look more suspicious than it already is. Tell the others too. I don't think I can explain a forty-car caravan going in the same direction without raising some questions that we don't have time to answer. If you get off this exit, take 218. It reconnects about a mile ahead. I'll let you know when to get back on."

Rick Engleheart, Lacey, Matthew, and Easton's communal silence revealed their nervousness. Gabe could sense their anxious spirits so he tried to reassure them. "Nobody worry. Just stay in your seats and zip up those lips. Matthew."

Everyone responded with a silent, but uneasy smile. There was nothing they could do. They were heading straight for the police stop, and as the flashing red and blue lights became larger and larger, they realized they could be heading straight into the hands of the enemy. Gabe was the only one that was not burning calories with stress.

Gerald Green comfortably sat and waited in the police patrol car. As an overly-confident man, he was his nonchalant self. Under the surface, though, he was nervous. He had failed his last mission, lied to his superiors by explaining that strong winds must have made him miss the target, and now was given a chance to make up for it. All he had to do was act as backup - a relatively easy task and one which he could do with his hands tied behind his back. He was picking at his fingernails

[185]

when his partner-by-default spoke up.

"Here they come, Green."

"Are you ready?" he asked out the open window.

"Of course," Koehler replied.

The minivan slowly approached the traffic block and came to a gradual stop a respectful twenty feet from the perpendicular facing police car. The flashing red and blue lights looked even more ominous against the near pitch-black backdrop. Koehler smiled at the driver before walking toward his side of the vehicle. Gabe returned her cold smile with a much warmer one of his own.

"Good morning," he said, after cranking down the window. "Feels strange to say that when it's still dark out. What can I help you with, officer?"

Koehler did not acknowledge his small talk or even greet his kindness. "Just a DWI check, sir. License and registration please."

Matthew leaned close to his younger brother and whispered that it was against Gabe's constitutional rights. Easton paused for a second, and then replied, "But I don't think he's a citizen."

Green, who was still lounging in the patrol car, could not get a good look at the driver of the stopped minivan. Even though he was backup, he still took the mission seriously. Casual was just his way of working. Retrieving the flashlight from his belt, he clicked it on, shining it in the direction of the minivan. Upon getting a clear view of the driver, Green's heart stopped for half a beat. Then, his insides did a somersault.

"No way," he whispered, in dreaded thought. "How can it be? Who is this person?" Green had been through three tours of duty overseas and had been in his position with the National Guard and as a private contractor for five years. Never in his life had something rattled him so much as shooting a man in the head twice only to see him walk away with not so much as a scrape. The same man sat in the driver's seat of the minivan. Green knew what Koehler was supposed to do, and in turn, knew that it wasn't going to work. He had to act, and act quickly.

Calmly, Gabe fetched a driver's license from his back pocket as well as the minivan's registration from the compartment under the center console's armrest. The passengers watching were surprised, but then secondarily remembered Gabe's stories of coming to their dimension and being provided with everything he would need to complete the mission. Koehler took the license and registration and walked back to the police car. She was met with a very grave and serious look from her partner. Once she was in her seat, Green closed the two open front windows using his door's control panel.

"We have to abort," he declared, with urgency.

"What?" Koehler asked, with surprise and disgust.

"This isn't going to end well, trust me. Just let them through."

"No. What are we going to tell our superiors?"

"I don't know, we'll figure it out. Just believe me, this won't end well."

"I can't believe you're getting cold feet now. After all of the heroic stories I heard about you, I gotta say I'm disappointed. Look, I'm going to go finish the assignment. When it's all over, you don't have to apologize. Besides, they're watching us," she said, looking up into the night sky. "If we let them through, we'll be dead before we can even think of an excuse."

Koehler quickly climbed out of the car. Green's right hand clutched his gun as his adrenaline and training switched on. Something distracted his attention, though. A string of lights traveling along the neighboring roadway seemed odd. Maybe it was their faint and faded yellow glow, or the sheer number of them, but something about a long line of cars traveling virtually in the middle of nowhere in the very early hours of the morning under the cover of night seemed irregular. Green didn't need his training to tell him that. Something was amiss. He could feel it. He was captivated by the lights as they danced in the dark every time the cars hit a minor bump in the road. There was something peacefully ominous about their sight. It evoked an unprecedented feeling inside of Green. Out of discomfort, he looked away, returning his gaze to Koehler and the minivan. He assumed his stare would last for at least thirty seconds, before business started to go down. But his assumption was greatly miscalculated. As soon as Koehler handed back the license and registration, the minivan peeled away, leaving only the dull and foul malodor of burnt rubber.

"After them! After them!" Michael Willard yelled, in command.

Koehler ran across the road and slid into the driver's seat, closing the open door with her left hand in one urgent, but graceful motion. Green tried his best to talk her out of it in the few seconds he had, but Koehler was in control of the car and her mind was already made up.

"We're in pursuit," she calmly and sternly said into her wrist.

"Green!" Victor grabbed his attention. "Shoot out the tires."

"Do it quickly, soldier," Michael Willard added. "That's an order."

Koehler gave the car more gas, trying to catch up to the minivan, which was already nearing its top speed as it passed the entrance ramp to its right. The ramp, which connected Route 218 back to the highway had bumper-to-bumper moving traffic on it, as Gabe had instructed the convoy to get back on a few seconds before he took off.

"Shoot out their tires, shoot out their tires," Gabe said, hurriedly, but matter-of-factly.

Koehler and Green noticed the on-ramp as they raced closer and closer to it. The longer they took to pass it, the more their chances of capturing the minivan decreased, for twenty cars were already in between the cat and the mouse. And more vehicles were flooding onto the highway.

"Do not kill. I repeat, do not kill," instructed Gabe. They are humans. They have families. Just shoot the tires."

In the minivan's rear view mirror, Gabe and the others could see the police car's lights flashing in the dark, their sight getting closer and their sound getting louder.

"Go! Go! Go Gabe!" Lacey yelled.

"Everybody get down! They might be shooting," Gabe commanded over the roar of the old engine.

Almost on cue, the minivan's passenger side mirror was blown off.

"Listen to me," Michael Willard dictated to both Koehler and Green. "Do not, I repeat, do not let them get away without carrying out the mission. I don't care if you have to kill the driver and the other passengers. Capture Lacey Hassle and Rick Engleheart!"

Green was standing up in the car, his upper body outside and above the open sunroof. A sniper scope was attached to his Desert Eagle .50 caliber. Under normal circumstances, shooting out the minivan's tires would be a menial task, but the roadway was bumpy, the car's acceleration was fluctuating, and there were other vehicles for the bullets to avoid. The conditions were not ideal.

"Come on, push through this!" Green yelled down to Koehler.

Like a fan trying to get closer to the stage at a sold-out

hardcore show, Koehler bumped into the other cars and got hit a few times as she shoved the others out of her way. Finally, clear from the traffic, she put the pedal to the floor.

"Shoot them!" she screamed up to Green.

There was only one last obstacle in their way. Fifty feet in front of them, an old station wagon was traveling directly behind the minivan, acting as its moving shield. Koehler wanted to tell Green to shoot through the minivan's rear window because it was in clear view above the station wagon's roof. But she never got the chance. The driver of the station wagon opened his door, and using it as protection, gracefully peeked around it with a gun in hand. With a stern, serious, and focused look, he fired his shot. Less than a second later, the police car's driver-side front tire blew out, sending the speeding vehicle out of control, off the road and onto the shoulder. Green was thrown out through the sunroof, and at over seventy miles per hour, his body collided head first into a telephone pole. The car wrapped itself around the same pole before lighting up the darkness with a fiery explosion. The last noise that Koehler heard was unprecedented to her ears, but it was incredibly loud and sounded like the breaking of crystal. Both Green's and Koehler's bodies were essentially disintegrated, but their spirits were never before at such perfect peace.

"The war has begun once again," Victor said, with a serious smile.

Michael Willard slammed his hands down on the table in front of him. "No!" he screamed, bowing his head in defeat.

After a few seconds, he abruptly rose up and started walking toward the door.

"Where are you going, Will?" Victor asked.

"I'm getting the gravity gun ready. Do you see how many people are headed this way?"

"It's still in the testing phase," Victor protested.

"It's a risk we have to take. Get Emerus' army prepared for an invasion. We'll squash them before they even get close to the boy. I'll meet you in the center silo in ten minutes."

Victor watched his friend leave the room and then spoke into his wrist commanding one hundred troops to be prepared in the center silo in eight minutes.

***

The overall mood inside every vehicle in the convoy was somber. For the most part, the two casualties were innocent puppets being used by the underground government at Emerus. It would have been almost effortless to kill them at the traffic stop, but Gabe held back. They were humans, living their lives and obeying their superiors' commands. It was sad, but Gabe and the other angels knew of the place Green's and Koehler's spirits were and they did their best to convey it to their respective passengers. But the truth was that the magnificence of it all was nearly impossible for human minds to even conceive. Hearing it described, even by angels, was like looking at a square millimeter on a painting the size of the United States. All they understood was that both casualties were in a better place than Earth, and that was enough to help put it behind them. There was a far more important task to focus on.

Gabe reminded his passengers of his strict instructions and the other angels did the same. The time had come. Gabe pulled off the highway and began driving over the hardened, dry dirt. "43.2 degrees north and 107.7 degrees west. That's the entrance point," he said out loud.

"How are we going to get in?" Matthew asked.

"We have someone on the inside," Gabe replied. The minivan bumped along for another ten minutes. "Here." He put the minivan in park and shut if off. The rest of the convoy followed suit, making a forty-car circle around a single point. As soon as the 160 were gathered, the ground was raised in the shape of a small sand-covered trap-door.

"Michael."

"Gabriel," Michael Willard said, with a sly smile.

CHAPTER 29

"Did you bring what I asked?" Michael quickly inquired.

Gabe took out a jackknife from his back pocket. "Here ya go," he replied, tossing it under-hand to the dark-skinned man who had just come up from the under the Earth.

Immediately, he opened up the blade and skillfully and carefully dug out the tracking chip in his wrist. "Now they can't see or hear or find me even if they try. I'll be just like all of you. We'll be flying under the radar from here on out."

"Join the club," Lacey declared.

Michael turned in her direction and smiled wide. "Lacey Hassle," he stated, as if a lost city was finally being revealed to his eyes. "My goodness. Look at your light." He let out an immensely satisfying sigh. "Beautiful."

Lacey was slightly embarrassed by the direct attention. However, she continued her eye contact with Michael and allowed a smile of her own to commandeer her face. Gabe, as if sensing her discomfort came to her rescue.

"So Michael, everything is still on point? The plan is still in place?"

"You bet. The countdown clock is near zero. We're ready."

"Gabe," Rick Engleheart spoke up. "Is this another angel?"

Michael smiled at Gabe, giving him the go-ahead to answer. "Yes. Yes he is," he replied, answering for everybody. "And without him, none of our plan could be carried out. Michael has been working on this mission for more than a decade. Every angel has his and her own earthly tasks. Some last a few moments, some a few days, and in Michael's case, many many years. This is just another example of human imperfection needing angelic intervention. It just so happens that it is more important than usual. This one carries as much weight as the Enlightenment, Renaissance, and the American Revolution combined."

Everyone was silent.

"Hope you're all ready," Michael announced, with a comforting smile.

"But there's no reason to be anxious whatsoever," Gabe proclaimed, correcting his and Michael's diction. "Just follow your leaders' instructions. Stick with who you came here with. Do not wander off, not if you value your own life. This is a dangerous place. And there aren't just humans here. Stay with the group."

"The sun will be up soon. Ten minutes. Let's get moving," Michael said.

Group by group, they descended down into the Earth. The sight was reminiscent of Noah and his ark. Raphael and his group went first. Quietly, other troops followed the hum of the faint, orange glow. Michael and Gabe greeted each group before their descent down the ladder and into the unknown, instructing them to stay at the bottom round room upon landing. After the thirty-nine angels and each of their four humans made their way down, Gabe and his four comrades began their single-file descent.

"What are we going to do about all the cars?" Rick Engleheart asked. "A little suspicious. Don't you think?"

Gabe stopped and looked at the large circle of cars, all parked around a center point in the middle of nowhere. "Don't worry about it, Rick. They'll all be gone before anyone notices."

Michael followed Gabe, but before descending, he took a deep breath. Smiling, he took it all in. Then, an expression of sadness came over his face. He took another deep breath as he closed and locked the hatch before descending back down to Emerus.

Once everyone was convened in the large round room at the base of the narrow ladder, Lacey's heart began to beat a little faster. Perhaps it was the soft orange light, or the hazy hum it made, but Lacey felt more close to Johnny than at any point since the last time she saw him - five days ago. Her surroundings were unprecedented, and they put her on edge, but she learned to use those nerves, use those negatives and turn them around into sharp focus while envisioning positive outcomes. Michael, who had lived and worked in Emerus for over a decade, said that Johnny would escape in a few minutes. Similar to Gabe, there was simply something strange about his demeanor that could only be described as trustworthy. It was a quality the likes of which Lacey had never been exposed to before, but which convinced her to leave her house with a stranger, the most important decision she would ever make. It gave her an overall sense of peace being in his presence, hearing him talk, and watching him go about life's simple tasks. The way he blinked, the way his eyes smiled, his stride, the inflections put on certain words - all of these and more mesmerized Lacey. Wondering if he had the same effect on someone like Easton, she leaned in and asked the eighteen year-old.

"What do you think of him?"

"Who? Michael?"

"Yeah," Lacey replied.

"I don't know. How do you mean?" Easton was nervous about the unrivaled task that lay in front of him. So he added more fuel to the conversation simply for the sake of it taking up more time.

"I mean he's just like Gabe. It's kind of weird, right?" Lacey whispered.

Easton smiled back. "Yeah, they're a lot of like. It's like they're fraternal twins, but have the exact same personality."

"I know, right?" Lacey replied.

Both she and Easton wished their conversation lasted longer because the truth was they were slightly frightened of what was may or may not going to happen in the next couple of hours. Talking to each other somehow delayed the inevitable, even if only mentally so. But Gabe, Michael, and Raphael, who seemed to be the leaders of the group, addressed everybody in the circular chamber.

"I know some of you are afraid and anxious," Gabe announced. "But I'm telling you that as long as you listen to your group chief and do exactly what he says, you are going to come out on the side of the victor. So don't worry about what may or may not happen, just focus on what you need to do in each moment and you'll find everything working out." As Gabe finished up his opening statement, he directed his gaze, and therefore his words at Lacey and Easton. They each smiled back, silently thanking him.

"Gabriel is right," Michael contributed. "Trust me. I've been down here for a long time. It is dangerous. There are people who will want to capture you, probably even kill you. And there are extra-dimensionals that look like humans. Do not trust anyone you do not recognize. But if you listen to your group chief, you'll have nothing to worry about. I can't stress that enough. This isn't a time to go off on your own. Just because they can't track you does not in any way mean they cannot see you with their eyes or hear you with their ears. If you do exactly as we say, we will come out victorious. Obey your commands with haste and act with focus."

"They're ready," Raphael stated, so everyone in the half-crowded room could hear his confidence. "Give them their arms."

Michael agreed with his fellow comrade. He turned around, and facing the dark concrete wall, placed his right hand in a specific spot. It was peacefully cold to the touch. After a few seconds, the wall began to silently slide open, from the ground up. Michael squatted down like a catcher and began reaching into the dark hole, retrieving unloaded black Ghost TR01's. Simultaneously, Gabe, Raphael, and the other group chiefs fetched small magazines loaded with the exclusive bullets Gabe had discussed. Each leader had his own briefcase full of them. It was a systematic assembly line of sorts. Michael continued passing the Ghost TR01's around the circle while each leader loaded them as they passed, sending it on all the way to the circle's endpoint. It only took a few minutes until everyone was armed. Michael retrieved the last gun from its hiding place within the wall and gave it to Raphael, who loaded it with the last magazine, and handed it to the last one in his group without a gun.

"Now they're ready," Gabe announced.

***

Johnny had been watching the dull, gray numbers on the countdown clock for the better part of two hours. Vigilantly, like a marine commissioned for a stake out, he watched the numbers tick down. He was mesmerized by them. Normally, an eighteen-year-old would be more than rattled by the past few days. On the contrary, though, Johnny never felt more alive. It was a grand combination of empowerment by virtue of his beautifully mysterious dreams, multiple mind-bending miracles happening right before his eyes, and the ethereal presence by which he constantly felt surrounded. He never forgot the chorus of the angels in his most recent celestial experience. How beautiful their song!

His soul held tightly to the words. It was ingrained into his mind. It was as if he knew as sure as the sun would rise, something was going to happen. It was on the horizon, and there was nothing he or anyone else could do about it, so he embraced the rarefied implications. He embraced them wholeheartedly.

The steel door reinforced to impede a potential escape was a double edged sword. To break it down, the people at Emerus would need at least two minutes. And that was time they simply did not have, for the countdown clock displayed *0:00:40* and Johnny would be long gone by the time the door opened.

***

Michael was the primary leader of his group of 161 . He knew
the ins and outs of Emerus - the secret rooms, the untouched tunnels,
and the secluded passageways that they could travel throughout to go
unseen and undetected. They moved like owls flying silently in the
night, stalking their prey. Half of the group went one way at the first
fork, the other half the other way. Only Michael knew where they were
in context of the grandiose underground habitat. He led one half of the
group, and Gabe led the other half. Before they split, Michael
instructed his fellow comrade on where to go - one of the countless
hidden rooms, which would be a thousand paces along the dimly-lit
meandering tunnel on the right hand side. Before splitting up, Michael
and Gabe touched their open hands, pressing them together for a few
seconds before confidently hugging goodbye.

Gabe, Rick Engleheart, Lacey, Matthew, and Easton, along
with eighty others quietly pressed onward with the help of the orange
light's soft glow. Gabe was out in front, Rick Engleheart behind him,
gun drawn.

"Gabe, I have a question," he whispered softly.

"Yes?" the angel whispered back.

"I know we're trying to do all of this with zero casualties, but
what if...what if one of these kids does die? What are their families
going to be told?"

Gabe stopped walking, which in turn caused everybody else to
stop along the three-person-wide line. "Rick," Gabe said, below a
whisper. "They have no families. All of these kids...they're orphans. It's
part of the grand plan, trust me. They have had no families their whole
lives, but they do now."

Rick Engleheart's heart sunk. With that, though, things began
to make more sense in his mind. He felt as if he was a few steps closer
to understanding. And right then and there, as they resumed their quiet
trek, Rick Engleheart made a solemn promise to himself that he would
treat all of the children as if they were his own because in a way, they
were.

It wasn't long before Gabe stopped again, this time arriving at
the destination. He looked up at the eight-foot wall to his right as if

recalling recently disclosed information. He pressed his hand into the concrete, held it there for three seconds, and the wall began to ascend. One-by-one they crawled into the secret room. Gabe entered last, pulling the wall downward, and shutting it behind him. The room was a large, disc-shaped chamber. There was a ovular table the same shape as the room with a beautiful blue light emanating from it. Many of them sat down, quietly relaxing. Some took a seat on the open chairs, others on top of the thin, oval console. Lacey was nervously pacing around, waiting for Gabe to finish talking to the other angels. She watched and noticed how normal they all looked and realized that unless she was told, she would not have recognized them as extra-dimensional supernatural beings. It made her think of all of Gabe's fascinating stories of angels intervening at just the right time, disguised as humans.

After his conversation, Gabe turned toward Lacey, as if he knew she needed his attention. But something else caught it first, something unseen. Half a second after he turned toward her, he looked quickly upward and to his right, like he saw something that immediately appeared. His eyes widened.

"What Gabe? What is it?" Lacey asked, slightly frightened.

Gabe smiled. "It's Johnny," he said. "He's activated."

CHAPTER 30

Johnny watched as the dull, gray countdown clock expired. As soon as nothing but zeroes returned his stare, the eighteen-year-old, who was anticipatingly sitting on the edge of his bed, stood up straight. With his head down and his eyes closed, Johnny inhaled deeply. He held his breath for a few seconds beyond the comfort threshold. After exhaling, he opened his eyes and confidently raised his head toward the door. There was something different about himself that Johnny could sense; it was something intangible, something that did not need to be thought upon, but rather something that simply was. Its characteristics were unearthly and empyrean, and they empowered Johnny. He inhaled again, this time fully taking in his newly discovered spirituality. Smiling, Johnny began walking in the direction of the door. Without slowing down as he drew closer to the composite material reinforced by twelve inches of steel directly on the other side, the gap quickly closed. Feet turned to inches and inches to centimeters. He knew what he was about to do, and in an ethereal way, he could already see himself on the other side. Fearlessly, Johnny continued toward the door and upon taking the final step, he became something uniquely anew. A different being indeed.

He was only inside the strange composite material for less than a second, the steel for only two. It was an extraordinary and remarkable sensation subsisting within solid matter, and even though it lasted for less than three seconds, Johnny possessed a heightened awareness of both himself and his surroundings. There was a different consciousness and energy inside each material, which he immediately picked up on, and because of their distinctiveness, they had a different temperature as well. Due to their different densities, the steel was much warmer than the composite wall. To Johnny, it felt like walking through two contrasting, achromic air currents.

Finding nobody on the other side, the setting was exactly as he remembered it. However, at this time, the usually-bustling super silo was eerily quiet. The transparent, high-tech city that created, harbored, and proliferated the world's most baffling technology stood resolute before him. It was strange. Their motives, schemes, and intentions had been in the dark to Johnny. But upon his most recent spiritual transformation, it was as if a brilliant light had been shone upon his captors' objective. It was put on Johnny's heart. He smiled.

"Oh, how disappointed they are gonna be," he quietly said out loud.

Just then, a man appeared to his right, rounding a corner and stopping at the sight of the escaped eighteen-year-old. Both Johnny and the man stared at each other for a few seconds before either of them spoke. Then, the man grinned.

"Johnny," he said, warmly.

"Michael," Johnny replied, smiling.

It took him a couple of seconds, but Johnny doubtlessly recognized the man standing before him as one of the angels in his most recent dream. Michael had stood in front of all the others as he, along with the choir of angels sang to Johnny in beautiful harmony. He thought back to the way he felt in his dream, and all of the wonderful emotions came rolling over him like a tidal wave, permeating his soul. He again thought back to what the choir had sung.

At the dawn of it all, we will come and rescue you.

A single tear of joy filled with hope that had finally come to fruition welled up in his right eye and began to stream down Johnny's cheek.

"Follow me," Michael commanded, with an earnest smile.

Obeying with an anticipatory smile of his own, Johnny did as Michael suggested. They walked quickly and they walked quietly, stopping to hide when necessary.

"Where are we going?" Johnny asked after a couple minutes of stealth.

"You'll see soon." Michael's lips did not move. Alternatively, Johnny heard the voice in his head. He stopped walking, rather abruptly, in awe of what had just transpired. He thought for half a second and then continued silently moving.

"So this is one of the gifts?" Johnny's heart did a somersault at the amazement of his newly found telepathic ability. Michael looked back and gave a sanguine nod.

They were finally out of the inverted super silo's core, undetected. Michael opened a door using his handprint and upon its opening, he led Johnny onward through an intricate labyrinth of twisting and turning tunnels, the likes of which would make a claustrophobic person twitch. Just thirty seconds after entering the tangled and tortuous tunnel system, Michael and Johnny had made over two dozen right and left turns. If it was not for the soft orange lights emanating from their designated spots on the concrete walls every twenty-five feet, Johnny would have ended up face-planting the calcified tunnel walls countless times. Michael, on the other hand, navigated the elaborate web with ease. It was as if he saw the maze from a bird's eye view. And he did. He and Johnny entered the square-shaped labyrinth near the top left corner. There were multiple options on where to go, but all of them except for one led to a dead end. The intersections were countless, the twists and turns dizzying. It took a special mind to get to where they were going, and without Michael's guidance, Johnny would have probably died of thirst because there was a zero percent chance he could find his way out of the bewildering intricacy.

Michael's goal was to get to the middle of the large square. There, he had half of the 160 in a confined room, awaiting his return, which he promised would be accompanied by Johnny Engleheart.

"We're almost there," he said in Johnny's head.

The eighteen-year-old was utterly relieved, not knowing how much longer he could last in the complicated labyrinth. With the negativity still existing but waning, asking him if he was ever going to make it out, Johnny had secretly been panicking for over a minute. He refused to tell Michael, out of embarrassment. But it looked as though their arrival was going to happen just in time, for which Johnny could not be more grateful.

"Good," he quietly replied out loud, forgetting his recent blessing of telepathy.

Michael snaked around for ten more seconds. The curved concrete walls and ceiling reminded Johnny of being in the Bahamas as a child when he and his cousins rode tubular water slides day-in and day-out. He silently chuckled to himself. That did not seem like it was too long ago, but oh how much his world had changed. From his only cares being trivial and meaningless, such as deciding whether or not to wear sandals to the water slide tower, his concerns had transformed into heavy burdens laced with epic implications. But all of his life's struggles and the rollercoaster ride therein - the ups, the downs, the victories, the disappointments, the proud moments, the sad moments, the death of his mother, and everything leading up to his most recent

spiritual transformation were simply stepping stones preparing him for
what was to come next. And he was ready.

Michael stopped and immediately placed his hand on the
curved concrete wall. It silently lifted up from the bottom, before
stopping to allow enough space for both him and Johnny to duck
through. In the crowded elliptical-shaped room, Johnny immediately
noticed many teeangers around his age, recognizing none. He could,
however, identify the men in the room as some of the angels in his
choir dream. Similar to Michael, they looked different from their form
in the dream, which Johnny assumed was their true condition -
transparent, incredibly muscular bodies with pure white wings
stretching twenty feet at their full wingspan. In the Earthly dimension,
they looked just like everyday citizens. They were still taller than the
average man, though not nearly as tall as in the dream. There was
something inherent about their faces, specifically their eyes - pure and
trustworthy - and that is how Johnny recognized them so easily.

"Let's get moving," Michael announced out loud.

"Where are we going now?" Johnny asked, slightly confused.
He thought they were where they needed to be. Little did he know,
however, that his father, his two cousins, and Lacey were waiting in
another, much larger room, along with another group of angels and
eighteen-year-old rebel spirits.

"We're meeting up another group who came here to carry out
the plan," Michael responded. Reading Johnny's mind and anticipating
his subsequent inquiry, he continued before the eighteen-year-old
opened his mouth. "The plan will be announced when we get there.
Two minutes out. Let's roll."

The group of 82 quietly exited the room, spilling out into the
tunnel system and lining up against the near wall like a class of obedient
first graders. Michael led the way, and two-by-two the troop silently
trekked onward through the confusing concrete intricacy. To Johnny's
delight, this particular journey was much more short-lived than the last
one. But he barely had time enough to catch his breath, and panic
began to set in sooner than previously. Something, however, started to
alleviate his anxiety. With each and every step, the nervousness was
replaced with the opposite. Delight. Anticipatory joy. Happiness.
Hope. Every step, without exception, brought a new efficacious
emotion to his mind, body, and soul. It was as if there was an unseen
energy connecting him to someone or something waiting for him,

pulling him closer and closer. Soon, Johnny could not wait to arrive at the new destination. All of the emotions were bunched up inside of him to a point where they could hardly be contained. He felt like he was going to explode with pure elation. Michael stopped, and before placing his hand on the curvature of the calcified wall, he turned toward Johnny.

"I just want you know why you are feeling this way," he stated, putting his hand on the eighteen-year-old's left shoulder. "Someone is inside here that you have a strong connection to. A connection that is going to be the central part to our plan."

"Who?" Johnny confidently asked, succeeding at containing his excitement.

Michael placed his hand on the wall instead of answering the question. The wall began to open from the bottom-up, like just before. As soon as there was just enough space to fit through, Michael looked at Johnny and smiled.

"Go get her," he said.

Johnny's heart began racing a marathon a minute. He knew about whom Michael was talking - the girl who had changed his world, captured his heart, and gracefully haunted his mind, and who now apparently had made a near-cross-country trip to help rescue him. The wall was still rising, but there was enough space for Johnny to fit through, which he hurriedly did. Upon entering, he could not believe his eyes.

There, standing right in front of him, just a few feet away was Lacey Hassle. Next to her, his cousin and one of his best friends, Easton. Standing next to him was Matthew - Johnny's older best friend and cousin. And behind them all stood a teary-eyed Rick Engleheart, his arms open, ready to embrace his son.

"My boy," he managed to get out, before succumbing to raw emotion. He began bawling his eyes out in the sheer joy and jubilation that his son was still alive and well. Johnny passed Lacey and his two cousins and fell into his dad's open arms with tears of happiness of his own.

"I thought I'd never see you again," he said, through gasps of joy.

"I know, Johnny. You're alive. You're alive...you're alive..." Rick Engleheart continued repeating the words out loud, so he could hear his voice proclaim the truth.

The father and son held their hug for nearly sixty seconds, their souls smiling at the significance of their embrace. Johnny loved and respected his father more than any other man he had ever known. Being in his clutches felt so peaceful and safe for the eighteen-year-old.

"Thank you, Dad. Thank you," Johnny said, rubbing the tears away from his eyes.

Rick Engleheart patted his son's back, nonverbally telling him the embrace was soon ending, for there were other important matters to attend to. Johnny patted him back, squeezed his father's broad shoulders and thanked him one last time before letting go. Slowly turning around, he was greeted with Lacey's forest green eyes, possessing all the love Johnny would ever need from true romance. A smile of unbelief commandeered his face.

"You're here," he said, skeptically.

"Saving your ass," she replied, with tears welling up in her immense, beautiful eyes.

The two passionately enveloped each other, breaking the chains of long, lost love. Cherishing being in each other's arms once again, they hugged, keeping their bodies touching from head to toe.

"Alright, that's enough out of you two," Matthew interrupted, with a sly smile. Johnny ignored him, keeping his attention on Lacey and the way her sun-kissed skin looked so touchable next to her blue jeans and white tank top, but most of all focusing on the way his soul felt cradled next to hers and how he so desperately desired to make her feel the same way. He succeeded, for she had never before felt so loved by another human being. They held their embrace for a few moments longer before slowly releasing their grip.

Johnny took turns hugging both Matthew and Easton. With sincerity, they echoed what Rick Engleheart had said. A rock began to form in the back of Johnny's throat as he started to get choked up.

"Are you ready for this?" Matthew asked with anticipation, stopping his cousin's emotions in their tracks.

"Ready for what?" Johnny asked, grinning.

Gabe spoke loudly so everyone could hear. While Johnny was preoccupied with his family and Lacey, Michael had ushered in the other half of the group, and now all 162 of them comfortably fit in the elliptical room. Johnny looked around and saw mostly strangers, but he immediately recognized Gabe as the angel who showed up multiple times in his strange, ethereal dreams, and concurrently he also recognized the tall, everyday-looking men in the room as the angels in his choir dream. He smiled, and looked up at Gabe. The blue light emanating from the table illuminated his face in a very mystical way, entrancing everyone listening.

"Now. We all know we're all here. It begins. Before we go forward with the plan, which I will announce very soon, you all need to know something. Something very serious. There is a natural disaster that is about to strike the United States, forever changing not only the country, but the world at large. I'm afraid it is imminent and cannot be avoided. But that is precisely why we are here, and not up there."

Almost on cue, the room began to shake and shudder, followed by a deep, rumbling roar, the sound of which rattled everyone's bones. No one in the room had ever heard a sound so apocalyptic before, and inherently, they all immediately understood that it spelled disaster.

CHAPTER 31

Victor was on his way to The Source. He had been instructed to meet with the leader of Emerus as soon as possible, orders which he hastily obeyed. He had never met Emerus' leader, just heard stories. Apparently, the man never showed his face to anyone, but was the mastermind of the super silos' construction and all of Emerus' projects, commissioning others to carry them out on the threat of personal and familial death. He, along with Emerus' higher-ups assumed great power, reaching as far as the upper echelons of the superpower governments across the globe. So Victor walked briskly. Something was amiss. He could sense it. Michael had not returned to his post with the gravity gun, like he was supposed to. And what's more, Victor had never been ordered to go to The Source, let alone meet Emerus' leader. Yes, something was wrong. Victor was sure of it.

The Source was at the very bottom of Super Silo Six, off the beaten path of the main super silos and their inhabitants. Victor was in the elevator, descending farther and farther down into the crust of the Earth.

"What is going on?" he thought, in fear.

Finally, after a longer-than-expected elevator ride, he arrived at his destination. The Source was nothing like he imagined. In his mind, he had built it up to be a place that was on the receiving end of Emerus' newest technology, with newfangled gadgets and advanced telecommunications and mechanics. However, it was nothing like that. In fact, it was immensely less modern than any other place in Emerus, including Victor's living quarters. He felt like the elevator had brought him back in time. The hallways, the doors, the walls, the floor - they all looked like the interior of a university's administration building. It was nearly eerie to be in such an unfamiliar setting.

The wrinkles on Victor's face showed that he was in thought. He pondered what he had been called to The Source for, wondered where Michael was, and most of all, speculated on the new plan regarding Lacey Hassle and her latent gifts. Sure enough, he had millions of questions, but somehow doubted he would receive the answers. He missed his family, and a day did not go by without him fantasizing about his old life, or at least a life that did not escape on the bewildering tangent he found himself on for the past decade. Victor walked with tragedy within himself, carelessly listening to his personal GPS, which was leading him to the meeting place. After two lefts and three rights, Victor found himself looking up at the numbers *621*, gold-plated above the door. He had arrived. Sighing, he turned the old, brass knob and entered.

"Hello, Victor," a voice announced, immediately greeting him.

The room was much smaller than he imagined. Like an office belonging to an everyday real estate agent, the chamber was incredibly basic. With an inelaborate desk against the far wall and eighteen feet from the door, it was the only semblance of furniture, besides its two wooden chairs, in the uncomplicated den. One chair, on the other side of the desk was occupied; the other one, nearest Victor, was empty. But it was strange. The small, square room was darkly lit in such a way that Victor could not see the man sitting at the opposite side of the desk. Rather, he could sense it. His half of the room was normally light, but as he walked closer and closer to the empty chair, Victor found that the light was peculiarly fading. The desk itself could barely be made out, the chair hardly visible. The remaining eight feet to the wall were completely black. Upon entering, Victor thought he saw the back wall, but now wondered if his eyes had been playing tricks on him. Gazing into the darkness, he surmised that it could have gone on forever. It looked like space, except without the stars.

"When was the last time you saw your family?" the man asked. His voice was deep and he spoke slowly, a tone perfect for the medium of radio.

Victor was caught off guard. Notwithstanding the oddity of being a few feet from someone he could not even see, the question he had just been asked was extremely loaded. He had not even sat down yet. So, before his body's bottom half found the chair, he halted and stood in silence.

"Please, have a seat," the man said.

"I'll stand," Victor replied. Defiance was not his goal, but there was something about the man's inflection and incendiary tone when he mentioned Victor's family that instinctively put the Doc on the defensive. Like a lioness protecting her cubs from a big game hunter, Victor huddled around his precious thoughts and memories.

"I told you," the man said, slowly and steadily, "to have a seat." Victor obeyed.

"Now, that wasn't so hard, was it? I will ask you again. When was the last time you saw your family?" The man's words still possessed a steady and in-control pace.

Victor pretended to think for a couple seconds, although he knew the answer immediately. "A little more than ten years ago," he replied into the darkness.

"Yes. Yes. That's right. So by now, you know the way things work. Well, Victor. What if I were to tell you that there was a way out? Suppose you could leave this place, go back to normal life, and return to being a father and a husband? Would you like that?"

"What are you saying?" asked Victor, cautiously.

"I am offering you a choice," the man replied. "Quite frankly, I'm surprised you are not jumping at the opportunity like a starving pig receiving food in its trough." The man had an insulting cadence woven throughout his words.

"What's the catch?" Victor asked. "An offer like that won't come without a price."

"There's the mind we recruited all those years ago." Victor could imagine a sinister smile behind the words. After pausing, the man continued. "You see, Victor. Something is about to happen. Something catastrophic that will shake the United States and the world for generations to come. Are you familiar with the Yellowstone supervolcano?"

Fear and adrenaline began to race through Victor's veins. "Somewhat, umm...yes," he replied.

"Well, the world's most dangerous geological hot spot is preparing to blow," the man said, matter-of-factly. "The planet's largest known supervolcano is long overdue, and it is angry, Victor. Very angry. The cauldron of magma that sits beneath Yellowstone's surface is the size of Mount Everest. Most volcano's tops are visible to the naked eye, like the top of a mountain. Well, this one is different. The caldera, the epicenter of the inevitable eruption, is so vast that it can only be seen from the air and is large enough to hold the city of Los Angeles."

"Oh my God," Victor pondered, perilously.

"Imagine, something a million times more powerful than an atomic bomb starting a series of other smaller, but still disastrous eruptions fifty miles around Yellowstone. A hurricane of hot gasses 800 degrees spreading out in all directions and 80,000 feet in the air; pyroclastic flows taking out everything in their path, two thousand square miles buried, hundreds of thousands dead in the first few days. And that's not even the worst of it. Two-and-a-half trillion tons of ash will create devastating effects. The sun will be blocked out for years, global temperatures will cool, significantly killing off all tropical plant life. Agriculture worldwide will fall into deep depletion. Both animals and humans will have no choice but to breathe in the ash with every inhalation. There will be widespread starvation and mass death across the planet. Trust me when I tell you this - there has not been something on this scale in the history of man. The human race will be nearly completely wiped out over time. Geologists and historians will look back on it and see a bottleneck of the species. Millions upon millions will perish, animals will go extinct, plant life will cease to exist. There is a chance that nothing will survive, and half a century from now Earth will have no life left."

Victor breathed a sigh of hopelessness. "It can't be stopped? There is absolutely no way?" he asked, assuming that he was going to be commissioned to somehow at least delay the inevitable so citizens could be warned.

"It is unavoidable. Mother Earth is fed up, Victor."

"What does this have to do with me and my family?" Victor asked, curiously. "If I delay the eruption, saving millions of lives, I'm rewarded with leaving Emerus and am allowed to return to my family?"

The man completely ignored the Doc's inquiry with his answer. "Someone once said, 'Never let a serious crisis go to waste' and this organization has lived out those words. Every natural disaster, every domestic tragedy, all overseas conflicts - never have we ever let any one of those go to waste. There is always the opportunity to take away liberty in the name of security. And this time, we, under the cover of the United States' governance will become a global government, in control of every nation. America has been the policeman of the world for over a hundred years, and this will be the end result. Earth's population, or what remains of it, will need us to survive. Finally, the goal of every American president since Teddy Roosevelt will come to fruition. It just took an enormous natural disaster disrupting lives across the globe to do so."

Victor nodded his head in agreement. "But what does this have to with my family?" he asked once again.

"It seems that Michael Willard has gone rogue," the man quickly replied. "We have it from a high authority that he is helping the invading group of people not susceptible to our technology. Trouble is, we can't track him, and have no idea where he is or what he and the others are up to. But they must be stopped. Our fate and the fate of this organization and all it's ever stood for depends on it. There is no mind down here quite like yours, Victor. You are the only one who can stop them. We'll give you whatever you need - high tech-weaponry, an army, whatever it takes. You'll be in charge."

"Michael is my friend," Victor stated, confused and hurt.

"Maybe at one time. But I assure you, he is doing everything he can to be the north to your south."

"What authority do you have that intel from?"

Victor's question enraged the man in the dark. He became upset and slammed his hands down on the desk in a loud bang. He must have leaned forward as well because Victor caught a glimpse of his hands. They were a light gray - almost sickly white. Perhaps it was the stark contrast to the pitch black void, but the man's skin did not look human.

"I am the authority!" the man yelled, angrily. "And if you want to see your family again, and return to normalcy, my offer still stands. Stop the opposition and you are free to leave."

"How will my family's safety be guaranteed? They live in Missouri. They'll never make it."

As an answer to Victor's question, the wall to his right lit up in a single, sustained flash. His eyes widened and his heart raced. There on the other side of the glass wall stood his family - his beautiful, fair-skinned wife and two gorgeous daughters, all of whom had aged like fine wine. It was not a two-way mirror because their reactions were almost identical to Victor's. He ran to the glass and pressed his face and hands against the cold, smooth surface. The three women did the same. The family of four called out to each other, together in fright and in desperation. Tears began to race down all of their faces upon hearing the voices of memories long lost and nearly, but never forgotten.

"I'm sorry. I'm so sorry!" Victor yelled, through gasps. His wife just kept repeating his name, with love and understanding in her voice. His two daughters fearfully and skeptically echoed the word 'Dad' over and over again. And then, their holding cell went dark, the sound of their voices silenced. Angrily and in alarm, Victor turned back toward the other side of the desk.

"Now that I have your attention," the voice calmly said, "Sit back down."

Victor thanked the man and obeyed, for if it weren't for the chair, he thought he might faint. His hands were shaking uncontrollably, which the man noticed.

"Now now...No need to worry. Your family will be safe, well fed, and taken care of. This I promise. But I also promise you something else. If you fail, your last image of them will not be pleasant. Just use your imagination, then think of something ten times worse. Do you understand?"

Victor could barely speak. "Yes," he managed.

"Victor, I need to know you are on board with this. Do you realize what I'm offering you? Are you going to help us or not?"

Victor straightened up, sharpening his focus. "I'll have an army. I'll have advanced weaponry. And I'll have trackers."

"And don't forget that beautiful mind of yours."

Victor once again sharpened his focus and localized his thoughts. And looking straight into the darkness, he solemnly said, "You want them stopped? I can do better. I am going to kill Michael Willard and all who are with him."

Just then, a low rumble began to permeate the airwaves.

"And so it begins," the voice quietly announced.

***

The rumbling eventually subsided, and ever since, all of the group leaders were buzzing around like honeybees. Clearly, they were in a hurry. And even though they were moving about rapidly, their kinetics were calm and with purpose. Gabe and Michael were unmistakably the co-leaders of the group at large. They instructed their fellow comrades on where to go, whom and what to take with them. It was certainly a sight to see. Every angel left the main chamber with the four humans they brought with them, each armed with pistols containing a silencer connected to their ends. Upon leaving the large elliptical room, each group of five took off in an eerily quiet jog to their designated post within the complicated maze. The task was simple. If there be any movement after everyone was equipped at their post - any movement at all - the orders were to shoot on sight. There was simply no time for questioning or for series of interrogation. No, all shots were aimed to kill. Once the army that was coming after them was eliminated, then the band of 162 would take Emerus by storm.

Michael embraced Gabe goodbye like a pitcher and a catcher hug upon culmination of a complete game. There was an odd celebratory aspect to it that surprised Johnny and the other remaining onlookers. Gabe's job was to stay put in the center room, guarding both Johnny and Lacey, along with Rick Engleheart. Matthew, anxious to enter the maze, which served as the battleground's front lines, exited the room with Michael. Easton followed. Before they left, though, the Engleheart family members enveloped into a close huddle. No words were said, but unspoken confidence combined with a sense of desperation took up the epicenter. Ten seconds later, they split up.

"Gabriel," Michael said, before he entered the maze. "Stay in contact."

Gabe replied with a nod of assurance, then shut the door. He turned around and smiled at Johnny, Lacey, and Rick Engleheart. They reminded him of three poor children from New York City in the 1920s that he was commissioned to save one winter's night. They were sitting on the curb with their feet in the gutter waiting to freeze to death. The three humans staring back at him in the mission, about a hundred years later, had the same faces. They looked like they needed answers.

"Come now, children," he said, in comfort. "Ready to go up?"

"Go up?" Rick Engleheart asked, confused.

"Well, no. Not all the way up. Not yet. Trust me, you don't want to see what's out there. This room, I meant." Gabe walked over to the wall next to the door. Leaning close to the dusty concrete, he closed his eyes and calmly and happily inhaled. Then, opening his eyes, he breathed into the wall. Stagnant dust scurried in every direction before dissipating in the air. Three seconds later, the room released from its bay and began to slowly ascend into the air.

"Whoa," Lacey said.

"You see, what makes this maze so complex is that it is a multiple level labyrinth," Gabe stated, to everybody. "Four levels to be exact. And each level is entirely different. Michael built it, in secret of course. If a human attempted to undertake a project so vast, they would be found out in a heartbeat. But every time they tried to track him, their technology faltered, and was interrupted by good old fashioned static."

"So why are we going to the top?" Rick Engleheart asked.

"The enemy here does not know of the multiple levels. If they ever get to the center room, which is a slim chance, they will find it empty. So we will be safe up high. And that's not all." As a physical continuation of his words, all at once the walls, ceiling, and floor became transparent. The elliptical concrete room had suddenly transformed into a floating ovular glass-like disc. Except the exterior was not glass. Instead, it was a strange type of composite material, stronger than steel, but as transparent as oxygen. "Don't worry," Gabe assured. "No one can see us. Think of it as a two-way mirror."

"Wow," Rick Engleheart declared, touching the room's warm walls, which began to glow a deep forest green.

"So we'll get to oversee the whole thing," Johnny stated, slightly in awe.

"Exactly," Gabe replied. "If for some reason the enemy starts to figure out the maze, we will see them coming, and can stop them before they even get close."

The room slowly stopped ascending, and settled into another bay. The table and connected chairs were still humbly shining their deep, brilliant blue, providing a mesmerizing contrast to the green for the room's inhabitants. The captivating color danced throughout the space and filled the room with an intensity unlike anything Johnny, Lacey, or Rick Engleheart could ever imagine. They shot a gracious look at Gabe, but he was not looking in their direction. His eyes were closed again, but is head was tilted up toward the Earth and his arms were outstretched wide. An ear-to-ear smile advanced across his face.

"What is it, Gabe?" Lacey asked, in whispered wonder.

Gabe lowered his head, retaining his smile. It was difficult to tell for sure in the glowing and swirling colors, but a single tear of pure joy was slowly sliding down his flawless face. He sniffed in an emotional inhale.

"People are waking up. All across the Earth, they are activating."

<u>EPILOGUE</u>

Doug Carson had not dealt with his best friend's kidnapping well. The suburban town of Windsor had been up in arms ever since, and that, combined with the sad news of the mysterious deaths around town, was not helping. Doug missed Johnny incredibly, and only recently began to accept that he would never see him again. It was one of the most difficult things he had ever had to do.

Doug could not sleep. It was nearly five in the morning, and he had to be at work - the local YMCA's youth camp - in an hour and a half. Checking the refrigerator, he was disappointed to discover that he had unnoticingly run out of root beer. "Might as well go to the corner and get some," he thought out loud. Thankfully, the bank's ATM was open twenty-four hours because his wallet was empty. Doug retrieved his car keys, slid on his sandals, and walked out of the house, softly shutting the front door behind him so as not to wake his parents. It was very warm for the time of day, so every window of his midnight blue Jetta was down on the two minute drive to the ATM. Pulling up to the right wall of the bank, he slid his bank card into the lit slot. What happened next was all a flash, but was the defining moment of his life.

Doug didn't see the two men dressed in black with their hoods up until a gun was pressed into his left temple. The man holding the gun to his head told him to empty out the maximum amount. The other man stood in front of the car, also holding a gun, and pointing it straight at Doug's face. Both of them had winter ski hats on, which only revealed their eyes and lips. Doug was larger and more muscular than the average eighteen-year-old, and the two men were slightly smaller than him. Normally, he would fight, but their advantage lay in their guns, and even though Doug's life had taken somewhat of a wrong turn, the last thing he wanted to do was die.

"Hurry up!" the man outside the driver's side window yelled.

Doug complied, but was nervous. Anxiety took over, and for the life of him, he could not remember his PIN. The two men were not buying it, and Doug quickly understood that if he did not type in the four digits that were so frustratingly eluding him correctly, then his life would soon be over. Tears welled up in his eyes as he accepted that his memory was not good enough. Hope was running out, but he had something that served as the light at the end of his tunnel - the element of surprise.

"Oh, look at this pansy cry," the man outside his window mocked. "He…"

The man's sentence was abruptly cut off as Doug rapidly and in one motion took the gun away, slammed open the door, and ducked down to avoid the incoming fire. He heard them screaming something to one another, but soon gun shots consumed the sound waves. Staying ducked down, Doug floored the gas pedal. He winced, preparing to run over the man in front of the car, but the man had moved. Twenty-eight feet later, the car ran into a group of orange barrels filled with water. It came to a sudden stop, and if it wasn't for the seat belt still secure, Doug would have gotten seriously hurt. A few bruises would form in the next couple of days, but he had no sign of injury. The car was jammed among and in between the barrels and a dumpster, and if he had more time, Doug could have pulled his car out with multiple tries. But time was simply a luxury he did not have. Remembering that he still had the man's gun, Doug aimed it out of the window, and undoing his seat belt, hurriedly climbed out of the car.

"Crash!" the back window was blown out with a bullet.

Doug walked in the shot's direction, spotting the man in the faint orange glow of the streetlights. He couldn't believe what he was doing, but his instinct had chosen fight over flight. He noticed the other man, from whom he had taken the gun, in pain on the ground near the ATM. The car had run over his legs, breaking both femurs. The other man tried to shoot again, but the gun had run out of bullets. He ran to his partner in crime. But so did Doug, accidentally dropping the gun along the way. They arrived at the same time and entered into an all-out brawl. It wasn't long before Doug noticed something, though. To hit the man, he didn't have to touch him. In fact, proximity was not even an issue at all. As long he could see him, Doug could punch the air and land one right on the man's cheek. Left jab, right hook, left jab, right uppercut. The man was on the ground, frantically crawling away, backwards.

"What are you?" he yelled, in fright.

Doug answered with a hard kick to the man's chin. Blood projected out from his lips. Doug was not a murderer, and didn't plan on killing the man. He stopped his animalistic instincts in their tracks. Feeling compelled to say something, he felt his spirit oblige him to speak to both men on the ground. "The best revenge is living well."

Walking away, he again punched through the air twice, landing a sharp right hook into the men's ribcages. Doug wanted to find out what the heck had just happened. He looked down at his body. Nothing had changed externally. Internally, however, was an entirely different story. He felt empowered, as if he could fly. He was about to test his newfound ability when something unexpectedly interrupted him. It was the town's emergency siren system. The last time it sounded, a hurricane had come up the east coast, and killed hundreds of Rhode Islanders. Something was wrong. Doug ran the mile home as fast as he could, into the sunrise, humming a song he had heard in his most recent dream, the words and melody of which he could not get out of his head.

At the dawn of it all, we will come and rescue you.

BenjaminDeerBooks.com